RAZOR'S TRAITOROUS HEART

THE ALLIANCE BOOK 2

S.E. SMITH

ACKNOWLEDGMENTS

I would like to thank my husband Steve for believing in me and being proud enough of me to give me the courage to follow my dream. I would also like to give a special thank you to my sister and best friend Linda, who not only encouraged me to write, but who also read the manuscript. Also to my other friends who believe in me: Julie, Jackie, Lisa, Sally, Elizabeth (Beth), Laurelle, and Narelle. The girls that keep me going!

And a special thanks to Paul Heitsch, David Brenin, Samantha Cook, Suzanne Elise Freeman, and PJ Ochlan—the awesome voices behind my audiobooks!

—S. E. Smith

RAZOR'S TRAITOROUS HEART: THE ALLIANCE BOOK 2

First E-Book Published June 2014
Cover Design by Melody Simmons

Summary: Razor's duty is to settle the conflict that Kali, the woman he needs to claim, is so deeply involved in, forcing him to choose between the Alliance and his heart.

ISBN: 9781500156725 (kdp paperback)
ISBN: 9781078746670 (BN paperback)
ISBN: 978-1-942562-13-9 (eBook)

Romance (love, explicit sexual content) | Action/Adventure | Science Fiction (Aliens) | Fantasy (Urban) | Post Apocalypse | Contemporary Paranormal

Published by Montana Publishing, LLC
& SE Smith of Florida Inc. www.sesmithfl.com

CONTENTS

SYNOPSIS

An alien warrior is supposed to forge a peace, but all he really wants... is her.

We sent messages into space to find out if there could be someone out there, listening. Then six years ago, Trivators came to Earth. They wanted to bring Earth into the Alliance of Star Systems, but worldwide there was such violent panic at the unexpected visit that the Trivators were forced to take control. It's not going well.

Razor is a High Chancellor for the Alliance who has been sent to finally bring order to Earth – by any means necessary. Chicago, a city torn apart by two factions, is an extremely important target to quell the chaos, and it is there in Chicago that a female warrior saves his life and disappears.

Kali has devoted her life to her brother's cause. After all, Destin is the only one has Chicago's best interests at heart. Colbert just wants power, and he certainly has become a powerful enemy. It wasn't always that way. Once he was someone they trusted above all others, but that time is past, and now Kali will do whatever it takes to bring peace to their people, even if that means battling giant alien warriors who stuck their noses into Earth's business six years ago and never left. One night though, Kali sees someone who will die if she doesn't act, and then discovers mid-rescue that he's a Trivator!

Razor has never failed a mission, and his reputation of ruthlessness is well earned, but for the first time in his life, he finds himself torn between duty and something he is unfamiliar with, his heart.

1

"Prepare the cleanup," Razor's deep voice ordered as he watched the fires burning in the remains of the city far below. "I want reconstruction of the city to begin within the month."

"Yes, sir," the male standing behind him replied.

"Was this really necessary?" the human male standing next to him asked in a shaken voice.

The huge Trivator warrior, known only by the name of Razor, stood in rigid silence on the bridge of the observation warship. The advanced command ship was overseeing the demolition of the city below. The human city that was once called Mexico City was now a pile of burning rubble. All life, all buildings, everything had been wiped clean.

Razor had earned his name. He cut through the resistance like a fine scalpel slicing through a life-giving artery. He was brought in when all others failed.

He was one of three High Chancellors for the Alliance and was in charge of the vast military structure. He was also one of the most controversial members among the council. It was his job to oversee the vast number of Trivator troops that made up the security forces of the Alliance. Their job was to initiate first contact, subdue any fear, and establish a safe environment for additional members of the Alliance to begin the process of bringing the new world under their protection.

He was used to the fear when they first made contact with a new species. Most beings soon realized that the Alliance was there not to harm or control, but to help bring them into the larger and often more advanced star systems surrounding them. For young, unprepared planets such as this, it could be frightening and some resistance was to be expected. Still, the humans had been surprisingly stubborn to the point they would rather destroy their world than accept the visitors they had unwittingly invited through the messages they sent out.

Razor's eyes narrowed on the ruins below him. This was a perfect example of the waste of resources and life. He had no regrets for his actions. The humans below had been warned that the Alliance had reached the end of its patience with those that continued to rebel against them.

The Alliance had finally decided it was no longer willing to waste time and resources to bring the last of the major cities on the planet under control. The rebels were warned to cease fighting and work with the new world government that was established or be erased. Those controlling the city below had refused the twelve hour grace period. Exactly one minute after the deadline, demolition ships began flattening the city.

Razor stared calmly down at the destruction. Since his arrival on the planet six months before, he had already resolved the issues with the rebels on the other side of the world that continued to resist integration into the Alliance. The small rebel groups in Cairo, Paris, and Riyadh had agreed to lay down their arms and the cities were currently being rebuilt. Of course, those agreements had come after he had ordered the Ukraine's city of Kyiv leveled after rebels there opened fire. He had warned them what would happen. Those that refused to leave at first had fled in desperation as the huge destroyers began demolition of the city. Those that continued to resist died.

"Yes," he replied coolly to the human representative that had been assigned to the region.

"You should have..." the man began.

"Resistance will no longer be tolerated. It is time to accept that your world is no longer alone in the universe. The Alliance's decision is final. It is time to rebuild your world and move forward."

Juan Rodriguez, the new Mexican representative to the Alliance, swallowed as the large alien next to him turned and walked away. His eyes moved to the city where he had been born. It had taken less than an hour for the city to be leveled. The power and precision behind the destruction left him shaken.

His eyes moved to the dozens of large Destroyers that scanned for remains. A shiver of fear ran through him. It was hard to believe it was only six short years since the alien warships appeared in the skies around the planet. Since then, he had moved from being a simple, newly graduated University of Mexico student in Political Science to being the representative for his people.

His eyes clouded as he remembered his passionate plea for peace. He had been shocked when the Alliance heard of him and approached him about being a representative for his people in the New World Government. They said they were impressed with his determination to calm those that continued to fight, his courage to face his opposition head on, and his willingness to face the council.

"What have we done?" he wondered under his breath as he gazed down at the devastation and thought of the men and women who refused to leave. "They should have listened to me when I warned them."

Silence was his only answer. Around him, members of the Trivator troops worked seamlessly to guide the command ship over the remains. He glanced at the massive males that towered over his own five foot nine frame. Their bodies were built for killing. He knew from experience that they were fast, agile, and deadly.

His eyes swept over the leader of the Trivators. Razor… no surname… just Razor. He was actually slightly shorter by comparison, if you could call being close to seven feet tall short. There was something about him that made him seem more threatening than any of the others. There was a coldness, a stillness that spoke of barely controlled violence.

Juan turned back to stare down at the fires and sighed. If this is what the man was like when he was calm, he hated to think of what he could do if he ever lost control. He wouldn't be surprised if the world did come to an end then, this time from the aliens instead of mankind.

God in heaven, he thought as he remembered the cold yellow-gold eyes, *I feel sorry for anyone who makes him mad.*

2

"What was this city called?" Razor asked the human pilot sitting beside him.

He glanced down at the darkened ruins. Cutter, his second-in-command, had given him a report on it, but a new issue on the way to the area had taken priority. He had arrived earlier that day to meet with other members of the Alliance council.

He had been furious to discover the number of details that had been deleted from the previously submitted reports. Badrick, the Usoleum council member who had formerly been in charge of this star system, had a lot to answer for as far as Razor was concerned. Badrick was lucky to be alive after he discovered the bastard had approved many of the falsified reports submitted to the Trivator generals and the council over the past six years.

Badrick's interference, compounded with his incompetence, was a big reason the Earth was still in such a mess. It was only because most of the evidence was circumstantial that he was unable to remove Badrick and ship him off-world. Badrick had done an excellent job of blaming others for his decisions. It was a slow process, but Razor was working on unraveling the Usoleum Councilman's lies.

"Chicago," the pilot responded through the headset. "Colonel Baker is in charge of this area. There are two groups of rebels fighting for control. The fighting has heated up over the past few months. They've divided the city in half between the north and south by building a huge-ass wall, reminds me a bit of the Great Wall of China only it's made out of rubble. We call it the Great Wall of Chicago," the pilot joked.

Razor didn't reply. He could see the twenty foot high by thirty foot wide wall that cut the city in half. The ghostly figures of cranes towered over sections of it like silent sentinels in the night. There were dots of light, probably from small fires, glowing faintly in the dark. He silently calculated how long it would take to level the city if the two opposing sides refused to lay down their arms.

"How much further to the base?" Razor asked.

"About forty-five minutes," the pilot replied.

Razor was silent. He would have preferred to have brought his own transport, but an emergency pickup for several wounded Trivator warriors was needed outside the city. He had ordered his own pilot to assist with the evacuation. The commanding human officer on location had offered the use of their own transport so that he could continue to his meeting with Colonel Baker. A journey that should have taken a few minutes had stretched into over an hour so far.

He slid his finger over the tablet in his hand to read over the report Cutter had given him. A picture of Chicago before the destruction showed a fairly modern city for the level of advancement of this species. He skimmed through the facts. Two men, Colbert Allen and Destin Parks, controlled the region. Intel suggested the men had at one time worked together before splitting. Allen took the southern half of the city while Parks took the northern half. The fighting had intensified over the past six months.

He touched the screen and a new image appeared. Several pictures, taken with a long distance, high resolution imaging device showed several groups of people. The top one was marked as being Colbert

Allen. He was a tall, slender male with short blonde hair and cold blue eyes. He was surrounded by several men that reminded Razor of some of the lower class miners and pirates he had encountered during his years as a warship commander. His gut feeling told him the male would not be easily persuaded to lay down his arms.

His eyes moved to the next image. A dark-haired male, shorter than Allen stood surrounded by a group of men who were listening intently to whatever he was telling them. Destin Parks was the direct opposite of Allen, not only in coloring but in his expressions. Concern, intelligence, and something else - Razor enlarged the image so he could study the male's face more closely. He raised an eyebrow in surprise - sadness - if he had to guess, he would say the male was sad.

A dark frown creased his brow as the shadowy face of someone standing off to the left of Parks suddenly caught his attention. He would have missed the person standing in the shadows if he hadn't enlarged the image. He touched the screen again to enhance the face of the human.

Shock ricocheted through him as the delicate features of a female came into focus. She had a rounded face framed by short, dark hair. He bit back a silent growl of frustration. She was standing too far back in the shadows for him to make out the color of it. It was either a dark brown or black like his.

Her eyes were focused on Parks. A dark intensity in them told him that her eyes probably were the same color as her hair. She had a small, smooth nose that was surprisingly appealing to him. Her lips were firmly pressed together in a straight line that told him she wasn't happy with whatever Parks was saying. He couldn't see what the rest of her looked like as Parks and his group blocked her body. He focused back on her eyes. This time the growl of frustration he released wasn't silent. Fear and worry shone clearly back at him.

"What?" the pilot started to say before a curse escaped him as an alarm sounded. "Fuck! The son-of-a-bitches have fired on us. Hold on."

Razor's eyes jerked up to the primitive display. The tracking of a ground-to-air missile moved across the softly glowing display. His mind was calculating the time to impact even as he was calling out a warning as the dark frame of a crane appeared in front of them. The pilot, intent on using defensive measures to miss the missile coming at them, had swerved to the left and reduced altitude. He tried to correct their flight pattern, but Razor knew the machine they were in would not be able to react in time.

"Brace for impact," he growled out as the helicopter violently shook.

The sound of screeching metal on metal echoed loudly through the helicopter. He gripped the bar near his head as the aircraft swung crazily around before it tilted and started to fall. He ignored the sickening feeling in his stomach as he stared out the windshield as they began falling toward the ground. His body jerked forward when the tail caught in the cabling of the crane. The straps holding him to the seat strained as he hung face down. He thought for a brief second that he might actually live through the crash unscathed. That slim hope disappeared when the air-to-ground missile struck the top of the crane holding them. The explosion above ripped through the metal, sending small, deadly fragments raining down around them. The hot shards sliced through the thin metal skin of the helicopter. An explosive curse burst from his compressed lips as the jib of the crane crumbled under the heat and weight, sending them plummeting downward. The helicopter rocketed into the remains of a skyscraper. Darkness descended as his head slammed into the windshield.

Kali drew in a deep breath, forcing the cold night air into her starving lungs. She bent over with her hands on her thighs, drawing in the clean, fresh air before standing straight and looking up at the stars.

She was near the downtown area tonight. She loved escaping the confining spaces of their current headquarters. She loved being outside. She always had.

She had climbed to the top of the Harrison Hotel Electric Garage. She wanted to go higher, so she walked over to the steel framing that held the partial remains of the sign, high above the city. At over twenty-one stories, it wasn't the tallest structure still standing, but it was close. She didn't bother going up to the top of the crane mounted on top of the building. It was a left over from BTA, before the aliens. It was too windy tonight to chance climbing it.

Kali scaled the metal girders holding the lettering of the sign like a monkey. She'd had plenty of practice over the past few years. She didn't stop until she reached the top of the 'H'. Most of the other letters had fallen away, but this one still stood proudly against the inky skyline. The letter was wide enough that on a calm night she could stand up on it and raise her arms to the sky. If she closed her eyes as a gentle breeze swept by, she could almost imagine she could fly. Tonight it was too dangerous to stand up. Instead, she contented herself by sitting on the edge and looking out over the city she called home.

"I wonder what it will look like in the future," she murmured as she gazed out of the ghostly remains. "When Destin reclaims the city, we'll rebuild it even better than it was before."

Kali didn't want to admit in her heart that she was afraid that would never happen. If Colbert... if Colbert was successful in killing her brother and overtaking the northern half of the city, she knew it never would. She lowered her head as she remembered how the young boy she and Destin had befriended as kids had betrayed them in the cruelest way.

"Why?" she whispered as she ran her fingers over the scar on her wrist. "How could he do this? To us? To our own people?"

She shook her head and blinked back the tears of anger. It had been almost two years since Colbert had turned on them. Destin hadn't believed her at first when she expressed her concern over Colbert's increasingly irrational behavior. He thought it was the stress they were all under. He often told her it wasn't easy trying to rebuild a world amid all the destruction and uncertainty of their future, that some people handled it differently than others. Destin had embraced the chance. He was determined to use the skills he had been learning as a mechanical engineer before the world went crazy to build a city like the ones they saw in the Sci-Fi movies they used to sneak into.

Colbert… Colbert saw a chance to rule through power and he wanted Destin by his side. Colbert saw what he thought was a chance to rise above the street kids they had been and become the absolute leader. Only one person stood in his way. One person who knew his weakness. One person who knew who he really was inside and what he desired most next to power.

Destin had almost died because she had been afraid to speak up. She had always known that Colbert loved her brother. When she was younger, she thought he loved Destin like she did, as a brother. When she was sixteen, she caught Colbert looking at Destin with a silent hunger that she recognized as anything but brotherly. Colbert had been eighteen to Destin's twenty at the time and was the leader of one of the most dangerous gangs in their neighborhood. He didn't like that she and Destin chose a different path. Kali knew Colbert blamed her for that. Destin would never have allowed that type of danger to come near her and he told Colbert as much. Both she and Destin had other dreams they wanted to follow.

Colbert's obsession with Destin remained hidden from her brother, but once Kali had glimpsed the hunger in his eyes that day, she had quietly watched Colbert from a distance. Two years ago, she caught Colbert spying on her brother when he was with one of the women who had joined up with them. Kali finally broke down and told her brother about her suspicions.

Two days after her meeting with Destin, the woman was found dead. The woman, Maria, had broken her neck when she supposedly fell through a weak spot while on patrol with Colbert and Johnson, Colbert's second-in-command. Colbert swore that he tried to save Maria but Kali had been suspicious and asked Doc do an autopsy on Maria. Doc said that the bruising around Maria's neck indicated she had been strangled and that additional bruising and blood under her nails showed she had fought against her attacker.

Colbert overheard Kali telling Destin the results. At first, Colbert had denied it, claiming the cuts on his arms and face were the result of retrieving Maria's body from the building. When Kali presented the evidence from Doc and asked for a blood sample to see if it matched the blood under Maria's fingernails, Colbert exploded into a desperate, jealous rage. The knife aimed for her brother's heart had cut a deep path across her wrist as she stepped between them to protect Destin.

Destin's call for help was answered by Jason and Tim. They had subdued Colbert, but his treachery ran deeper than either she or Destin knew. His followers helped him escape the makeshift jail they had constructed. Several good men died that night. Men that had families. All because Destin didn't love Colbert the way Colbert loved Destin and refused to join him in ruling Chicago.

"What a screwed up world we live in," she murmured as she leaned back and stared up into the night sky again. "Why can't people just learn to live together?"

She gasped as the dark lit up when someone from the southern half of the city launched a ground-to-air missile. Her eyes followed the path as it streaked across the night sky. Her low cry of denial was carried away on the wind as she saw the target. A Black Hawk helicopter flying low dipped to the left, heading toward her.

Kali watched as the helicopter approached in slow motion. It took a moment for her to register that it was heading straight toward her. She rolled backwards and flipped over the side of the sign. She scrambled down the metal frame, jumping or sliding as fast as she could. She was almost to the bottom of it when the sound of the helicopter grew louder and she swung around to look. A hoarse curse burst from her lips and her eyes widened in horror as she recognized the shapes of two men in the cockpit.

Time appeared to stand still as the pilot swerved again. It was obvious he didn't see the outline of the large rooftop crane sticking up like a greedy hand. Kali jumped off the sign's metal frame as the tail rotor caught in the thick metal cables of the nearby crane. The horrific sound of screeching metal echoed above the wind. She hit the ground and rolled as another sound mixed with the doomed aircraft. The whistle of the missile ended with an ear-shattering explosion.

Kali continued to roll until she was under the metal overhang of a fresh air intake duct mounted on the roof. She curled into a ball and covered her head as flaming shards of hot metal rained down around her. Fear threatened to engulf her as a part of the helicopter's main rotor blade snapped and several large sections flew wildly through the air. One long piece, approximately six feet long, pierced the metal duct inches above her head.

She lay breathing heavily as the sounds of creaking metal and the snapping and popping of flames continued to fill the air. Cautiously raising her head, she looked around at the wreckage. She was amazed that she was still alive. Rolling until she was on her hands and knees, she slowly crawled out from under the impaled duct. She knelt on the gravel and tar-papered roof staring in shock and horror at the destruction.

The crane that had been installed to replace some of the lettering before the alien invasion now stood twisted and disfigured, as if it had been made out of papier-mâché instead of steel. The 'H' was broken in half. The section that was missing had taken out a good ten feet or more of the short wall surrounding the roof. Long ropes of steel cabling hung like the remains of a spider's web blowing in the breeze. Sparks and small fires continued to burn, lighting the darkness so she could see the hideous outline of what remained of the helicopter.

Kali walked slowly toward the edge. There was no way anyone could have survived such a crash. The tail boom was shredded with large chunks missing from it. The tail rotor was completely gone. She glanced around and saw what she thought were pieces of it sticking out of the building across from her. Climbing over the rubble, she raised a trembling hand to push the hair that blew into her eyes back behind her ear and looked over the edge of the building to see if the helicopter had fallen all the way to the ground.

She drew in a surprised breath when she saw that it hung suspended two floors below her. Her eyes followed the tangle of steel cables that barely held it. She jerked back when the whole thing shifted as the crane tilted and bent under the weight of the helicopter. Scrambling backwards over the broken brick and mortar from the building, she turned and headed for the back corner where the metal fire escape was attached to the side of the building. She doubted that the two men were still alive, but she needed to confirm it. She couldn't leave them if they were hurt.

One thing is for sure, she thought as she climbed over the edge and began working her way down through the narrow caged ladder to the floor below. *If those men did survive the crash I have to help get them out because that crane sure as hell isn't going to be able to hold them for long.*

3

Razor blinked several times in an effort to clear his vision. He remained perfectly still as he ran an assessment over his body. Every part of him felt bruised and beaten. He ignored the throbbing in an effort to assess what was minor damage and what could be life-threatening. A low curse echoed through the cockpit when he realized that he was still face down. The only thing holding him in place was the seat harness. There was nothing else between him and the ground far below. The windshield of the helicopter was missing on his side.

He slowly raised his hand to wipe at the blood that kept blurring his vision. A deep cut ran just above his right brow. His arms were fine, but excruciating pain in his left leg hazed his vision when he tried to move it.

Drawing in a deep breath, he lowered his chin until he could look down at it. A shaft of metal, over six inches long, was embedded in his upper thigh. He turned his head so he could look at the pilot. The male hung lifelessly from his harness. A thick metal rod protruded from his chest.

"Hey, is anyone alive in there?" a soft voice called out from behind him. "Oh God!"

Razor turned his head as far as he could, but from the position he was in he couldn't see who had called out. He could only feel it. A deep heat mixed with the pain running through him. Frustrated, he closed his eyes and wrapped his hand around the top of the metal in his leg and pulled in another deep breath in preparation for the pain that would come with removing it.

His eyes jerked open when he felt slender fingers close around his wrist. "Wait," the husky voice whispered next to his ear. "Let me make sure it didn't hit an artery. If it did, you'll be dead before I can get you to safety."

Razor turned his head and breathed in the sweet scent of wildflowers. A low moan escaped before he could contain it. The heat inside him flared again, rushing through him at such a speed that he had to close his eyes again to calm the dizziness.

"I am dead either way," he murmured as the metal around them creaked and shifted again.

"Not on my watch you aren't," the voice replied with a trace of amusement. "Now, keep your pantyhose on. I'm going to reach around you and attach a strap to you so I can release the harness and free you. Is your other leg good?"

Razor's eyes jerked open and his breath hissed out when the most beautiful almond-shaped brown eyes, mere inches from his face, looked back at him with a combination of humor and fear. The first thought that went through his mind was that this was the female from the image he had been studying right before the crash. The second and most disturbing was that she was in imminent danger.

"Leave me," he ordered with a dark growl. "It is too dangerous. The whole thing could collapse at any moment. Get out now. I will get myself out if I can."

Kali ignored everything around her, but what she was doing. If she thought about it, she would do exactly like the alien demanded. Hell, if she had known that there was an alien on board the damn 'human' helicopter, she would have left his ass to die instead of risking her neck to save him.

No, you wouldn't have, her good side argued silently with her bad side. *You would have helped anyway because you are a sucker for those in need.*

"Yeah, and look where it has gotten me," she muttered under her breath.

"What?" the alien male demanded before he let out a curse as the helicopter shifted again. "Get out!"

"Shut up!" she snapped back, quickly tying the thick cloth of a rolled up fire hose around his waist.

"You…" Razor's voice died as the helicopter shifted violently.

This time the entire thing dropped several feet. A large section of the tail boom opened up and fell to the ground far below. The shift caught Kali off-guard as she adjusted her feet to get into a better position to unhook the straps holding him to his seat.

She screamed as the footholds she was using dropped from under her feet. She tilted and would have fallen through the opened windshield if his hand hadn't shot out as she fell and wrapped around her arm. She slid down until his fingers clamped down with an iron grip around her wrist. Looking down, she stared at the ground wondering briefly if this was the way she would die.

"No," the voice growled out.

Kali looked up at the face of the male who held her life in the palm of his hand. Dropping her gaze to his thigh, she studied the metal for a moment before deciding that unless they were built vastly different, the metal should have missed all the main arteries. She looked back up to see sweat glistening on his brow and his eyes glazed with pain, determination and anger.

"Well, I think the metal in your leg missed your artery. It's still going to hurt like a bitch when I remove it," she replied grimly. "You can't pass out on me when I do, you hear me? I need you to keep it together until we are out of this mess."

"Are you crazy, female?" his deep, rich voice asked in disbelief as he stared at her hanging from one hand over certain death. "You are going to get yourself killed!"

"Not tonight, I'm not," Kali replied in a husky voice. "Just… don't let go of me yet. I'd hate for you to prove me wrong."

Lifting her legs up, she found a good foothold and reached up to grab the back of his seat. The move had her straddling his legs and her forehead pressed firmly against his. She knew that he was going to be pissed with what she was about to do, but there was no time for making the task at hand any easier. The moment he released her hand, she gripped the metal shard in his leg and pulled it out as quickly as possible.

"I'm sorry," she whispered, staring into his eyes. "I'm so sorry."

She dropped the blade of metal, letting it fall through the shattered glass to the ground below. Readjusting her position, she reached into her back pocket and pulled out the bandana that she sometimes used to hold her hair back. It was barely long enough when folded diagonally to wrap around his thigh.

She hated having to hurt him, but some instinct told her that they were running out of time if they were going to get out of this alive. She needed him to be able to move and he wouldn't be able to with a spear of metal in his leg. She glanced up as she finished tying the strip of cloth.

His head was pressed back against the seat, not an easy thing to do considering he was hanging by a few straps. His face was pale and his lips were pressed together so tightly they were almost white. His eyes had turned to a darker gold. It was the look of pain, anger and exhaustion shining in them that pulled at her sympathetic heart. She knew all too well what those feelings felt like.

She reached up and touched his cheek before pressing her lips lightly against his. It was the only thing she could think of to give him a moment of comfort. Resting her forehead against his again, she reached down and grasped the buckle holding the straps together.

"Are you ready for this?" she asked softly. "I'll help balance you. Use your good leg to brace against the dash. I'll act as your left leg. Try not to put too much weight on it if you can. We don't want it to give out and have you collapse. The shift might take the whole thing down. Once we get on the back side of the seats the side door is open. If we get to the opening and the crane gives way, don't worry about falling. I have the hose around you and it will hold you. Let it swing you down to the lower floor. The windows are all gone and I've kicked out the rest of the glass so just let the momentum take you to safety."

"What..." he started to say hoarsely as the buckle opened and he gripped her as she wrapped her arms around him to keep him from falling. "What about you?"

"Don't worry about me," Kali whispered in his ear. "Tonight isn't my time to die."

4

Razor's mind rebelled at the thought that any night would be her time to die. Gritting his teeth, he braced his good leg against the instrument panel. He kept one hand wrapped around the strap tied to his waist to help steady him and his other arm around the waist of the slender female.

They moved in a slow, painful synchronized dance over the seats toward the open door. He tightened his arm around her when the helicopter shifted again under their weight. He could feel it as it began to tilt. The sudden knowledge that things were about to change quickly hit him at the same time as it must have hit her.

"Hold on," he ordered as he bent both legs and pushed off, ignoring the burning pain as he pulled on the jagged cut on his leg.

For a moment, time stood still as they were suspended in the air. Razor felt the female's warm breath against his neck as she buried her face against it. Her arms had moved from around his waist to around his neck. He turned at the last minute so his body could take the force of them hitting the brick building. They briefly bounced outward, but her hold on him never loosened. He rolled as they came back against the side so his back was to the falling debris that was dragged down under the weight of the helicopter.

He bent his head forward as she splayed her hands protectively over the back of it. It took several seconds before he realized that she had wrapped her legs around his waist and was pulling him closer to the building. He groaned against her shoulder as she held him tightly against her.

"I think… we… made it out of the helicopter," her trembling voice whispered against his ear.

"Yes," he muttered, pulling back.

He watched as she tilted her head upwards before looking down, then returning to look into his eyes with a small grin on her lips. He felt her body relax against his as she stared at him in curiosity. He saw her frown as she studied the cut above his eye.

"You're going to need stitches for that one as well," she murmured before meeting his eyes again. She tightened her legs around him as she raised one hand to gently push his hair back from his face. Her expression changed as she rubbed it between her fingers. "It's soft."

"Can we discuss the softness of my hair when we are not hanging almost sixty meters above the ground," he muttered through his teeth.

He didn't know if it was pain or exhaustion causing the confusion swirling through his mind, but he was finding it almost impossible to concentrate on anything but the female wrapped around him. It wasn't like him to allow anyone, much less an alien female, to distract him from his mission.

"Sorry," she muttered, releasing his hair.

If it wasn't for the fact that she was still in danger, he would have demanded that she continue her exploration. His arm tightened around her waist when she slowly lowered her legs. Fear that she was about to fall swept through him.

"What are you doing?" he bit out as she let go of him.

She raised one delicate eyebrow at him. "Like you said, we can't just hang from the side of the building. I'm going to turn around so my back is to you. Hang on to me and I'll walk us along the edge until we get to the window. Once I'm through, I'll pull you in and take a look at your leg. Will any of your people come looking for you?"

"No and yes," Razor snapped out in frustration.

"No, no one will come or yes, they will?" she asked in confusion, even as she twisted nimbly in his arms by holding onto the hose that ran above his head before it ran down his back and tied at his waist. "Hold on."

Razor gritted his teeth until his jaw began to throb. The irritating female didn't listen to anything he said, had no concept of survival, and needed her ass thoroughly whipped for putting herself into such a dangerous situation. He didn't bother trying to hide his opinion either.

Soft laughter filled the air around them as she gripped the jagged bricks and scooted along the narrow lip that separated the different levels. He refrained from making any more comments, afraid he would distract her. Right now, his arms around her and his body pressed against her back were the only things keeping her from falling to her death.

"Have you no concept of survival, female?" he asked as she pulled them closer to the window.

"Of course I do. Just be thankful I was here to help you," she replied softly. "I've done this before without help, you know."

A soft, rich growl escaped him at her comment. "Where is your protector? Your male should not allow you to do such things."

He felt her body tremble. At first he thought it was because of fear of what her male would think of her risking her life. A flash of hot rage swept through him at the idea of her belonging to another male. A male like – Destin Parks. It took a few seconds for him to realize the trembling was caused by her chuckling.

"I don't have a 'male' as you put it," she replied as she gripped the open frame of the window and stepped through. He grasped her hands when she turned and held them out to help guide him through the opening. He used his good leg to steady his body as she pulled him inside. "Even if I did, he wouldn't have much say about what I do."

Razor rested his hands on her shoulders as she worked at cutting the thick cloth from his waist. "I would," he answered in a surprisingly husky voice.

Her head jerked up in surprise at the change in his voice. He caught the soft gasp on her lips. He pressed his lips against hers like she had done earlier. He did not understand what it meant to do this. He just knew he wanted to feel her lips again. His people did not press their lips to another. Their sharp teeth and aggressive behavior made it too dangerous, but her teeth were smooth. He groaned as her tongue tentatively touched his lips.

He had an overwhelming urge to rub his nose along her neck and face. He wanted to leave his scent on her so others would know that she belonged to him. He wanted to mark her as his. He tore his mouth free from hers as the thought ripped through his mind.

Mine, he thought in shock as he swayed. *She is mine.*

"Hey, big guy. Hold on to me," she was saying as she wrapped her arm around his waist. "You're beginning to crash from shock and your injuries. Let me check your leg, then I'll see if you are hurt anywhere else."

"I… You are…," he muttered before he slid down the wall she had backed him up against.

"Yeah, I am," she teased in a light voice. "Destin has a tendency to mutter the same thing whenever I'm around."

Razor's eyes cleared for a moment at the mention of the other male. "Who is he? What is he… to you?"

Slender fingers tenderly ran down his face before cupping his cheek. "He's my brother," she replied simply.

Exhaustion, pain and his injuries darkened his vision, even as he tried to fight it. The feel of her slender fingers tenderly caressing him felt unbelievably good. He had never before experienced such a sense of rightness like he felt now at her touch.

"Mine," he muttered in a slurred voice. "What are you called?"

Her soft, warm breath caressed his face as she leaned forward to hear what he was trying to say.

"I'm called Kali," she chuckled. "Kali Parks."

Razor tilted his head back against the wall behind him. "You are mine, Kali," he whispered faintly.

"Whatever makes you happy, big guy," she chuckled again as his eyes closed. "Whatever makes you happy as long as you don't die on me."

Her words registered like a gentle breeze in his mind. A small, unfamiliar smile tugged at his lips as he closed his eyes. He had a feeling that having her under him would make him very happy.

Mine, he thought as darkness descended around him. *My Amate.*

5

"Razor," the deep voice quietly called out from behind him.

Razor didn't bother to turn. His eyes were focused on the three figures running, or should he say 'jumping', through the ruins of the city below. He was following one figure in particular. The slender form in the front was covered in black and slipped in and out of the shadows, at times disappearing from his view. He cursed under his breath when that happened and quickly switched to infrared so he didn't lose her. His gut tightened when he saw another human rise from behind a destroyed transport and open fire on the group.

"What is the current report?" he growled as his second-in-command approached to kneel beside him.

His eyes continued to follow Kali as she flipped in midair, sailing over a burnt out shell of another transport while pulling two firearms out from her waist. She landed and rolled, coming up on one knee, before firing the weapons in her hands in rapid succession. He released his breath when she hit both targets.

"The fighting between the two factions has escalated. Intelligence information states the two males identified as Destin Parks and Colbert

Allen are fighting for control of Chicago, as you know. It would appear some of Parks men may have been responsible for the theft of the military equipment used to shoot down the helicopter you were in," Cutter said quietly as he raised his viewer to his eyes to watch the conflict below. He whistled under his breath when he saw the figure take out the two men with a clean shot to the head. "Nice shooting. If nothing else, some of these humans would make good warriors."

Razor ignored the comment as he continued to observe the figure as it rose. Kali. His. That was all he could think about over the past two weeks since she vanished after flagging down several members of the search team looking for him and leading them to where she had left him. Since then, he had ordered every piece of information available on her delivered to him.

Tonight, there were two other men with her. He watched as she turned and called out to them. They knelt next to the dead men, talking for several minutes. Frustration ate at him that he could not hear what they were saying.

He reluctantly lowered his viewer as they turned and began moving away. It was the same each night. He was slowly piecing together a pattern of her movements. Kali frequently traveled with one or more men. Jealousy flared at the thought of other males near her. He wondered if these males meant something to her. He had seen them with her on more than one occasion. It wouldn't matter. He had already made his decision. She was his.

"Wasn't that the female who saved your life?" Cutter asked suddenly, turning to look at him with a puzzled expression.

"Yes," Razor bit out in a low, savage voice.

Razor scanned the area once more before standing. Since he regained consciousness in the medical unit aboard his Flagship, the *Journey*, two weeks ago, he had been studying both forces with an intensity he hadn't felt since he took command of his first warship. While each side was fierce and methodical in their attacks, there was a clear difference in their styles. Destin Parks' followers routinely protected and worked at rebuilding the city, using more of a defensive rather than offensive strategy while Colbert Allen waged a war of terror and destruction. Those fighting under him were aggressive and ruthless; uncaring of the collateral damage done during their attacks.

This was why he found it difficult to believe that Parks was responsible for the attack on the helicopter. Something was missing, he could feel it in his gut. It didn't make sense.

The question that continued to bother him the most was from the Intel he had read through during his recovery. Human military aircraft had routinely been crossing the area for the past six months and none had been attacked. Why would they fire on the human helicopter now? What were the odds of the rebels picking one that was flying an unscheduled flight, at night, with him on board, and attack it?

Only a handful of humans were aware of his sudden change of transportation. A handful of humans… and members of the council. An immediate report was filed every time a Trivator warrior was injured or reported missing. He had learned a very valuable lesson thanks to his younger brother's new sister, Jordan. Hunter had informed him four months ago on his journey here that information proving Dagger may still be alive had come to light. A rescue mission was currently in progress.

The incident two weeks ago left too many unanswered questions. He wanted answers, especially for the one burning a hole through his chest every time he saw Kali Parks in danger like she was tonight. She could easily have been wounded or killed. Why would Destin Parks' allow his sister to constantly be exposed to such danger?

Watching Kali in action reminded him of some of the stories his brother, Hunter, had told him about the feats of his *Amate*. When Hunter told him about how Jesse had saved his life, not once, but twice, he thought his brother had been exaggerating. Now, after meeting Kali, he realized that Hunter's stories had probably downplayed what really happened.

He pushed aside his disappointment that he had only caught a brief glimpse of her tonight. He needed to find the answers to his questions – he had to because time was running out. He had already delayed his decision to level the city by using his injuries as an excuse. He knew it was because of the female and his reluctance to give the order confused him. There was no rational explanation for his reaction to her.

When he regained consciousness, he was sure he had been mistaken about his response to her. At first, he tried to justify his feelings as being due to his injuries. He had almost convinced himself that was the case until he caught her scent from the cloth lying on the table next to his bed in the medical unit. It was the one that she had tied around his leg.

Razor slipped his hand into the pocket of his pants and touched the soft piece of fabric. He carried it with him everywhere, even though her scent had faded from it, replaced with his own. Angered at the traitorous response of his body to her, he had set out on a ruthless mission to discover any information he could find pertaining to her and her brother. What he had found out about them had been disturbing.

Allen's forces outnumbered Parks' by almost two-to-one. Unless something was done, and soon, Chicago would have to be declared a hostile zone and he would be forced to order the Destroyers in. When that decision was made, all inhabitants that resisted would be immediately eliminated without prejudice. He had a feeling Kali and her brother would be two of those who would refuse to leave. He would not risk his men's lives in trying to negotiate with the remaining rebels; enough Trivator warriors had been wounded or killed over the last six years. Yet, the thought of ordering Kali's almost certain death had been more than he could do.

A frustrated growl escaped him as he stood. "I know the fighting has escalated. I want you to tell me something I don't already know, Cutter. I want a meeting set up with Parks," Razor snapped out as he slid the viewer back into the clip at his waist.

"Are you sure that is wise?" Cutter asked cautiously. "So far both sides have refused to negotiate. Allen is demanding he be recognized as the leader of Chicago and given assurances that neither the World Government nor the 'fucking alien bastards' as he likes to call us interfere. Parks refused to meet with any alien representatives, he didn't give an explanation as to why, but I found out Badrick made a personal call two years ago. He was his usual charming self I suspect."

Razor glanced at Cutter, noting a fresh cut on his face. "I will meet with Parks before I make a decision as to whether the Destroyers should be brought in. What happened to you?" he asked, nodding to the thin cut on Cutter's cheek.

Cutter grimaced and touched his face. "I got a little too close to a resident of the city on my way here," he replied with a slight curve to his lips. "I'll have to be a bit more careful next time."

"Did you kill him?" Razor asked as he stepped into the small transport and nodded to his pilot.

Cutter stepped in behind him and sat down on the narrow metal seat. He pulled the straps over his shoulders and hooked it. He was quiet for several long moments before he looked up to see that his commander and friend was studying him with an intense expression that made him wince. Razor always seemed to know when he was trying to think of a way to avoid answering a direct question.

"No," Cutter sighed, looking out the open door as the small, military transport rose off the roof of the building. "I need to know in advance if you plan to level the city."

"Why?" Razor asked bluntly.

Cutter turned and glanced at Razor with a penetrating stare. "I have to find someone."

"I assume it is a human female," Razor said with a raised eyebrow. "She will leave once it becomes clear the area will be cleansed if the two factions refuse to cooperate and lay down their arms. If we can get Parks to agree to a truce it will be easier to contain the southern half of the city."

Cutter shook his head and turned to look at the darkening city below him. A few scattered lights glimmered from burning fires, but that was all. Everything else looked abandoned.

"I don't think she will," he replied quietly. "These females... they aren't like any others I've met before. You saw what the female that rescued you did tonight. They fight right alongside the males, especially if there are young involved."

"If a female has young then she will be more willing to leave," Razor remarked, looking at the tablet in his hands as he pulled up the new information Cutter sent to him about the two men fighting for power. "She will want to protect her young so she will leave when the order to abandon the city is given."

"She can't," Cutter bit out. "The kids aren't hers. They are children whose parents have died or abandoned them. She will not leave if she thinks any remain behind."

Razor looked up at the hard tone in Cutter's voice. "How do you know this?"

Cutter touched the cut on his cheekbone. "One of the little devils she protects told me," he admitted ruefully.

Razor's eyes narrowed on the teeth marks also gracing Cutter's hand. "This female, she bit you?" he asked, an amused glint lighting his eyes for a moment.

Cutter chuckled as he turned his hand and looked at the tiny set of marks. "Yeah, she bit me. I was surprised how strong she was considering she was so small," he admitted. "Just so you know, I also found out that Parks protects them as well. From what one of the boys she protects told me, Parks has provided protection, food, and medicine for the northern half of the city for the past six years. It was only in the last two years that Allen made a move to take over the northern half of the city."

"Why?" Razor murmured, looking at the data on the tablet with a frown. "Why does Allen suddenly want the northern section of the city? He could have seized it six years ago by eliminating Parks when he had a chance."

Razor turned his gaze to look out over the remains of the city. He could clearly see the border separating the southern half of the city from the northern half. A crude barrier of collapsed building rubble had been piled up to make a twenty foot high wall that went in both directions as far as the eye could see.

It didn't keep all the intruders out. That was evident from the conflict he had observed earlier. Parks didn't have enough men to guard the entire length. Instead, small teams patrolled the line. Kali's group was one of dozens that moved through the shadows of the city.

For a moment, he became lost in thought as he remembered back to that fateful night two weeks ago when Kali had risked her life to save his. He resisted the urge to rub his leg where she had pulled the shrapnel out of it. The wound was already healed. It had been minor compared to what would have happened if she hadn't suddenly appeared. He would have been dead. He had no illusions of what his fate would have been without her assistance. For that he owed her a life debt, something that did not sit well with him.

"Razor," Cutter said, breaking into his thoughts. "Did you get the information that I sent to you?"

Razor gave a brief nod before he pushed his memories aside. He wanted to know what would drive two men who had been friends at one time apart to the point they were trying to kill each other. He also wanted to know how two men with such different views could have been friends at one time. The more he studied the situation, the more questions he discovered he had.

In frustration, he turned off the tablet and stared out over the ruined Earth city. He had seen the same countless times before on other worlds. The difference with this species was they were the ones who had destroyed their own cities as panic overwhelmed the population. They had refused to believe the initial first contact when greetings of peace had been given.

So far, he wasn't impressed with this species' ability to contribute to the growth of the Alliance. The humans still held too tightly to their various superstitions. This was one of the things that hindered their progress. The only thing the humans had going for them was their will to survive. They adapted, some faster than others, but they adapted. They had little choice now that they knew they were no longer alone in the universe.

6

Kali moved silently through the underground corridors of a fortified former mall that was the current headquarters of her brother, Destin. She nodded to the few people she passed, but didn't speak with them tonight. Her mind was focused on what had happened earlier.

Even though she was only twenty-three, she moved with a quiet confidence that spoke of strength and power. She was in charge of her brother's personal security team, in addition to helping patrol the perimeter that protected the people living in the northern section of the city. Those responsibilities left little personal time that she could call her own. She was constantly on the move, either meeting with the members of their security team, evaluating and planning defensive maneuvers or working out to make sure she was in the best condition possible if her brother needed her protection.

Over time she had come to know and care about those living out on the streets and in the inner city they had created. While the times and the world around them had changed dramatically, the people remained the same. They were still the ones that laughed and scolded her and Destin when they ran through the streets as children causing mischief and enjoying their freedom.

A small smile of remembrance curved her lips when she remembered their carefree childhood. She had never worried about what would happen. Destin, older by three years, always had her back as she had his. They were not only brother and sister, but best friends. In a crazy world, they had lived a crazy existence of freedom, roaming the streets and rooftops like the city was their personal playground. Her lips drooped before tightening when she remembered the only other person that she had trusted above all others at one time – Colbert.

He had begun to change long before the world had its first contact with aliens. They had reunited when that happened six years ago, but he had become a stranger to her and Destin. He ruled over the southern half while Destin took the northern half. It was easier to work together to protect and care for close to a million residents who refused to leave the city.

Kali had hoped they could become friends again when they banded together after the world dissolved around them. For a short period, it seemed as if they had, but everything changed two years ago when Colbert… Kali's mind shied away from the memories as her eyes burned. She refused to think about what had almost happened. Instead, she focused on the present.

She nodded to an older woman and young child, Mary Clark and her granddaughter, Beth. They both smiled back at her before turning a corner leading into the common area. Her heart pulled when she thought of all the destruction on the other side of the city. Destin was trying so hard to rebuild the city and the people living here while Colbert was tearing it further apart.

Kali cared about the people living here. She would do whatever she could to make their lives better. Unfortunately, her compassion came with a price. Her heart ached as she remembered the men and women who had died to protect those living here.

She had earned her position as Destin's chief of security by sacrificing a piece of her soul. Every time she sent one of her team members out and they didn't return, a piece of her died with them. What almost suffocated her, though, was when she took a life like she had tonight. Then, then the dark fear of what she was becoming threatened to choke her.

Knock it off, she admonished herself silently. *If I'm not careful, I'll become as crazy as William.*

"Kali, wait up," William called out from behind her.

Kali hid the grimace when she heard William call her name. *And that,* she added to herself, *is why I should never think such thoughts. William will invariably know.*

"Troy said you killed two men tonight," William stated breathlessly as he tried to keep up with her quickening pace. "Do you want to repent for it?"

Kali ground her teeth together to refrain from saying anything that would hurt William's feelings. William had decided to become a born again preacher who believed in every faith known to mankind a few weeks ago. At seventy-two, she didn't know why he bothered. If he hadn't found religion before now, and from what she knew of his past he had not, she honestly didn't understand why he even wanted to at this late date. The only thing she could think of was that he hoped it might give him an edge if Colbert broke through their defenses, not that Colbert cared about what happened to his black soul.

If that son-of-a-bitch does break through, he'll be the one needing to repent, Kali thought savagely as hatred burned like lava in her gut.

"I have some holy water that I found in St. James Cathedral over on Huron and Wabash," William added holding up a battered whiskey flask.

Kali bit back a derisive remark when she glanced at the hopeful look on William's face. The water in the flask was probably rain water from the spring showers that had come through a few days ago. With a shake of her head, she stopped and looked at the withered face of the former Bookie and street corner Hot Dog vendor turned evangelist. Taking a deep breath, she gently covered the hand holding the flask up.

"William, I have nothing to repent. I think you should stay closer to the compound. We ran into some of Allen's men tonight," she calmly replied. "I wouldn't want you to get hurt if you should accidentally run into any of them."

"I...," he started to argue before he clamped his lips tightly together at Kali's look of warning. "I'll see if Mabel would like for me to hold a prayer session."

"You do that," Kali encouraged him before turning back to the lower section of the building. "Just make sure you stay at least a foot away when you do. Mabel is likely to hit you again if you start tossing water on her," she called out over her shoulder as she walked away.

"I'll stay at least three feet from her," William called out behind her. "She's using a cane now."

Kali shook her head and chuckled as she thought of William's current love interest. Mabel was as chipper and optimistic as they came. At almost eighty, Kali suspected she just started carrying the cane to keep William from tossing water on her again.

Turning the last corner, she pushed open the double doors, noting with satisfaction that Jason and Tim were standing alertly by the thick metal door leading to her brother's office. She nodded to them, murmuring her thanks when Jason opened the door for her. She brushed past him, ignoring the way his eyes lingered on her. She knew he was interested. Unfortunately, she wasn't.

She had no desire to complicate her life by getting involved with anyone. She had made a promise to herself after the Earth was invaded that she would not think of her own desires until it was free again. What she hadn't expected was that it would be the humans who would cause all the chaos and destruction. She realized now that she had been young and naïve.

It had taken two years for her to finally learn that the aliens had come in peace, not to conquer them. Even so, she still didn't trust them any more than she trusted – anyone, except for Destin. Her brother was the only one that she trusted to never betray her.

"Destin," she greeted softly as she entered the room. "We need to talk. Colbert's men are becoming more aggressive and… and I believe the Trivators are about to make a move into the city."

Her brother's frown pulled at the scar along his left cheek. He glanced at the door to make sure it was closed before he nodded toward the seat across from the battered metal desk he was sitting behind. Kali crossed the worn floor and sank down into the equally worn leather chair.

She knew better than to say anything until he finished with the report he was reading. She hid the grimace when the frown on his face darkened and he shot a fierce glance at her. Troy or Richard must have already submitted their report before she got back. While they had all been together on the perimeter check and when they encountered Colbert's men, she had stayed out a bit longer afterwards.

Kali shifted slightly in the chair as she thought of the reason for her delay in returning. She had known 'he' was watching again. Every night for almost the past two weeks he had been waiting… searching… watching.

She glanced down so Destin couldn't see her troubled eyes. He had enough to worry about without her adding her nagging feelings to the load he carried on his broad shoulders. It may have been a mistake to save the alien, but she couldn't leave him once she knew he was alive and injured. She just hoped it wasn't a mistake she lived to regret one day.

"Tell me," he demanded, his deep voice echoing in the quiet room.

Kali shuttered her feelings behind the calm mask that she had learned to hide behind after Colbert's betrayal. She lifted her head and stared back at her brother, noting the lines of fatigue around his eyes and mouth. She also saw the concern.

She released a sigh and tucked her short brown hair behind her ear. "You know about the three men tonight?" she said more than asked.

"Yes," he replied, tapping the report in front of him. "Colbert's growing brasher. You were lucky you weren't killed tonight, Kali. Troy said that you were caught out in the open."

"I knew they were there," she replied in a soft voice. "I caught a glimpse when we were topside, but lost them. They were almost five blocks inside the barrier. That is the farthest they've made it so far. I wanted to know how they were getting through. We followed them, but lost sight again as we got closer to the line. I couldn't let them get back across."

"So you used yourself as bait?" Destin bit out. "I need you alive, Kali. Foolish decisions like that won't keep you that way."

Kali's mouth tightened at her brother's quiet reprimand. Her fingers curled until her hands were fisted in her lap. She fought and won the battle with her temper. She didn't lose it often, but when she did, shit usually hit the fan.

Instead, she counted to ten and drew in a deep, calming breath before replying. "We needed to find the weak area. I did, in the form of a traitor. Jeffrey was with them."

Destin's head snapped back in shock before his eyes narrowed in rage. Jeffrey was a relatively new member of the city who claimed to have found his way here after coming down from Canada. He had recently been assigned as a perimeter guard.

"Damn it. I should have known," Destin cursed out as he stood up. He ran his hand through his own short hair in frustration. "What did you discover?"

"There is an underground utility tunnel that we missed," she replied. "I've given the information to Mason. He and his crew are sealing it even as we speak. That's why I was late. There may be others. I've instructed Mason to go back through the archives to see if there are any more building plans available. From the look of the tunnel, I would have to say it was built at the beginning of the last century."

"Damn it! You went down there? Alone?" Destin asked, glaring angrily at her. "What if there had been more of Colbert's men down there? Kali, if Colbert gets his hands on you..."

Kali's eyes softened at the slight fear that crept into her brother's eyes as he remembered what had almost happened before. She stood up and walked over to him. Wrapping her arms around his waist, she rested her head on his chest. Her eyes closed as she listened to the steady beat of his heart. They only had each other and it terrified both of them when they thought how close they had come to losing each other.

"He won't," she promised as he held her close. "He isn't smart enough, and he knows if I ever get near him again, it will be to shove a knife through his heart."

Destin's soft chuckle pulled a smile to her lips. "You've turned into a blood-thirsty little demon," he remarked before he sobered and released her to step back. "You have to be more careful."

"I will," she teased as she returned to her seat. She was glad she had when he answered her next question with one of his own. "So, what are you going to do about Jeffrey?"

"I should kill his ass, but I'll probably just have him escorted out of the city," he replied tiredly as he returned to his own seat and sat down. "Now, when are you going to tell me about your encounter with the Trivator warrior and why you think they are going to be making a move on the city? I've been waiting two weeks and you still haven't submitted your report on that incident."

"Shit!" Kali exclaimed in irritation. "You weren't supposed to know about that."

7

Razor walked through the corridor of the facility he had been given. He nodded to several warriors and human personnel as he strode through the long corridor toward his office. Irritation burned in him as Cutter explained that Councilor Badrick from the Usoleum Star System was waiting for him.

"Three humans from the northern section of the city have requested a meeting with the leaders of the Alliance, specifically the Trivator commanders," Cutter muttered. "I don't like this. Badrick is here and has demanded your presence when he heard they were here. He said they wanted to negotiate with us to secure the city."

"There is no negotiation. Is Parks one of the men?" Razor asked impatiently as he walked into his office. Since he arrived on the planet he could see what part of the problem the Alliance continued to have with the humans were - each faction wanted to make their own rules and demands instead of learning to live together as one species.

He stared intently into the nervous brown eyes that turned to glance at him in shock as he stepped into the room. "You will cease fighting immediately or those who continue to fight will be eliminated. The Alliance will select who will oversee the rebuilding of the city."

Razor watched nonchalantly as the human male swallowed several times. The male to the left of him nervously shifted while the male to the right glared back at him with hatred. Razor knew immediately which male would fight and which ones would back down. The male doing the talking was not the leader of this group of supposed representatives and none of them were Parks.

He and Cutter both smelled the faint odor of explosives when they walked further into the room. He ignored Cutter as his friend and second-in-command moved to the side so he could circle around the third male.

Badrick, the stupid, arrogant fool that he was, had walked into a deadly trap. Now, he and the human military officers in the room were in danger. This is why the Trivator were in charge of the military for the Alliance and not the Usoleums. His arm swept up as he pointed the laser pistol in his hand at the head of the third male staring back at him with loathing.

"Concede," he growled in a low, dangerous voice.

The male's hand moved slightly toward his belt. Razor didn't wait. He pulled the trigger. The two males standing in front and to the side of the human jumped in panic as the male collapsed. Coarse expletives filled the room as the human military grabbed the remaining males. One of the human officers reached for Razor but backed off when Razor turned the pistol in his hand toward him.

A loud sigh filled the air. "Was that really necessary, Razor? The negotiations were going well," Councilmen Badrick remarked sardonically, looking with distaste at the dark blood staining the finely woven carpet on the floor.

Razor turned his eyes to the slender male with long white hair and faint blue-tinted skin. There was no love lost between the two of them. He knew Badrick didn't always approve of his methods. In fact, he had been the lone dissent on the Alliance Council asking for Razor to step in.

The council really had no other choice. Razor had already informed them that no more Trivator warriors would be sacrificed on this world. Either they allowed him to end the last areas of rebellion, or he would pull the warriors and let the Alliance security teams deal with them alone. Six years was longer than it had taken to bring any of the other worlds the Alliance had inducted under control.

"Yes, it was necessary. Your species does not have the sense of smell a Trivator does. If you did, you would have smelled the explosives on the male. Did you not have your security team check the humans before you agreed to meet with them?" Razor asked in a cool voice.

Badrick looked down at the dead male with disdain. He shrugged his slender shoulders as he looked back at Razor. He was very careful to keep his true feelings hidden. He was well aware of the Trivator warrior's opinion of him.

"I will talk to the security team. I had assumed they would have checked the humans before allowing them inside the building. Are you sure he had explosives on him?" Badrick asked in a calm voice.

"Press the detonator button he has at his waist and let me know if I'm wrong," Razor replied before he looked at the two remaining rebels. "Who sent you?"

The male who had originally been doing the talking swallowed several times as he looked at the laser pistol now pointed at his head. He paled and began to tremble violently as he opened his mouth to speak. He stumbled several times before he finally choked out one name.

"Parks," he whispered.

Razor pulled the trigger before he turned it to the last man. "One last time," he snarled in a low voice. "I want the truth this time. Who sent you?"

The other man's eyes widened for a moment before he shoved the MP holding his arm. He reached for his waist at the same time as Razor pulled the trigger. A bright stain of red spread over the front of the male's chest as he collapsed.

"Well, at least we know which side to contact now," Badrick remarked as he wiped a small splattering of blood from his cheek.

Razor's eyes turned to coldly observe the other councilman. "He was lying. Parks did not send them."

"Of course Parks did," Badrick said with disdain. "The human admitted it before you killed him. Parks obviously does not want Allen to receive additional support. He probably knew that our forces were going to join with Allen so he wished to eliminate you in the hopes of blaming it on Allen."

"Do you really believe the shit coming out your mouth or are you just that stupid?" Cutter asked under his breath.

Badrick turned and coldly looked Cutter up and down. "You are dismissed. In fact, all of you are dismissed. This is a matter between Chancellor Razor and myself. Your presence is not required," he stated with contempt.

"Now, wait just a damn minute," Colonel Baker, the human commander for the area interrupted. "I'm in charge of this district. I want to hear Councilman Razor's observations on the matter."

Razor watched as Badrick turned sharply and took a step threatening step toward the human. His eyes flickered to Cutter who nodded. They both knew how volatile the Usoleum male could be when he didn't get his way.

"The human stays," Razor stated with an underlying tone of warning. "Control yourself Badrick. The Alliance Council granted that it would cooperate with the human military. Colonel…" Razor's eyes shifted briefly to the human male before turning back to Badrick who stood clenching his fisted hands at his side. "… Baker is within his rights to remain."

Badrick drew in a hissing breath before his cold eyes turned back to Razor's challenging stare. He forced himself to relax. Stepping back, he briefly bowed his head to show he recognized the quiet threat in Razor's voice.

He shielded the hatred in his eyes even though he knew the Trivator could smell it. The cynical amusement in Razor's eyes were like claws ripping through his gut. It perturbed him that he had not known the human male had an explosive on him. He would be having a conversation with his new security team as soon as he got rid of the two Trivator warriors.

"My apologies," he said with a fake smile. "Of course the human may remain. Perhaps we should retire to the Colonel's office while your second oversees the removal of the bodies?"

"Agreed," Razor replied. "Cutter, see if you can discover where the explosives came from and review the documented images to determine which side of the city the men belonged to."

"Documented images?" Badrick asked with a frown. "You have images of the men on each side?"

"I like to know who I am fighting against. It helps to know how they think and move to minimize the amount of threat to my men," Razor briefly answered.

"Of course," Badrick muttered, turning to walk through the doorway leading to a back corridor.

Razor paused when the human Colonel stopped next to him. He glanced at Cutter who raised his eyebrow in inquiry before turning slightly toward the human male. The man's troubled eyes were not on him but on the back of Badrick. Suspicion darkened the already dark brown eyes until they looked almost black.

"He refused to let my men search them," Baker muttered under his breath. "He also had them by-pass the security scanners. I don't trust that bastard, neither should you."

"I don't trust anyone but my own men," Razor replied.

Baker nodded in understanding. "I know what you mean," he agreed. "Did you really order the destruction of Mexico City?"

"Of course. They refused to concede," Razor replied as he turned toward the corridor to follow Badrick. "As I said before, I do not negotiate."

Colonel Baker stared after the huge alien male as he walked confidently down the hallway. He swallowed as he ran his eyes over the thick muscles straining against the dark fabric of the alien's black uniform. He had been in the military for almost thirty years and was looking forward to his retirement when the Trivator warriors first appeared six years ago. All military personnel had been called to active duty and all retirement suspended until the threat was over.

Unfortunately, they had been expecting the threat to come from the aliens, not the citizens. At least not to the magnitude it had. When rioters, government reformers and religious zealots poured out, they were split in half. He had quickly moved up the ranks from Staff Sergeant to Colonel due to the lack of resources and his experience as more men and women were called to action.

It soon became clear that while there were more humans, the Trivator out-powered them, had far superior technology and extremely well trained soldiers, or warriors, as he later learned they called themselves. When the United States Commander-in-Chief ordered a cease-fire, the military followed those orders; unfortunately, the civilians did not and so the fight continued. Only this time, it was citizen against citizen in a world gone crazy. In desperation, governments around the world met and agreed that if humanity was to survive, they would have to accept not only the aliens who came to Earth at their innocent invitation, but each other.

I just hope that bastard knows what he is doing, Baker thought as he followed Razor down the corridor. *I sure as hell don't want to be the one to stop him like I've been ordered to do if he tries to flatten the damn city.*

8

Kali breathed a sigh of relief as she escaped her brother's office. He had questioned her for over two hours, pulling everything he could out of her before she convinced him it was better for them to review every inch of their defenses, weapons and evacuation routes for those living in the city just in case the Trivator did decide to attack. By the time they were done, she was more than ready to get out for a while.

"Hey Kali, wait up!" Jason called out from behind her.

Kali quietly groaned under her breath. She wanted to run. She needed to run. Right now, confusion and frustration were making her antsy and she needed to escape to a place where she could be alone to think about the discussion and strategies she and Destin had just gone over.

It still shocked her that her brother knew about her rescuing the alien. His question had thrown her off guard at first before she realized that a helicopter crash and three Trivator rescue ships hovering above the barrier dividing the city wasn't something she could easily hide. An incident like that would immediately be brought to his attention, as he so eloquently pointed out to her.

The first hour he had grilled her about what had happened and why she felt like the Trivator might be taking a more definitive stance compared to their previous actions. He also wanted to know everything she could tell him about the warriors she had seen.

She told him what she could, without, she hoped, revealing how much her encounter with the male had shaken her or the fact that she had been on Colbert's side of the city. She hadn't been able to stop thinking about the alien male and it was beginning to piss her off. It was only when she was running that she able to lock him away for a short period of time. Even that wasn't a guarantee anymore.

The last couple of days, the feeling that she was being watched – even followed - had grown worse, and the irritating male's dark face kept sneaking back into her thoughts when she least expected it. She knew he was watching her. She could feel it. Tonight, that distraction had almost gotten her killed. She didn't know what he wanted, but it was time she found out before the stupid lout ended up causing her to make a really dumb mistake.

"Kali, wait!" Jason called her again, this time a little more sharply.

Kali paused and turned to glare at Jason, a look of annoyance on her face. He flushed slightly at her raised eyebrow and tight lips. She wanted to make it obvious that she wasn't happy that he was interrupting her.

"What do you want, Jason?" she asked coolly.

He flushed again and came to a stop a few feet from her. "Are you going out again?" he asked bluntly.

Kali stiffened at the disapproval and suspicion in his voice. She didn't answer to anyone but Destin. From Jason's tone, it sounded like he was about to try to take his interest to a new level. It was time she nipped that idea in the bud.

"What I do is no one's business but my own and Destin's," she replied.

She watched as he shifted from one foot to the other before his jaw stiffened in determination. She knew she had made the right guess when his eyes flashed. It was time to set him straight.

"I heard about what happened earlier this evening. I can't believe Destin would allow you to put yourself in danger like that. You shouldn't be going out on patrol," he bit out in a low voice. "It is too dangerous. I said as much to Destin. He agreed with me. I've also told him of my interest in you."

Kali took a step forward, stopping when she was only a foot away from him. The temper that she had been fighting to control snapped like an overstretched rubber band. Hot fury poured through her. She was furious that not only did Jason think he had the right to talk to her brother about her behind her back, but that Destin had neglected to tell her about it.

"No one tells me what to do." She pushed her finger into his chest hard enough to knock him back a step as she spoke. "You have no right to talk about me behind my back. *I* am the head of Destin's security team. *I* am the one who decides what is and what isn't too dangerous," she snapped out coldly before dropping her voice lower in warning. "And *I* am the only one who decides who I shall or shall not be with."

Kali cursed silently to herself when Jason grabbed her wrist and yanked her forward. She remained unmoving, impassive as he crushed his lips to hers. She knew she could fight him. She even had a good chance of beating him, but she also knew that remaining unresponsive to him would have a greater impact than arguing or fighting. She knew she had made the right decision when he tore his lips away and released her.

"I want you, Kali," he muttered in a low, angry voice. "I plan to have you. We would make a good team."

Kali remained rigid, a calm mask hiding the trembling inside. She hated confrontations. While she had learned to deal with them, deep down they always left her feeling uncomfortable and shaky.

"You're a good man, Jason. I respect you, and we need you, but I'm not interested in a relationship with you or anyone else. There is too much uncertainty in the world right now," she continued, softening her tone when she saw the brief flash of hurt cross his face. "I made a promise that I would protect my brother and the people under him for as long as it took to rebuild our world."

Jason swore and reached out to cup her face between his hands. "We can do that together, Kali. Just give me a chance. Let me in," he responded in a low desperate voice. "Don't… don't say no. Not yet. Think about it. I'll give you time… just, think about it. Life is too short to live it alone."

Kali lifted her hands and wrapped them around his wrists, pulling them down and letting them go before taking a step back. She shook her head when he started to take a step forward. She didn't need time. She knew that the moment his lips touched hers. All she could think about was the feel of another man's lips pressed against hers. A man who refused to leave her alone. A man who wasn't human.

"I have some things to take care of," she murmured, turning away. "I'll be back in a few hours."

Kali could feel Jason's eyes on her back as she hurried away. A part of her wished she could feel something for him, even if it was just a small attraction. The frustration she had felt earlier grew even stronger the closer she got to the entrance to the former mall.

She pushed through the heavy doors, ignoring the four men standing guard on each side of the re-enforced barrier protecting the front entrance. She was already thinking of where she was going to go. She knew he would be there. She could feel it in her bones.

Kali broke into a run, heading away from the makeshift compound Destin had created and toward the place where she hoped she could lay to rest the feelings threatening to overwhelm her. She would go back to the place where they first started. She would lay to rest her foolish thoughts of an alien male once and for all.

9

Razor landed the compact Skid gently down on the rooftop of the building. He climbed off the small bike-like transport that was perfect for moving quickly over congested areas. He scanned the surface of the rooftop as he did. The twisted remains of the rooftop crane bent awkwardly over the side of the building. The broken remnants of the sign that once proudly displayed the name of the building were mixed with pieces of brick, mortar and helicopter fragments.

"What were you doing up here that night?" he murmured quietly, looking up at the remains of the sign.

"Thinking… dreaming… wishing," a soft voice responded from the darkness behind him. "I love staring up at the stars. On a calm night, I would stand up on the top of the sign, close my eyes and imagine I could fly out over the city."

Razor turned sharply, inhaling deeply as Kali's slender shape stepped from the shadows of a large section of the crane. He watched her as she warily approached him. His eyes swept over her figure, memorizing every inch of her now that he could think without his mind being hazed with pain and shock.

She stopped several feet from him. A soft, nervous laugh escaped her as she stepped to the left of him to circle around so she could see the Skid he had ridden. He watched her thoughtfully as she knelt down to look at the transport. She whistled under her breath in appreciation as she studied it.

"You can if you wish," he replied as a sudden idea took hold in his mind. "I could take you over it, over the city, on the Skid."

Amusement tugged at Razor when he saw her eyes widen in delight before suspicion darkened them again. She bit her bottom lip before she shook her head and stood. He twisted to follow her with his eyes as she put more distance between them.

"Thanks, but no thanks," she replied in a husky voice. "Why have you been watching me?"

"Why did you save my life?" he responded instead.

He stepped closer to the Skid as she took another step away from him. It took a moment for him to appreciate that she had strategically placed his transport between them as a barrier while he was distracted. She was standing near the spot where the helicopter had been hanging from the crane two weeks before. While she didn't turn her back to him completely, he could see she was looking at the remains of the helicopter far below.

"What happened to the pilot?" she murmured as she stared down at the twisted skeleton far below before she turned to look at him with sad, troubled eyes. "Did he have a family? A wife? Sister? Brother? Parents?... Children?" she asked in a strangled voice that faded on the last word.

"His body was returned to his people. I do not know if he had a family," Razor admitted with a frown. "Why did your brother order an attack on me?"

He watched as her eyes jerked up to his in surprise before she frowned and shook her head. "Destin didn't order an attack on you. We don't have… it wasn't us. The rocket came from Colbert's side of the city," she finished. "I want to know why you have been watching me. I want you to stop. It's… I want you to stop."

Razor stepped around the Skid, pausing when she moved back a step. "Be careful; that area is not stable," he bit out sharply. "Why did you save my life? You could have left me to die, but instead you risked your own life. Why? Why does your brother continue to refuse to meet with me?"

Kali stepped to the side, keeping a wary eye on the huge male. He seemed even bigger tonight then he had the night of the accident. She had been lying on the roof of the fresh air intake near the bottom of the crane when she saw him approaching. She knew if she stayed perfectly still it would be difficult, if not impossible, for him to see her since she was dressed all in black as well.

She hadn't been able to stop herself from answering his softly spoken question. She didn't know or understand why she had told him about her fantasy. It had just slipped out.

Drawing in a deep breath, she decided there was no harm in telling him the truth. Hell, she had never been a good liar anyway. Her mom and Destin always knew when she was telling a fib.

"I couldn't leave you," she finally admitted, glancing at him to see his reaction. "I mean, I didn't know that you were in the helicopter. I thought it was a couple of human guys. It wasn't until I was in it that I realized that you were a… you."

"You still could have left me," he commented, stepping to the side and walking toward the edge so he could look down at the wreckage. "When you realized that I was on board, you could have just left. Instead, you almost died."

Kali gave a short laugh and reached up to grab one of the metal support beams above her head. She curled her legs up under her so she was hanging from it before she put her feet back down on the roof and leaned back. She thought for a moment as she stared at his profile before she decided she was in too deep to stop now.

"I told you it wasn't my night to die," she teased quietly before she sobered and continued. "You might be an alien, but you are still a living being. I knew I couldn't leave you and I knew the crane couldn't hold that much weight for very long. Waiting for your people to show up wasn't an option. Once I saw that you were injured, well, that just sealed it. I was the only one there and you needed help if you weren't going to end up like yesterday's road kill."

"Why does your brother allow you to be in such danger? Tonight…." He drew in a deep breath and his eyes flashed a dark yellow-gold before he continued. "Tonight you were almost killed."

"You saw what happened? I was right then. You have been watching me," Kali breathed out, this time pulling herself up so that she was sitting on the narrow bar that she had hung from a moment ago. "I knew it. I could feel it. How long have you been watching me?"

"A week and a half," he bit out, taking a step toward where she was sitting. "Answer me! Why would your brother allow you to be in such danger? Does he not care what happens to you?"

Kali's eyes briefly flashed in outrage at the contemptuous tone in his voice when he said Destin's name. He knew nothing, absolutely nothing, about Destin. If he did, he wouldn't be siding with Colbert.

She hissed as she remembered what the other alien male had told her and Destin two years ago. The aliens were one of the reasons Colbert had increased his attacks. They were the ones supplying weapons, granted human weapons, but weapons all the same to Colbert in an effort to defeat Destin and take over the northern half of the city.

"You know nothing about my brother!" she hissed out angrily, standing up on the bar. "If you did, you would know he loves me more than life itself just as I love him. Why are you supporting Colbert? Don't you know what he is like? Don't you see how he doesn't care about the people living in the southern half of the city? Every day we take in refugees seeking a safer way to live. He doesn't care about anyone or anything."

Razor's mind caught her accusing words even as he moved forward to capture her waist when she turned to climb higher on the bent framing of the sign. His hands wrapped around her, almost touching as he pulled her back against him. He ignored the short, frightened cry she emitted as he wound his arms around her to prevent her from escaping into the darkness.

"Calm," he murmured in her ear as she struggled against him. "Be still, Kali Parks. I mean you no harm."

Kali froze in his arms. "Then let me go," she whispered throatily. "You owe me that. I saved your life. Let me go."

Razor moaned softly and rubbed his nose along her neck. A low rumble escaped him, surprising him as he caught the faint scent of another male on her. He stroked his nose along her jaw as she tilted her head so she could look up at him.

"Another male has been near you," he growled in a dark voice. "Who is he to you?"

Kali jerked in surprise and tried to move away from him when he rubbed his nose along her jaw again. A shiver ran through her, startling her. She didn't know what in the hell he was doing, but it felt… right.

"Let me go," she demanded.

She turned her face away from him, ashamed that what she really wanted to do was relax back into his arms. She pushed back against him. This wasn't what she wanted, she told herself fiercely. She had come here to resolve her confusing feelings, not create more.

"Who is he, Kali?" Razor demanded.

"I don't know what you are talking about!" she snapped.

Kali wiggled against the hot body holding her, trying to work her arms loose from where he had them trapped by her side. She froze when a soft purring suddenly filled the air. If that wasn't enough to make her realize the potential danger she was in, the feel of a very aroused male pressed against her backside was enough to set off every built-in set of survival alarms that she had cultivated over the past six years.

"Who is he, Kali?" the husky voice asked again.

"I… I… It must be Des… Destin you… smell," she stammered. "I… I gave him a hug. Or it might be…"

"Who?" he growled in a deep voice that sent shivers racing through her. "Or it might be… who, Kali?"

"Jason," she choked out as he ran his nose along the side of her neck again. "It could be Jason. He… he grabbed me and…"

Razor spun her around in his arms. His hands wrapped around her wrists even as he pressed her back against the metal upright support. He pulled her arms up above her head, forcing her to look into his glittering eyes.

"And," he pressed in a low menacing voice.

"He kissed me," she whispered, staring up into his eyes wondering how they could glow like that. "Did you know your eyes glow when you are mad?"

Razor closed his eyes and breathed in deeply, fighting to calm the primitive rage that swept through him at the thought of another male touching his female. It took a moment for her words to sink in, when they did an unfamiliar sound escaped him - laughter. It started out as a low, rusty sound before turning to a deep, mellow chuckle. He opened his eyes to stare down at her upturned face.

"You do not belong to him," he stated firmly.

"Who? Jason?" she muttered in surprise. "Of course not! I told you before that…"

Razor leaned forward and rested his forehead against hers. "…even if you did belong to a male, he would not have much say about what you do."

"You remember that?" she asked in surprise.

"I remember everything about you," he admitted with a sigh, releasing her arms so he could slide his hands down to her waist. "I do not understand the effect you have on me. No female has ever caused me to feel this way before," he confessed reluctantly.

"Feel what?" she asked in curiosity before she shook her head fiercely from side to side. "No, don't answer that! I don't want to know. I came here tonight because I had a feeling that you would be here. I just wanted to find out if you were watching me and to tell you to stop. I don't like it. It… it is distracting me, which is dangerous," she finished in a faint voice. "What are you doing?"

"Mm?" he hummed in a low, distracted voice. "I'm marking you."

"Marking me!" she squeaked as he ran the bridge of his nose up along her left cheek. "What on Earth for? You aren't like giving me some weird alien disease thingy, are you? I swear if you are, I'll chuck your ass over the side of the build…"

Her voice died as his lips brushed against hers. "What is this thing? You did it when you pulled the shard from my leg. I like it," he murmured, touching his lips against hers again.

Kali pulled back to stare up at him in disbelief before a mischievous glimmer darkened her eyes. She gazed at him for several long seconds trying to decide if he was serious. When she noticed the slight crease between his eyes and his intent gaze, she shook her head in amazement.

"Are you telling me you don't know what a kiss is?" she asked with a raised eyebrow.

"Of course I do. I studied your language on the way here. A human kiss is when you press your skin to another. It is the same as on our world. We brush against a female to show affection and to mark her," he growled. "I am marking you as mine, so other males will know my intentions."

"You know what?" Kali said, tilting her head to the side and staring up at him in amusement. "You may have studied the language, but you don't have a clue about the meanings."

"Then tell me," he demanded.

Razor's eyes narrowed in frustration as he tried to understand what was going on. Since he first met this human female his mind and body had been acting illogically. He couldn't focus and just the thought of her lips against his were enough to send his body spiraling out of control.

He hadn't had to seek relief by his own hand since he was an adolescent. Three times! Three times in the past week since he was healed, he had found the need to relieve the pressure from his loins. He thought seeing her, confronting her, would help him control his raging desires. Instead, he was more perplexed now. His frustration grew when she muttered under her breath before stepping closer to him.

"Oh hell, I have totally lost my frigging mind." Her softly spoken words echoed in his ears.

He was about to ask her what she meant before he became lost in the rush of heat sweeping through him as she ran her hands over his shoulders and rose on her toes to press her lips firmly against his. His lips parted as she moved her mouth against his at the same time as she touched her tongue to them. The moment he opened for her, she pressed forward, winding her arms tightly around his neck.

A deep moan escaped him as she splayed her hands through his short hair and pulled him closer. His arms tightened around her as he pressed her body along the length of his larger form. He needed to get closer to her. He needed to feel her under him. He needed to be *in* her.

A shudder escaped him when she changed the kiss to a slower more exploratory one. If he thought he understood humans based on the documentation that had been recorded over the past six years, he realized he was sadly misinformed. Nothing she was doing had been in the recordings. Nothing that he was feeling when they touched made sense to him.

He started to protest when she slowly pulled back. His hands slid down to her ass and lifted her up against him. He buried his face in the curve of her neck as she wrapped her legs around him. Taking a step forward, he pressed her back against the metal upright beam again.

Raising his head so he could look into her eyes, he lifted one trembling hand to thread his fingers into her short straight hair. Never before had he felt such an explosive reaction to a female. The primitive feelings of possessiveness, the need to mark, his need to claim her burned like the hottest star inside him.

"You are mine, Kali Parks. I claim you as my *Amate,*" he growled in a voice laden with desire and need before he captured her lips again.

10

"Let her go," a low, furious voice snarled from out of the darkness.

Razor stiffened as he partially turned. He kept one arm wrapped protectively around Kali as he glared over his shoulder at the male who stood in the doorway of the roof access. His eyes narrowed on the weapon in the male's hand. He released a dark growl of warning and flashed his sharp teeth.

"Jason! What are you doing here?" Kali hissed in surprise as she looked over Razor's shoulder.

"Trying to keep you from making the biggest mistake of your life," he snapped. He jerked his head at the huge Trivator that still held her. "I told you to let her go."

"He's right. You'd better let me go," Kali whispered with a chagrined sigh. Razor's head snapped around so fast that she jerked back in surprise, hitting the back of her head on the metal beam. "Ouch! Damn it."

"Kali," Jason started to say, taking a step forward.

"Stay back, human," Razor snarled in a menacing voice. "You are the one who dared touch my female. For that alone I should kill you."

"Your… who the fuck is this guy, Kali, and what the hell were you doing kissing him?" Jason demanded angrily.

"He's…." Kali paused as a look of dismay crossed her face. She looked at Razor and grimaced. "What's your name?" she muttered under her breath.

"You don't even know his name yet you're wrapped around him like some bitc…."

Kali stumbled and would have fallen if not for the beam at her back as she was suddenly released. She blinked in surprise several times as she stared at the back of the man she had just been kissing. One second he was holding her in his arms, the next he had Jason by the neck. Jason's feet dangled almost three inches off the roof. He had one hand wrapped around the wrist of the Trivator warrior while his other hand, the one holding the weapon, was being held in a crushing grip.

It took several seconds for it to dawn on Kali that Jason wasn't struggling as much as he had been and his eyes were beginning to roll back in his head. She rushed forward and grabbed the arm holding Jason. She turned her head, about to order the male to release Jason but the words died on her lips at the cold, ruthless look in the Trivator's eyes.

She drew in another breath before forcing the words past her lips. Her eyes went back to Jason's face even as she pulled fruitlessly on the arm holding him by his neck. She had never seen anyone so strong before. A silent curse flowed through her mind as she realized just how stupid she had been to forget that he was an alien.

"Please," she whispered, tugging on his arm. "Please, let him go."

"He touched you. He pressed his lips to yours," Razor snarled.

"Listen… what is your name?" Kali asked in desperation as Jason's head fell forward as he lost consciousness. "Please don't kill him. He's my friend. We need him. *I* need him. There aren't enough of us as it is to defend the northern half of the city. Please, I'm begging you. Please let him go."

Razor glared down at Kali for a moment before he dropped the male in disgust. He reached down and pulled the weapon from Jason's limp fingers. Turning, he tossed the gun across the roof where it skittered into the dark shadows. A dark foreign curse, at least that was what it sounded like to Kali, echoed in the air. Strong fingers wrapped around her arm and pulled her away from Jason when she bent to check on him.

"I am Razor. I am the Chancellor for the Alliance's Defenses and Commander over the Trivator Forces," he informed her in a cold, furious voice.

Kali jerked away from him in shock and fear. She slowly backed away from him, shaking her head in disbelief. She had heard of him. Talk spread fast around the world thanks to the large number of Ham Radio operators who shared what was going on.

"You...," she swallowed and stumbled backwards when he took a step toward her. "You ordered Mexico City and that other city destroyed."

Razor's eyes glittered as he took another step toward her. Fury built inside him as she stumbled away from him in fear. His nose flared and his mouth tightened when she glanced beyond him to the male lying unconscious behind him. She claimed she had affection for the male. That would end, along with her living in a constant state of danger. It was now his right to care for and protect her. She was his.

"Just as I will order Chicago leveled if the fighting does not stop. I will not allow any more Trivator warriors to be wounded or killed in the battle between your brother and Allen," he stated ruthlessly.

Shock, then fury, combined with the bitter taste of fear, began to boil inside of Kali as she stared into the cold, ruthless eyes of the male standing in front of her. She swallowed and desperately pulled on the mask she used to hide behind when she was nervous or frightened. She was Destin's protector, head of his security. She would do whatever she had to do to protect him and their people. She had to warn Destin who was coming.

"When do you plan on sending in the ships to destroy the city?" she asked in a voice that held a slight tremble in it.

"Now that I have you, I will give a twelve hour notification to lay down arms. Your brother and Allen will turn themselves in to the human leader of the area," he stated, watching her reaction.

"And… and if they… don't?" she asked in a husky voice.

"Then they and every other human who resists will die," he replied softly.

"No!" she gasped.

She swayed as the faces of William, Mabel, Mary Clark, little Beth and the thousands of other residents in the northern half of the city that depended on them flashed through her mind. She stumbled over a small pile of rubble as she took another step backwards. She had to warn Destin. He had said something… now that he had her… her troubled eyes cleared. If he didn't have her, maybe he wouldn't attack. She shook her head in denial. He would never have her. She would stand by her brother's side and fight, even if it meant giving her life for those she had sworn to protect.

"I will not allow you to put yourself in danger any longer, Kali. The fighting has gone on long enough. It is time for your world to begin the process of healing. Groups like your brother and Allen must be dealt with. I was brought in by the Alliance and given the authority to do whatever was necessary to end the conflicts so that your world could once again grow and prosper. Enough of my people have been wounded or killed over the past six years. I will not allow that to continue."

The other alien had warned them that a Trivator warrior named Razor would come and destroy everyone, everything, if they did not lay down their arms. He said he could prevent it if Colbert was given control of the city. The strange light blue alien had made a deal with Colbert, weapons for women, an offer he had made to Destin first. According to many of the refugees who fled the area over the past two years, females fourteen to forty were being rounded up and taken away.

She remembered the sick feeling in her stomach when the male first approached Destin. He had demanded a private meeting with her brother. Her skin had crawled when he had run his gaze up and down her with a licentious appraisal. Destin had agreed, knowing that she would not be far from his side. She had hidden inside a small closet in his makeshift office and listened to the offer the horrid male had proposed. Destin not only turned the male down, he had Jason and Tim escort the male from the north side of the city with the promise that he would kill anyone, human or alien, that tried to harm one female under his protection.

"Leave," she choked out as she shook her head again and pushed the memories away. "Leave our planet then. Leave us alone. We didn't ask you to come here. We don't need you. Your people have caused enough pain and death to us. Just… leave!"

"Your people did ask us to come. The messages were sent long ago, but your people reached out and we answered. It is too late to deny the existence of others outside of your world, Kali. Most of the death and destruction to your planet was caused by your species. Humans are in danger of dying out as a species if preventive measures are not immediately taken. Your people need the Alliance if you are to survive," he added cruelly.

Kali's hand went to her stomach as it rolled. She knew all about the talks of global warming before the Trivators came. She knew that the climate of the world was rapidly changing. She couldn't do anything about that, but this… this was something that she could fight against.

I have to stop him somehow, she thought in despair. *I can't let him destroy everything I know and love!*

She *had* to warn Destin! Pivoting on her heel, she refused to think of anything else but escaping back to her brother. She let instinct guide her when she heard the menacing snarl echo behind her as she darted for the edge of the building. She might not have a fancy transport like him to fly over the city, but she wasn't above creating her own wings.

She felt her muscles tighten as she neared the edge. She sent a small prayer of thanks that her eyes were adjusted to the darkness. She jumped, stretching out for the tangle of metal cable hanging like ghostly vines in the night. The palms of her hands burned and she could feel the skin tear on the steely threads, but she ignored the pain as she let the momentum carry her across to the roof of the building next to the former Harrison Hotel.

A cry of frustration escaped her when she realized that she would not make it. The distance was too far for her to try to safely land. She twisted her body as the pendulum of momentum shifted and she found herself swinging back toward the building she was trying to escape.

She blinked as the dark shadow of a window caught her attention. She twisted as she made contact with the frame. A small scream of pain tore from her throat as a jagged piece of glass cut a long path along her shoulder before she released the metal cable and crashed to the hard floor of a former hotel room.

Panic swept through her, driving her to her feet. She ignored the burning pain and the warm moisture that was running down her back. Cursing when she ran into a small side table that had been knocked over, she raced for the door. Pain poured through her arm when she gripped the door handle and tugged on it. If she wasn't so desperate to escape, she would have cried in frustration when she found she had to unlock it before she could open it.

Kali stumbled through the doorway and turned to the left. At the end of the long corridor there was the staircase. She knew the set on this side of the building were still intact until the second floor. She would have to switch to the east side staircase to get to the first floor. She just hoped she could make it down the stairs and escape into the maze of streets before Razor did.

"Oh God, please let me make it," she whispered as she pulled the door open to the stairwell and raced down the steps. "Please don't let him catch me."

11

Razor's eyes narrowed as he stared over the side of the building. His heart thundered in his chest as rage and fear fought for supremacy. The first emotion he was familiar with; the second he was not. The rough edge of the broken mortar bit into his palms as he watched Kali's dark form swing through the air. He wanted to cry out a warning when he realized the impossible feat she was attempting to accomplish.

He sucked in an uneven breath when she twisted in midair as she was pulled back toward the building. A low expletive escaped him when she hit the side of it and disappeared into the darkness. The sound of breaking glass and a muttered cry carried faintly above the icy wind that was beginning to build. He pushed away from the edge of the building and turned back toward the roof access. His mind raced ahead as he tried to think of every scenario.

He knew without a doubt that she would do everything she could to escape back to her brother. He had learned a lot about her over the past two weeks, both from the Intel submitted to him and his own personal observations. She was proud, protective, and courageous. All traits that he admired. He also knew without a doubt that she would fight.

Yes, she will not give in easily, he thought with a sense of pride.

His eyes swept the area where the human male should have been. A dark scowl crossed his face when he realized he was gone. The thought of the male reaching Kali before he could retrieve her shot a rush of adrenaline through him that he hadn't felt in years. The primitive need to hunt down his prey and capture it rose inside him. This is what made his species excel as warriors. While the Trivator had learned to control their primitive side, they were genetically designed to be predators.

He turned toward his Skid. She would have to leave the building. He would capture her before she could escape. He climbed onto the sleek air bike. Skimming his thumb over the control, he rose silently into the air. Leaning forward, he depressed the accelerator and shot over the roof toward the back side of the building. A long, narrow road ran between it and the next building.

He circled around the corner and hovered approximately six meters above the ground. He programmed the auto-pilot to maintain its position and snapped the small remote securely to the thick wristband he wore. Swinging his leg over, he silently dropped to the ground below. He knelt for a moment, listening and scenting the air. Once he was satisfied no other humans were close, he straightened before crossing over to where a service door stood ajar.

Kali grabbed the wall to stop from falling as she reached the bottom of the stairwell. Her legs felt shaky and she knew she was running on empty. The last week of interrupted sleep, combined with blood loss and the intense physical demands from her escape were threatening to overwhelm her. She shook her head in an effort to clear it. She couldn't stop yet.

"Kali," a quiet voice called out to her.

Kali jerked around, pressing her hand to her chest and her back to the wall as she strained to see. A shuddering breath of relief escaped her when Jason stepped out from the shadows. She weakly held out her left hand to him.

"Jason! Thank God you are okay," she whispered back in a faint voice. "We have to get out of here. I have to get to Destin."

Warm fingers wrapped around her hand and pulled her forward into his arms. A smothered whimper escaped her as the cut on her shoulder and back pulled apart at the pressure. She shivered as additional warmth ran down her spine.

"What's wrong?" Jason asked in a strained voice. "Did that bastard hurt you?"

"No, he didn't hurt me. I'll be okay once I get back to our base," she mumbled. "We have to move. I don't know where he is. He could come down the stairs at any moment."

"Are you sure?" Jason asked, straining to see her face. "If you're positive you're okay then let's get the hell out of here. That bastard is one scary son-of-a-bitch and I personally don't relish meeting up with him again," he added, rubbing his tender throat.

Kali nodded and leaned on Jason when he wrapped his arm around her waist as she swayed again. She started to protest when he pulled his hand back with another curse when he felt the sticky moisture of blood coating the back of the black sweat shirt she was wearing.

"Don't...," she started to say.

She grimaced when he ignored her and reached into his front pocket and pulled out one of the small flashlights they all carried. He looked at his hand before flashing it on the wall behind her. A crude expletive escaped him when he saw the dark smear on it.

"Turn around," he ordered in a rough voice.

Kali touched his face with the tips of her fingers. "We don't have time, Jason. We have to get back to Destin. If that..." She drew in a deep, shaky breath before she continued. "His name is Razor. He plans on flattening the city just like he did Mexico City. We have to warn Destin.

He said he is going to give the order to wipe out Chicago. Once the order is given, Destin and Colbert only have twelve hours to turn themselves in. If they don't... if they refuse... Razor said anyone who resists will die."

"Fuck!" Jason cursed.

"Jason, if I don't make it," Kali started to say before the words died on her lips as Jason laid his fingers against them.

"You'll make it, Kali," he whispered. "You are the strongest, most beautiful, most stubborn woman I've ever met. You'll make it."

A weak smile lifted the corner of her mouth. She didn't respond. In truth, she couldn't over the lump in her throat. With a nod of her head, she wrapped her fingers around his as he cupped her hand again. She ignored the burning pain and pushed pass her exhaustion. He was right. She would make it. Failure was not an option. She had sworn to protect Destin and those who sought protection under him. She would do anything and everything she could to keep them safe. She refused to give up without a fight.

Razor stood in the shadows behind a long counter. His eyes narrowed on the two figures as they pushed open the doorway leading into the former reception room. The front entrance was blocked by fallen debris from the helicopter and damage from the building, making it impossible to escape through it. His assumption that the slightly opened door was how they gained entrance to the building was correct.

His nose flared in anger at the possessive way the human male was holding Kali. Fear and concern swept through him when he saw her stumble and cry out in pain. He stepped out from behind the reception counter as she whispered to the male that she would be alright.

"You are hurt," Razor growled. "You need medical attention."

Kali froze as Razor's voice echoed in the silent room. A shiver of apprehension ran through her. His dark shape seemed more menacing amid the clutter of debris and destruction, especially now that she knew who he was. Only the faint light of the flashlight Jason was holding illuminated the area. She closed her eyes and leaned heavily on Jason as defeat swept through her.

"I'll hold him off," Jason muttered in a dark voice. "Run, Kali. Get to Destin."

"Jason…" her voice died as Jason suddenly pushed her toward the shattered front doors.

"RUN!" Jason snapped as he charged toward the dark warrior.

Kali felt a sparse reserve of adrenaline rush through her as she turned. The front was blocked except for a narrow sliver of space barely wider than a couple of feet. It would be a tight fit, but she was small and slender enough to squeeze through it.

She forced herself to ignore the sound of the struggle behind her. Grabbing the twisted metal frame of the door, she stepped through and started crawling up the slated slab of concrete blocking the way to freedom. As the space became narrower, she dropped further down until she was lying on her stomach. Lying flat, she ducked her head and began inching her way between the thick sheets of concrete.

The sound of a vicious snarl reverberated behind her before it was replaced with the distinctive sound of a body hitting something hard. Kali's breathing had turned to deep gasping breaths as she clawed her way through the debris. Fear engulfed her when silence fell from behind her. There wasn't enough room for her to turn her head to see what was happening. She could only hope that Jason was able to hold Razor off long enough for her to get through the obstacle course so she could disappear.

That hope died when she felt a pair of steely hands wrap about her ankles. She cried out in frustration and pain as she clawed fruitlessly at the concrete in an effort to break away from the manacles pulling her back. Inch by inch she was pulled backwards away from the narrow chance of freedom.

"NO!" she cried out as the hands moved up her legs until an arm wrapped around her waist. "No, let me go!"

"Calm, little *fi'ta,*" the dark voice murmured. "Calm, Kali. You are bleeding again. I must get you to my healer."

Kali's head fell back in exhaustion as he gently turned her in his arms. She stared up at him with bitter tears of frustration, pain, and hopelessness glittering in her eyes. A low cry of denial burst from her lips as his arms tightened around her as he picked her up.

"Jason!" she whimpered, trying to turn her head to look for him. "Jason!"

"He will live but he cannot help you now," Razor growled. "I told you, Kali. I will no longer allow you to put yourself in danger. You are lucky you didn't break your neck! If this is the kind of care your males give to the females, it is amazing that your species has survived this long. This is another reason why your species needs the help of the Alliance."

"Jason, please… warn Destin," she whispered, ignoring Razor.

"Twelve hours, Kali," Razor murmured as he carried her back through the reception area, down the corridor and out the back door of the old hotel. "It is all I can give him, *fi'ta*. I have my duties. I am… sorry."

Kali turned her head into his shoulder and closed her eyes as he approached the Skid that was slowly descending toward them. God, she was so tired. So, very, very tired. She would fight him, but she needed a few minutes first to rebuild her strength.

She breathed deeply, unaware that her body was already shutting down in response to the warm arms surrounding her. It was as if her body knew she was safe while her mind fought against it. Her thoughts drifted as she breathed in the soothing scent of the male holding her. Images flashed through her mind like a kaleidoscope, turning and changing.

Images of her mom, tired, but always cheerful from a long day at the restaurant, flowed like a vivid movie behind her closed eyes. Carla Parks stopped by the small, shabby apartment they lived in so she could check on Kali and Destin for a couple of hours before she left for her second job at the local corner store. Kali and Destin running. Her mom would listen as she and Destin told her about their daily adventures. Carla was an innate free spirit who saw nothing wrong with allowing Kali and Destin to run through the streets as children, laughing along with them as they learned how wonderful it was to be free to run and discover new adventures.

A single tear escaped as she remembered coming home from visiting a friend when she was seventeen. There were half a dozen police cars outside the small convenience store where her mom worked nights. She remembered Destin turning when she called out his name. She had been surprised that he was home from his college classes so early.

"Momma," she murmured restless. "Why? Why?"

Two young boys, one the same age as her and the other two years younger sat in the back of one of the patrol cars. She remembered glancing at them before turning back to Destin when he called out to her.

"She's gone," Destin's strained voice explained. "She was handing them the money from the register when someone came in. The gun went off. The police said she died instantly."

"No!" Pain swept through her as the memories held her imprisoned in their sticky web. She turned back and stared at the two boys. She knew one of them. "Randy, why? You knew her. Why?"

She could see Randy's blank eyes staring back at her as if it was yesterday before he turned his head and sunk down in the back of the car, ignoring her. The images turned and twisted again as Destin lead her away from the scene.

Now, her world was dissolving around her again. She cried out, reaching for Destin but he continued to walk away from her as if he couldn't hear her pleas for him to come back. She was sitting on the roof of their apartment building watching as the skies filled with alien spaceships. They didn't own a television, it was an expensive luxury that her mom could never afford, so she hadn't known what was happening at first.

People filled the streets as news of the 'invasion' as it was being broadcast spread. From high above Chicago, she had watched as day turned to night and the city became an inferno as panic spread and the worst of human nature erupted like a festering wound. She stayed on the roof, packing only the necessities that she could carry in her backpack and a small box containing the few trinkets of her mother's life. That was where Destin found her three days later. It had taken him that long to make it from the city college downtown to the government housing where she lived. In two short months, her life had changed forever.

Kali shivered and stirred as a light rain began to fall. The icy moisture woke her from her restless exhaustion. She tried to move, but found she was trapped against a hard, muscled body. One arm was wrapped protectively around her while the other held the grip of the Skid. She gasped and struggled to sit up as she became aware of what was happening.

"Careful," Razor cautioned in her ear.

"Where are we? Where are you taking me?" she asked nervously, pushing her damp hair out of her eyes.

She gripped the arm around her waist tightly as they wove between the buildings. The cold rain was helping to clear her mind. She recognized that they were flying over a section of the southern part of the city. She looked down, but she could see very little in the darkness.

"Back to the base that has been set up for the Trivator forces in this area," he replied.

Kali shivered as some of the rainwater seeped under her shirt and down her back. She moaned as the water touched the deep cut in her right shoulder. She leaned forward and bit her lip as a wave of dizziness swept over her. The arm around her tightened, pulling her back against the warm body behind her. She shivered again, but this time for a different reason. Razor's warm lips were pressed against the side of her neck as if he were trying to comfort her.

"I have contacted my personal healer. He will be waiting to care for you when we arrive," he informed her in a husky voice against her ear. "It won't be long now."

"I want to go home," she muttered. "Doc can stitch me up."

"No," he replied.

Kali stiffened before forcing her body to relax. There was nothing she could do at this moment. If she were to fight, she would kill them both. For a brief second, she considered that as an option before shaking her head in disgust. Killing him wouldn't stop the plans to destroy the city. Besides, she wasn't in any hurry to die either. No, the best plan was to play along with him and the minute the opportunity to escape presented itself, she would be a distant memory.

"Has anyone ever told you that you have serious social issues?" she asked with a tired sigh. "Bossing people around, kidnapping me and trying to kill one of my friends, not to mention threatening my brother, after I saved your life isn't winning any brownie points with me," she added dryly.

A deep rumble and the sound of masculine laughter ricocheted through her like a speeding bullet making her want to squirm when she felt an unfamiliar heat low in her belly. She snorted her displeasure even as she snuggled closer to his warmer body. She grimaced as she put pressure on the cut on her back. At least being half frozen was beginning to dull the pain.

"We are almost there," he murmured.

"Yippee," she snorted grumpily.

She closed her eyes when he chuckled again in that damn sexy voice of his. Maybe she could just push him off the damn air bike. That would solve at least one of her problems.

12

"I can walk, damn it," Kali growled in a slightly slurred voice. She blinked several times as rain blurred her vision and glared up at the stubborn facial lines of the male carrying her. "I've got a cut, not a broken leg."

Razor's mouth tightened. She had more than a cut, it was a bloody slice half the length of his arm and at least a quarter inch deep. From the shivers wracking her body, it was more than the cold affecting her as well. She was beginning to go into shock from blood loss. Her face was white and her eyes, while angry, were wide with a glaze to them.

He cursed himself for not checking her over before he carried her away. His main focus was to get her to a place where he could protect her. He did not want to take a chance of anyone else surprising him.

Or give her a chance to escape before I could claim her, he silently admitted to himself.

"Razor, you are hurt?" Cutter asked, jogging out from under the overhang to them. "I was informed you requested Patch to transfer down to the planet."

"It is for my female," Razor stated bluntly. "Is he here?"

"There is a super-cell developing. The transport is just landing, but it wasn't a smooth flight. He isn't very happy with you. You know how he hates transporting down as it is," Cutter said, looking at Kali with a speculative look. "So, this is the female that saved your life when the human transport crashed."

"Yes, she is my *Amate,*" Razor replied sharply. "She is to be protected at all cost."

"I'm not a mutt," she snapped before she turned to the other male in the hopes of getting some help. "Tell him to let me go. He has no right taking me from my home."

Cutter's eyes glittered with amusement at her stubborn tone. "*Amate.* You are his *Amate.* That means you belong to him. I'm afraid he wouldn't listen me, little warrior."

"I don't belong to anyone," she muttered before exhaustion and the loss of blood became too much for her to fight against. "Bloody hell, does he boss everyone around? I just want to go home. I need to warn Destin," she whispered in a barely audible voice.

Razor felt the change in Kali as her head fell back against the crook of his arm. Her face twisted in pain as the movement put pressure on her wound. Her eyes were closed, and though she tried to hide it, he could see the tears of pain blending with the rain.

He strode under the covered walkway, picking up speed as she became more lethargic. He cradled her head when it rolled to the side. A muttered exclamation drew his attention. He knew what Patch must be thinking from the accusing look of disapproval on his face.

"I didn't do this," he snapped with an unfamiliar need to defend himself. "She jumped off a building and crashed through a window."

Patch's eyebrow rose and his mouth tightened into a flat line. He ran his hand over her throat, counting before he gently lifted one of her eyelids. Turning, he barked out a series of sharp commands to two men standing to the left of him.

"Why would she jump off a building?" Patch snapped out as he pushed through the door following one of the men. "And how far did she fall?"

"She didn't fall," Razor responded, ignoring Patch's first question. "She grabbed a cable and tried to swing to the roof of a building across from the one we were on. It wasn't long enough and she crashed through a window two floors below. It was a horizontal impact, not vertical."

"Again," Patch said, nodding to the bed in the makeshift medical room. "Why would she jump off a building?"

Razor tenderly laid Kali down on her side on the bed. A guttural curse in his native language ripped from his throat when he saw the actual wound across her back and shoulder. He stepped around to the other side when Patch pushed him aside so he could see it.

He ran trembling fingers along her pale cheek. "She was trying to get away from me," he finally admitted in a low voice.

Patch paused for a fraction of a second. His gaze narrowed in on the trembling in Razor's hand as he touched the human female. Pressing the sedative injector against her neck, he depressed the button. Once he was confident she was asleep and would not feel what he was about to do, he reached for a pair of shears to cut away her torn and bloody shirt.

"Now that I find that hard to believe. I don't think I've ever met a female that resisted your attentions before," Patch replied calmly as he opened the back of her shirt. "I need a cleanser and a sealer."

Razor listened as Patch ordered one of the resident medics to get him the items he needed. He continued to stroke Kali's hair and face as his friend and personal healer cared for her. He stared down at her face. This was the first time he had really seen her up close in the light. She was even more beautiful, more exotic, than he remembered.

"She almost died twice tonight," he murmured, touching the corner of her lips. "Several human males opened fire on her the first time."

Patch continued cleansing the wound. He pulled several small slivers of broken glass from the jagged edge. The wound was a good fifteen centimeters in length. While it wasn't deep all the way across, at least half of it was six millimeters in depth.

"Did you kill the males?" Patch asked as he applied another layer of cleanser to the wound to protect it from infection and to help reduce scarring. "Is that why you were on the building?"

"She did. She flipped over a burnt transport like it was a toy and made a clean kill-shot to the head," Razor replied with a touch of pride and admiration. "She takes too many chances with her life."

Patch raised his eyes to Razor's for a brief moment before returning to the process of sealing Kali's torn flesh. Fresh blood ran in thin rivulets, staining the pristine sheet beneath her body. There was something strange about the way Razor was reacting to this female. He was acting like she was his…

"I have claimed her as my *Amate*. I need you to mark us," Razor murmured, curling his fingers in her short hair. "She is going to fight me, but she is mine."

Patch's lips twitched in amusement. "Shouldn't you wait until she wakes? You know you could be committing yourself to a long, lonely and possibly very frustrating life if she refuses you."

Razor's lips twitched as well when he thought of the battle he was likely to have on his hands when Kali was feeling better. His body warmed and his damn cock hardened at the thought. He tenderly picked up her hand and turned it. A dark frown creased his brow when he saw her ravaged palm.

"It will be an exciting and rewarding life. It is a Trivator warrior's dream. One I can honestly say I never thought I would experience," he countered. "Her hands are damaged as well."

Patch muttered under his breath when he saw the ripped tissue. He carefully rolled Kali onto her freshly healed back. It would take a few more days for the flesh to be completely mended and it would be tender but she would live. She would also have a scar, but it would be a faint one, mostly where the deepest part of the cut had been.

He carefully cleaned each of her palms, spraying the cleanser on them, then applying the sealer to each cut no matter how small it was. He had been on too many planets where the smallest wound could prove deadly if not cared for.

"Are you sure about this?" he asked, staring at the pale face of the female before looking back up at Razor. "Once done, only death will free you."

Razor's eyes flashed in annoyance. His irritation must have shown clearly because his friend turned with a sharp nod and muttered he would return shortly. Several long minutes later he returned with a wide circular device.

Razor watched carefully as Patch programmed the device. It would embed his mark on her and hers on him. They would forever be tied together, or so he hoped. If she rejected him…

A shiver of apprehension ran down his spine. If she rejected him, Patch was right. He would be condemned to a long, lonely and frustrating life. Once a Trivator warrior gave his word to a female, she became his life, his future. He would give his seed only to her, meaning he would forsake all other physical release to prove his commitment to her and only her.

He pushed aside his doubts. She was his. Something inside him connected with her on a basic level that he did not understand. Frustrated at his lack of understanding ate at him. Pushing his feelings of uncertainty aside, he gritted his teeth and held out his arm.

"Do it," he ordered.

Patch slipped the opened device around Razor's left wrist and snapped it shut. He secured the lock mechanism and checked the programming once more before he looked up at Razor one last time. With a nod, he pressed the button, sealing Razor's fate to that of an unknown human female.

Ten minutes later, Razor gently picked Kali's unconscious form up in his arms once again. The dark marks around both of their wrists stood out, especially those around her pale, delicate wrists. Pride, and another unknown feeling, poured through him as he gazed at the markings for several long seconds.

He nodded to Patch as his friend mumbled that Kali needed to rest as much as possible over the next couple of days to fully recover from her wounds and to give her body time to replenish the blood she had lost.

"Good luck, my friend," Patch muttered, staring at Kali's relaxed face. "She is an unusual female. I hope you know what you are doing."

"Yes, she is, and I have no doubts that she is meant for me," Razor responded in a slightly husky voice before he cleared his throat. "Tell Cutter I want to see him in one hour. Plans need to be set into motion to end the conflict here. I have duties back on Rathon that require my attention and I want to leave within the fortnight."

"I will notify him. He was in the command center checking on the weather. This planet's weather is very unstable," Patch complained, returning the marking device to the medical satchel he had retrieved a short time ago. "If the weather is like it was on my way down to the planet, I'm not leaving. I hate flying as it is."

"It might be best if you remained close," Razor commented over his shoulder as he stepped through the doorway. "I have a feeling things are not going to go as smoothly as Mexico City."

Patch stared at Razor's retreating back with a look of dismay and resignation on his face. The rebels in Mexico City had fought fiercely before being overwhelmed. If Razor classified that as 'smooth' then he hated to think what this city was going to be like. Personally, he would have been happier remaining on board the *Journey*. These humans were some of the most stubborn creatures he had ever studied. Personally, he was ready for the return trip home.

He shook his head in wonder before he picked up his bag. He needed to find Cutter. Maybe he could explain what was happening to Razor.

13

Razor pushed the door to his personal quarters open with his shoulder. He was careful not to jar the precious bundle in his arms. He drew in a deep breath at his thoughts. Kali's sweet scent, tinged with her blood, filled his lungs and pulled on a deep need to care for her.

The sedative Patch gave her would keep her unconscious for several more hours, giving her some of the rest she desperately needed. The first thing he needed to do was clean her up and get her warm. Her clothes were still damp from the rain and every few seconds he could feel her shiver.

Laying her down on his bed, he wished he was back at his home on Rathon. There he could easily bathe and care for her in the spacious cleansing room adjacent to his bedroom. His quarters here were small and barren in comparison to his residence. He sank down on the edge of the bed and gazed at her relaxed features.

She was paler, softer than the females of his world. Her bone structure was smaller and more delicate as well. A smile curved his lips as he touched her short hair. It was straight and feathered around her face.

He carefully began peeling her ruined shirt from her. It was easy since Patch had cut it down the middle in the back. She was wearing a black restraint around her breasts. Her breasts, while not large, would easily fill his hands when he cupped them.

A low groan escaped him as a wave of heat flashed through him. He studied the garment for a moment before he realized that the release for it was nestled between her soft mounds. He quickly snapped the clasp. His breathing grew heavy as the black lace cups fell apart. Sweat beaded on his brow as he forced his eyes downward to the fastening holding her pants on. Standing up, he quickly removed the soft soled shoes she was wearing. Tossing them aside, he unfastened her leggings and pulled them and the lace panties covering her womanhood away. Once she was undressed, he grabbed the blanket folded at the end of the bed up and covered her.

"Oh *fi'ta,* I do not understand what control you have over me. I can only hope you do not take too long to accept that we belong together," he muttered under his breath as he turned and stepped into the small bathroom.

Ten minutes later, Razor grimaced as he gently lowered Kali's body into the warm water. He had filled the tub as high as it would go, but it still barely covered her. He grabbed one of the towels he had set out and used it as a pillow under her head.

Reaching for one of the washcloths, he quickly lathered it up before tenderly stroking it over her skin. He took his time, memorizing every inch of her. He noted every scar, every bruise, on her body. She had a long scar on one of her arms as if it had been broken at one time. There was another long scar just below her right knee.

Almost a dozen other scars, some small, some large, covered her delicate skin. She also had a large number of bruises. Guilt, another unfamiliar emotion, pulled at him. He should have had Patch do a thorough examination on her.

He ran his fingers over a large bruise on her right hip. She must have hit it as she went through the window. He bowed his head and closed his eyes as he remembered her body flying off the roof. Panic had held him in its greedy grip for several long seconds before he rushed over to the edge.

Locking the memory away, he continued to bathe her. Once he was finished, he pulled the drain and reached down into the water to lift her up. He balanced her limp body on the narrow counter as he swept up another towel and carefully wrapped it around her.

Picking her up, he returned to the bedroom and once again laid her down, this time under the covers that he had tossed back with one hand. He shifted her to the side closest to the wall before covering her again. Only when he was satisfied he had done what he could to make her comfortable did he take care of his own damp clothing.

He quickly shed his clothing, tossing them into the hamper by the bathroom door as he strode into the bathroom. Twenty minutes later, he stood by the bed watching as Kali lay curled in a small ball. He undid the towel at his waist, letting it fall to the ground, and pulled the covers back so he could climb in beside her.

"You, little warrior, are killing me," he muttered when she turned and snuggled against his body. He knew she was just seeking the warmth, but his body didn't care. "Rest, my stubborn human. I will protect you."

Razor knew he didn't have much time before he was to meet with Cutter, but Kali came first. He would turn up the heat in the room before he left to keep her from getting chilled. He pressed a tender kiss to the top of her head as she sighed in her sleep. A silly grin curved his lips and his arms tightened protectively around her as it sank in that he had an *Amate*.

"I will never let you go," he vowed in the silence of the room. "I will protect you and care for you and you will come to accept me as your *Amate*."

"How long is the weather expected to continue like this?" Razor asked in frustration.

He stared out at the thick sheets of rain mixed with sleet. An Arctic blast from Canada had intensified unexpectedly and was sweeping through the area. Several feet of early winter snow was expected. Right now, he could barely see a few meters outside the window.

He ran his hand through his hair in aggravation. He had been fifteen minutes late to the meeting he had ordered. It had taken every ounce of his self-discipline to pull himself out of Kali's arms and get dressed. His plans to return to Rathon in a fortnight were quickly beginning to look less and less likely to happen.

"Four, possibly five days," Cutter responded grimly looking out of the window with a worried frown. "This is going to put an incredible hardship on the humans in the city."

"Won't that make your job easier?" Badrick drawled as he stepped into the room. He looked with disdain at the cracked leather covering on the office chair before sitting down with a sigh of resignation. "They will be either eager to surrender or they will be dead. Either way, it will allow you to finish your mission here on this planet."

"Your compassion for this species is commendable," Cutter muttered sarcastically.

Badrick turned his icy blue eyes on Cutter and sneered. "Isn't there some duty you need to attend to? Perhaps cleaning the waste removal units?" he drawled.

Cutter took a threatening step toward Badrick. Razor shot his second-in-command a sharp look and shook his head. Badrick had arrived just before all transports were grounded. He wanted to know what the blue bastard wanted. He was tired of Badrick's lies and deceit. If the councilman wasn't careful, Cutter would be the least of his concerns.

"Enough, Badrick," Razor snapped. "What are you doing here?"

Badrick turned his gaze to Razor's intense gold ones. Within seconds, he shifted his gaze to stare out the window. After several long seconds he finally responded to Razor's question when he realized that neither Razor nor Cutter were prepared to continue their discussion until he answered the question.

"I heard that you captured one of the rebels. I thought perhaps I could be of assistance," Badrick finally answered. "I have dealt with these rebels before and thought you could use my knowledge to resolve the situation faster."

Razor heard the lie in Badrick's voice. He frowned as a brief memory flashed through his mind. Kali's accusing voice echoed harshly as he remembered her questioning him.

Why are you supporting Colbert? she had demanded. *Don't you know what he is like? Don't you see how he doesn't care about the people living in the southern half of the city? Every day we take in refugees seeking a safer way to live. He doesn't care about anyone or anything.*

"It was you," Razor murmured as his eyes narrowed on the councilman. "You are the one supplying Allen with the weapons, one of which was used to attack the helicopter I was on."

Razor watched as Badrick paled until his blue skin took on a sick pasty bluish-white tint. Cutter moved in behind the male when he tried to rise. Razor shook his head. No, the bastard was his. It was within his right as the Chancellor over the Trivator Forces to enforce the laws of the Alliance. No one was above the law of the Alliance, especially those sworn to uphold them.

"They… it was necessary to bring peace to the city. I was doing what I felt was in the best interest of the humans and the Alliance. Allen had the larger and more powerful force. It seemed natural that with enough weapons, the conflict would soon end," Badrick replied, sitting back as Razor stepped closer to him. "I was thinking of the Alliance," he repeated weakly.

"You better hope to the Gods and Goddess' that you were because if I find out differently, I'll gut you myself," Razor growled in a frigid voice. "I am in control of this area now. I will take care of the situation. You will no longer interfere."

Badrick's eyes flashed with fear and fury. He pushed out of the chair, turning as he did to put it between him and Razor. His eyes shifted nervously to where Cutter was now leaning against the wall by the door. A satisfied grin on his face.

"You were ordered to bring the humans under control. Instead, you have one of the rebels in your bed. I do not think that the Alliance Council will be pleased that you are protecting one of them," Badrick argued. "I demand you turn the female over to me. Kali Parks could be used to end the conflict."

Razor's huge body stilled. A primeval urge to kill the male swept through him at the mention of Kali. Badrick must have sensed the danger he was in because he took a defensive step closer to the door. Razor followed the other male's movements.

"How?" he gritted out in a low, dangerous voice. "How can Kali be used to end the conflict?"

Badrick swallowed nervously, glancing back and forth between Cutter, who raised an eyebrow at him, and the rigid face of Razor.

"She… Allen wants her. He will use her to force Parks to concede to him," Badrick replied. "He just needs some way to force Parks into negotiating with him. He assured me that if he had Kali Parks, that her brother would cease fighting."

Razor stepped forward. His fists clenched and unclenched at his side as he fought for control. His gut was telling him that Badrick was telling him the truth, but not all of it. There was more behind Allen's desire to get his hands on Kali.

"I want a detailed list of all weapons given to Allen," he snapped in fury. "You have put the lives of my men in danger by supplying weapons that can be used against us. I want to know what they have, where they got them and what you discussed with both men."

14

Kali blinked several times as she woke. A frown creased her brow as she tried to figure out where in the hell she was. She moved her right shoulder expecting to feel the intense pain in her back from the cut she had received when she went through the window but all she felt was a slight tenderness and...

She gasped when she turned her head and found a set of dark, yellow-gold eyes staring intently at her. Shock swept through her before fear and fury took its place. Razor... his name was enough to send a shaft of fear through her, as well as another emotion she didn't quite understand.

She nervously licked her lips. "Where am I and what in the hell are you doing here?" she demanded in a husky voice.

She would have climbed out of the bed in fury when she saw his lips twitch in amusement, but another realization swept through her that froze her in place. She wasn't wearing any clothes, none, nada, completely bare. That alone was enough to keep her frozen in place. Her eyes flickered down to his chest. A rosy blush flushed her face as she realized that she might not be the only one who was bare as the day they were born.

"You are at a temporary base set up for our use. You were going into shock from blood loss and needed immediate medical attention," he replied, rolling onto his side so he was facing her.

"Fine, I'm healed. Now, explain what in the hell you are doing in the same bed as me," she choked out as the sheet slipped lower.

Yep, something tells me he isn't wearing anything below the covers, she thought with a combination of dread and curiosity.

She scooted further back until her back was pressed against the wall behind her. Pulling the sheet tighter around her, she rolled onto her side so she was facing him as well. Her eyes briefly flickered past him to scan the room. It was very basic. A small table, a couple of chairs, a bathroom and the bed. Overall, it was very simple and functional.

The corner of his mouth curved upward as he caught her covert scrutiny of the room. Even if she tried to escape, she wouldn't get far with the weather outside. He raised his hand to brush a small strand of her hair that had fallen forward back behind her ear. A rumble of displeasure escaped him when she jerked away from him.

"You were cold, I was tired, the answer was simple," he replied, dropping his hand to the bed between them. "You are in my personal quarters."

"Why?" Kali asked with a confused frown as her eyes narrowed on his wrist that was lying against the pristine white sheets. She glanced at her wrist and her eyes widened even further. "What is this?" she asked, frightened, holding her wrist out in front of her.

Razor watched as she struggled to sit up. She kept the flat sheet tucked around her as she twisted until she was sitting on her knees. One hand held the sheet protectively against her while she stared at the intricate patterns of his language that graced her right wrist.

He twisted, sitting up on the edge of the bed as well. The bedspread fell to lay across his lap. Frustration ate at him as he studied her fearful expression. Dark brown eyes lifted to his. He could see the panic in them as she held her wrist up.

"What is this?" she demanded again. "What does it mean?"

Razor's eyes hardened with determination as he gazed back at her. He rose to his feet, letting the cover fall away as he reached for his trousers laying across a chair near the table. He kept his back to her while he stepped into them and pulled them up. He didn't bother fastening them all the way.

Running his hand through his hair, he turned back toward the bed. Kali had taken advantage of his turned back to slide off the end of the bed as well. The sheet was wrapped tightly around her and she was rubbing at first one wrist, then the other in an effort to remove his mark.

"They will not come off," he replied quietly.

Kali raised her troubled eyes to his face. "What is it? What does it mean? Is it some form of alien tracking device?" she asked, worry and fear clearly evident in her expression and voice.

"It is my mark. It means you belong to me as I belong to you," he responded in a soft voice. "I am Razor. I belong to Kali as she belongs to me. Forever will I tie my life to hers. I will care for, protect and give my seed only to her. She is my *Amate*. She is my life. I have taken you as mine, Kali. For always."

A look of growing horror twisted her face even as she shook her head in denial. Her lips trembled as she stared at him. Her eyes darted to his wrists as he held them up for her to see the marks circling them before they dropped to her own.

"No," she whispered in distress before raising her eyes to his again with growing anger. "No! I do not belong to you. I do not want you. I will *not* accept you," she continued in a voice that grew louder as her anger grew. "I want you to have it removed."

Razor strode forward, ignoring how she stumbled backwards. He pressed his hands on the wall on each side of her head. A burning jealousy ripped through him. He remembered the way the human male had held her and how she had called for him when he had taken her.

"I will not remove it. You are mine," he said grimly. "You will come to accept me. I will do everything in my power to protect and care for you. No longer will you live in fear and danger. Twice! Twice I watched as you almost died. Three if I count that stupid stunt of yours the night we met. I will not allow you to put yourself in danger. I cannot." His voice dropped to a darker, husky tone as he continued. "Nor will I allow another male to take you from me. You are mine, *fi'ta*."

He swallowed her gasp of denial as he pressed his lips against hers. His hands moved to cup her face so she could not turn away just as his body caged her between him and the wall. He drank deeply, kissing her over and over until he felt her tremble and begin to respond to him. Only then did he change the kiss to one that was more exploratory. After several long minutes, he slowly released her lips and ran his hands down along her side to pull her against him.

"Yes," he groaned as he ran his nose along her cheek. "You make me feel things inside, my *fi'ta*. You have started a fire that is threatening to engulf me."

It took a moment for him to feel the dampness against his skin as he rubbed his nose and lips along her cheek. His hand tightened slightly on her hip. He pulled back as the salty taste touched his senses. Tears glittered on her eyelashes. A second tear escaped to make a jagged path down her cheek. The single drop clung to her chin, drawing his hand up to capture it.

"No," she whispered, gazing up at him with a heartbreaking despondency in her eyes. "No."

Razor stood in his office staring out at the thick snow that was falling. The dip in the weather matched his mood. He raised the glass of dark red liquor to his lips and drank deeply. His thoughts on the human female in his quarters.

Her rejection of him felt like he had taken a blast from a laser rifle directly to his chest. If it wasn't for the fact that he could feel his heart beating he would have wondered if he still had one. He raised the glass once more even as the reflection of Cutter came into view behind him.

"Information from the *Journey* states the storm should dissipate in three to four days. I've also put a guard on Badrick," he commented as he walked over to the small bar and poured a drink. "The bastard is up to something."

Razor didn't respond at first. He already knew both pieces of information. Badrick had tried to leave, but the weather prohibited any transports from lifting off. At the moment, he was limited to ground transport and communications. He was being surprisingly silent about both.

"I want a meeting with Parks," he said.

Cutter walked over to stand next to him. They both stood silent for several long minutes, lost in their own thoughts. Razor finished the drink in his hand. He needed information. Information on human females. Information on stubborn, hard-headed females who refused to listen, who were fierce and proud. He needed help from someone who had experience with such a female. He needed to talk to his younger brother, Hunter.

Turning, he glanced at Cutter. "I want you to go back through every transmission Badrick has made in the last two years. I want to know who he contacted, who contacted him and where he has been. You are right, he is up to something and I want to know what it is," he ordered.

Cutter tossed back the drink in his hand. A dark smile curved his lips. He had never liked the bastard. It would be interesting to see what the male was trying to cover up.

"I'll work on both. I may know someone who can lead me to Parks. I'll also do some research on Councilman Badrick's personal files," he said, turning toward the door. "I'll report my findings as soon as possible."

"Very good," Razor said distractedly. "Cutter."

Cutter turned as he opened the door to look back. "Yes?"

"Ask Patch to stop by my office in an hour," Razor ordered.

"Are you unwell?" Cutter asked in concern.

Razor glanced over his shoulder and shook his head once. "I am fine. I just need to speak with him."

Cutter paused before he nodded his head. "I'll let him know."

Razor waited until Cutter closed the door before he walked over to his desk. Sitting down, he swiped his hand over the console before inputting his pass code. Touching the private communications link, he brought up his brother Hunter's call number. It took several long minutes before the link connected through the communication stations that had been dispatched between their worlds.

"Speak," Hunter's deep voice ordered.

"I need your assistance," Razor replied in greeting. His eyes narrowed on the sleeping form of the small child resting on his brother's shoulder. "He is growing fast."

Hunter shifted his son, Lyon, onto his left shoulder and gently patted his back. Pride and warmth shone in his eyes as he stared back at Razor. He was covering many of his older brother's duties while he was gone, as well as his own duties as part of the founding family of Julumont. He was part of the governing board and oversaw the safety of the region.

"He is," Hunter replied in a voice that was softer. "What do you need? I have everything under control here. The fighting in the Tellamon region is under control."

"What of Dagger? Has he been located yet?" Razor asked.

Hunter's face tightened into a stony mask. His eyes flickered over his shoulder as another figure came through the doorway. Razor watched as his brother turned toward the female entering the room. Shy eyes glanced at him and a nervous smile crossed his new sister's face as she brushed a kiss across Hunter's lips.

"Hello Razor," Jesse called out quietly. "How is Earth? Is there still a lot of conflict?"

"Greetings, Jesse," Razor said, bowing his head. "There are fewer and fewer each day. Lyon is growing. Is he walking yet?"

Jesse's face lit up as she turned her gaze on her son. "Yes and he is into everything! We have to watch him constantly or he'll disappear."

Razor studied the changes in his new sister's face. He had been doubtful when he first heard that his younger brother had taken a human as an *Amate*. While he'd had limited contact with her, his parents frequently kept him abreast of what was going on. The pride and admiration in their voices laid to rest many of his doubts about the success of their union. A smile curved his lips as he remembered some of the amusing tales of his youngest new sister.

"How are Jordan and Taylor doing? They have settled in well, I hope. Father said Taylor had graduated from her basics and applied for advanced training," he remarked politely.

Jesse's eyes grew sad and she bit her lip, looking at Hunter for several seconds. A silent look passed between his brother and his *Amate* proving that all was not well. Razor's eyes sharpened as he noted Jesse's suddenly pale complexion and Hunter's stony look.

"What is it?" he demanded sharply. "Has something happened to the little one?"

"No, nothing has happened to Taylor though I am expecting Saber to strangle her any day," Hunter replied heavily. "Jesse, please take Lyon while I talk to Razor."

"You'll ask him?" she responded in a hesitant voice, reaching for their sleeping son. "You said he could help."

"I will ask him, Jesse," Hunter promised, brushing his fingers along her cheek. "I promise."

Jesse turned worried eyes to Razor before she gave a brief nod and a strained smile. Both Razor and Hunter watched her walk out of the room; one with a look of love and worry on his face and the other with a speculative look.

Hunter turned back to look at Razor. He gave a tired groan as he sank down into the chair. He cursed that he was still having problems with weakness when he was overtired.

"What is wrong?" Razor asked bluntly.

"It's Jordan. She's gone," Hunter responded in a tired voice.

"When and where?" Razor asked, getting to the point.

"A month ago," Hunter admitted. "We believe she is safe. She is with Trig."

Razor's face darkened at the mention of Dagger's older brother. Neither one of the brothers were someone he would want around a female, especially one as fragile and delicate as a human one. Jordan's serious face flashed through his mind. He had only met her once, but she had a quiet vulnerability to her that had brought out the protectiveness in all the males in his family. Hell, she brought it out in any male who came near her.

The thought of her being with Trig sent a chill through him. He knew what Trig was capable of because he had used his services many times over the past fifteen years. Dagger wasn't any better. Both males had a dark, dangerous edge that qualified them as among the elite warriors often used for impossible missions. Trig had been in his class while Dagger had been with Hunter.

"What happened?" Razor asked harshly.

Hunter rubbed his hand over his face and leaned back. "I told you about Jordan finding a vidcom of Dagger in a fight ring. Trig went to get him, but he arrived too late. Dagger had already been moved. The previous 'owner' of the fight ring did not know where he was taken. He just wanted to get rid of Dagger because of how dangerous he was and the fact that Dagger had already broken one of his legs. A month ago, Trig returned after losing Dagger's trail. That same night, Jordan disappeared. I've been sending word to Trig, but haven't had a response yet."

"Surely Jordan left some type of clue behind," Razor replied in disbelief. "She can't have just vanished."

"She left a brief vidcom saying she had a lead as to where Dagger might be," Hunter admitted. "She said she had to go, that she knew she could find him if they moved him again. She..." Grief darkened Hunter's eyes as he thought of the pleading tone of the vidcom. "She refuses to give up. I have a lead, Razor. One of my sources says Trig was sighted heading for the Tressalon galaxy. I need you to go after Jordan."

Razor's mind calculated the time it would take the *Journey* to reach the galaxy. There were only a handful of habitable planets in the star system, but it was littered with Spaceports. The area was known for its hostility toward the Alliance and was a haven for those living on the outer edges of the civilized planets.

"I am bound here for at least a fortnight," Razor replied. "I will leave as soon as possible. I have one last city here to secure before I leave."

"I understand," Hunter said with a nod. "It will take Trig at least that long to get there considering his last location. That is one of the reasons I was hoping you could help us. Your Flagship is the fastest, most advanced warship in the Alliance. If anyone can get her out safely, it would be you. Now, what did you need my assistance with?"

Razor released a sigh and rubbed his jaw before leaning forward to stare intently into Hunter's eyes. He knew little about Hunter's *Amate,* other than she had saved his brother's life on more than one occasion. How such a delicate creature as Jesse could do something like that amazed him.

"I have an *Amate*," Razor stated bluntly.

Hunter's eyes widened in surprise before a huge grin lit up his face. "Who is she? Is she here? Father and Mother have not mentioned her."

"Her name is Kali Parks. She is human," Razor replied quietly. "She…"

Hunter's eyebrow rose as his brother's voice faded. He released a deep sigh and shook his head. He could tell from his brother's worried eyes that things were not going well.

"She isn't happy about your claim," Hunter guessed.

Razor gave a sharp, dry laugh. "Unhappy is putting it rather… mildly," he said. "She rejects my claim on her."

Hunter heard the low, almost desperate tone in Razor's voice. He remembered all too well his own panic when he thought that Jesse would deny his claim. There were times at night when he still woke from a nightmare, his fear of losing her choking him. When that happened, he would reach wildly for her, needing to hold her close against his pounding heart.

"Jesse did as well," Hunter admitted. "They do not understand the commitment that we make to them when we claim them as our *Amate*. Many of their males give out empty promises. They also do not believe that we can feel such deep feelings so quickly. Jesse..." Hunter paused for a moment and his eyes darkened with the memory of almost losing Jesse. "Jesse feared for her sisters. She is very protective of them and did not trust me at first. I was an alien, far different than any human male she had known."

"Kali is protective of her brother," Razor said heavily. "He is the leader of one of the factions I have to contain. If he refuses to lay down his weapons and work with the Alliance I will have no choice but to kill him and any other humans who resist. Too many Trivator lives have been compromised because of the extended fighting on this planet. This is the last major city that needs to be contained. There continue to be small groups in remote areas, but the largest areas of the populace have joined to rebuild their world. Once others see the progress being made, the smaller groups will cease fighting."

"Be patient, care for her, show her that you only wish to help her people, not harm them," Hunter recommended.

Razor looked into Hunter's eyes. "She will not forgive me if I order the destruction of her city, or…" His voice dropped as the weight of his duties surrounded him. "or kill her brother."

"If she is anything like Jesse, Jordan and Taylor, she will fight to protect him. I do not envy you your position, brother. If you kill him, she will not forgive you. If he does not cease his fighting, you have no choice but to order the destruction of the city. She must understand that what you are doing is not personal," Hunter replied with a shake of his head. "Unfortunately, the humans do not understand that."

Razor nodded in agreement. "What is it like? To have a human as your *Amate*? I did not expect the intensity of my reaction to her. I planned on choosing Rainiera when I returned to Rathon," he said wearily.

"Rainiera will not be pleased to discover you have chosen another," Hunter replied with a sympathetic smirk. "I have run into her a few times and she has asked about you. I believe she has already made plans for your union. She asked when you were returning so she could schedule the designers to come in and remodel your home."

Razor grunted instead of responding to Hunter's teasing. It was true, he and Rainiera had been lovers and he had thought to take her as his *Amate*. She was intelligent, attractive, and trained to deal with the demands of his position since her father worked in the Ministry of Defense.

"I will deal with her when I return," he said dismissively. "It is pointless now that I am committed to Kali."

"Well, all I can say is good luck, brother. Rainiera has nails and sharp teeth. Neither of which I would want buried in me," Hunter replied with a dry humor before he sobered. "Let me know what happens, both with your *Amate* and especially with Jordan. I do not like it when Jesse cries. She is very worried about Jordan."

Razor could hear the underlying strain in his brother's voice. Hunter was just as worried about Jordan as Jesse was. He bowed his head in acknowledgement as a soft knock on his office door sounded. Patch had arrived.

"I will keep you informed. Until we meet again, brother," Razor said in farewell.

"Farewell, Razor, and thank you," Hunter replied before signing off

"Enter," Razor called out when the knock sounded again, this time a little harder. "Patch, I have a request for you."

Patch's eyebrows rose at the hidden command in Razor's voice. A grimace darkened his face. Such an introduction could only mean two things; he was going to be doing something very dangerous and more than likely not part of the approved Alliance protocol.

15

Kali remained frozen against the wall, staring at the closed door for several long minutes before she sank down to sit on the floor. She closed her eyes and rested her forehead on her bent knees. A torrent of emotions turned like a whirlpool inside her, swirling around and around until she felt dizzy from it.

A shiver ran through her, more from the look on Razor's face when she told him 'no' than from the chill in the room. Drawing in a deep breath, she raised her head to glance out the window beside her. Several inches of moist snow had begun to accumulate on the windowsill. It was as if the weather was mocking her desire to escape.

She wiped at the dampness on her cheeks. Leaning her head back against the wall, she drew in a deep, steadying breath. She needed to think. She also needed to push the anger down and away. It would do no good; just distract her from her mission.

"Oh girl, you have really gotten in over your head this time," she whispered on a hiccup.

She was angry alright. Not so much with Razor as she was with herself. Emotions only broke your heart or got you killed. Over the past six years she had seen it happen over and over. That was another reason she made sure she avoided any attachments. She didn't want to love someone only to lose them or to leave the one she loved heartbroken.

She held her wrists up and studied the thin bands surrounding each one. The symbols on them were beautiful. They wove in and out, connected yet individual. She turned to see if she could make sense of it. Using the tip of her right index finger, she traced the lines. A confused frown creased her forehead as she followed the curving lines. They circled perfectly.

"It is like it goes on for infinity," she murmured in awe.

"That is what it is meant to symbolize," a feminine voice replied cheerfully from the door. "I knocked. When you didn't reply I became worried. I'm Chelsea. I'm the resident human nurse."

Kali stared up into the smiling face of a woman in her mid-forties. She was wearing a light blue scrub top and matching pants. Her black hair was pulled back into a ponytail, framing her rounded cheeks. She had a ready smile and dark brown eyes filled with warmth and humor.

"How do you know?" Kali asked as she stood up, holding the sheet in place so she wouldn't lose it.

"I overheard Dr. Humorless and the Scaryman talking. I put two and two together and it came up to four so it was a no-brainer," Chelsea said, shutting the door behind her. "Patch asked me to check on you. He was worried about how much blood you lost and didn't want you to be alone in case you crashed."

Kali shook her head in confusion. "Dr. Humorless and Scaryman? Who is Patch? Why would I crash?"

Chelsea chuckled as she guided Kali back to the edge of the bed. "Have a seat and let me take your blood pressure. Patch is the doctor or healer as the Trivator call them. He has almost no sense of humor. He reminds me a lot of that actor who played in those Sci-fi movies. That's why I call him Dr. Humorless. My significant other is always warning me to be careful around these guys. Thomas, my hubby and love of my life, is the civilian aide to Colonel Baker, who is in charge of the facility. At least he was until Scaryman came. I think that guy's name is Razor. Anyway, Thomas said the guy is like this alien killing machine that was brought in to settle any conflicts. I haven't had to deal with him, thank goodness. If you ask me, all those aliens are scary in a hunky, dangerous kind of way, if you know what I mean!" Chelsea said wiggling her eyebrows up and down suggestively as she wound the blood pressure cuff around Kali's arm. "Stay still, this won't take but a minute."

Kali's mind swirled with questions as she tried to understand everything that Chelsea was telling her. There was a human Colonel in charge. Maybe he could help her. If not, she would just have to help herself. She turned to stare outside the window. She was used to the cold weather that Chicago got. She could use it to her advantage. She just needed to know exactly where she was first.

"Where am I?" Kali asked in a husky voice.

"The US Army National Guard building on S. Calumet," Chelsea replied. "One of the reasons it is so damn cold is because we are right on the water. This is the time of year when I curse Thomas not being transferred to Florida or even better Hawaii. I could handle Hawaii."

Kali's heart skipped. She was on the edge of the divide between the Northern and Southern sections of the city. Interstate 290 was the divide. The line ran from the edge of the water all the way to South Branch Chicago River. It would be dangerous, but she could make it. The old Harrison Electric Garage was in Allen's territory, barely. Once she got there, she could use the old Metro lines to cross back over.

"Whoa, your blood pressure just spiked," Chelsea murmured. "I better get Patch to take another look at you."

"No!" Kali said sharply. She shook her head and reached for the mask she wore to calm her. "I mean no, I think it is just the surprise of knowing I'm still in Chicago. I thought we had traveled much further."

Chelsea looked at Kali's calm face for several long seconds before she nodded reluctantly. Pulling the cuff from Kali's arm, she folded it and slipped it into her front pocket as she stepped to the side to look at Kali's shoulder.

"If you're sure," she said. "It never ceases to amaze me how these guys can heal a wound. It isn't as fast as some of the science fiction movies I've seen, but it is pretty damn close. I tell you what; if you can get dressed and eat, I'll give you the okay. If not, I'm having the doc take another look at you."

"I need some clothes," Kali remarked with a blush. "Mine seems to have disappeared."

Chelsea laughed. "I have some you can have. They'll be a bit big for you, but at least you'll have something covering your ass. Will a pair of sweats be okay?" she asked, already moving toward the door.

Kali gave the other woman a grateful smile. "That would be great," she replied.

"Be back in a few. I'll take you down to the mess hall for dinner," Chelsea commented opening the door. "It'll be nice having another woman to chat with. Thomas works all kinds of strange hours so we don't get to eat together that often."

"Isn't there other women here?" Kali asked in surprise.

Chelsea shook her head. "About half a dozen, all married to human personnel. The Trivator have this old-school mentality about women working, especially in the military. I guess it is fine as long as they are not in any danger. Personally, I think us women could show them a thing or two, but I promised Thomas I wouldn't aggravate the aliens. He says they are bigger than him and he likes having a pulse. He couldn't fight his way through a Black Friday sale, so I don't know how he thinks he could protect me from one of those guys."

Kali giggled as Chelsea rolled her eyes. She waited until the door shut behind the infectious, good-humored nurse before she decided she needed to explore the room a bit. The smile died on her lips when she opened the bottom drawer near the bed. A small weapon of some sort lay in the drawer. Kali palmed the device, turning it over in her hands to study it. She swallowed as she carefully returned it to the drawer. Turning, her eyes caught on the hamper by the bathroom door. A familiar piece of black lace was hanging from the top of it.

Walking over to the hamper, Kali pulled out her bra. She blushed again when she saw her pants and panties mixed with Razor's clothes. For some reason, the sight of her clothes tangled with his made her feel hot and achy. Pushing the feeling away, she searched for her socks and shoes. She breathed a sigh of relief when she found them under the bed. She looked around for her shirt and finally found the bloody remains in the trash can in the bathroom.

At least most of my clothes survived, she thought ruefully, holding up the tattered remains.

She had almost everything she needed to escape. She had clothes that cover her ass and breasts, pants that fit and shoes for her feet. She would need whatever shirt Chelsea brought and a jacket. Her eyes narrowed on a wardrobe. Pulling it open, she grinned when she saw what was obviously Razor's jacket hanging in it.

"Checkmate," she whispered. "Now, to find a map of the layout of the base."

She turned when she heard the knock on the door. Tossing the clothes onto the bathroom counter, she walked over to the door and cracked it before opening it further when she saw it was Chelsea. She gratefully took the clothes handed to her and turned to head into the bathroom.

"I'll be right out," she called over her shoulder, feeling slightly guilty at the thought of deceiving the other woman.

"No problem," Chelsea responded, looking around curiously. "I didn't know this was Razor's quarters. What is he like? Is he as scary as he looks?"

Kali turned in the doorway and looked at Chelsea for a moment as she thought about the question. Was Razor scary? He had never done anything to her personally that was scary. True, he had knocked Jason out – twice – but he had also had her wounds healed.

"No," she said slowly thinking about Razor with a frown of confusion. "He is… different, but I wouldn't call him scary."

Chelsea shrugged and sat down on one of the chairs at the table. She grinned as she looked at Kali's confused face before her eyes dropped to the markings on Kali's wrists.

"Well, I hope you know what you've gotten into. Thomas was telling me about what happens when one of those alien's claims a female as his *Amate*."

"What do you mean?" Kali asked, holding onto the doorframe. "What happens?"

"The females are well and truly fucked, in the most pleasurable way," she laughed. "And honey, they don't have the word divorce in their dictionary. I overheard Patch tell Razor that once he marked you, only death could free him."

A shiver ran down Kali's spine. Only death could set him free. His death or hers, she wondered. Kali didn't say anything. Instead, she stepped into the bathroom and quietly closed the door. The sooner she put her plan of escape into action the better, and safer, it would be. She needed to get back to Destin and warn him.

But most importantly, she thought as she looked at her reflection in the mirror, *I have to get away from him before he really does claim me.*

16

Destin stared out of the front entrance of the building they had taken over. Bitterness and guilt threatened to consume him. Two of his best people were missing. One he considered a friend, the other was his flesh and blood. He had sent every available member he could spare out to search for them. He even had William out spreading the word to the residents that still remained in the northern section.

"Destin," a voice called out from behind him.

He turned as Tim came running up to him. He stiffened at the look of fury on his friend's face. Tim seldom showed emotion.

"What is it?" Destin asked tersely.

"Two members just brought Jason in. He's pretty beat up. Doc is with him now. They found him over on West Adams," Tim replied breathlessly.

"Kali?" Destin asked harshly.

Tim shook his head and turned to follow Destin who was already moving quickly to their makeshift infirmary. He quickly caught up with him. Speaking in a low voice so he couldn't be overheard, he shared what little he knew so far.

"Mike and Justin said Jason kept muttering for Kali to run," Tim shared. "When they asked him from whom, he just said one word… Razor."

Destin stopped and turned to stare at Tim in silence, then continued down the corridor toward medical. Razor. One name that chilled his blood. He knew who Razor was. The blue alien bastard that he had spoken to before had explained exactly who Razor was and what he would do if Destin did not agree to Colbert's demands. If that hadn't been clear enough, the reports coming in from Mexico City, Kyiv and dozens of other cities around the globe were enough to let him know that death came with another name.

He pushed through the door, nodding to Doc when he looked up. Jason lay on the examination table. It looked like his nose had been broken. Dried blood crusted around his nostrils. His top lip was busted and would need stitches. His face had several dark, painful bruises on them. Doc must have already set his broken arm as another one of the medics was wrapping a temporary cast around it.

"Jason," Destin said in a quiet voice as he stepped up to the side when Doc moved to give him room. "Where is Kali?"

Jason's head turned and his pain-filled eyes blinked several times as he tried to focus on Destin's face. He winced when he licked his cut lip. It took him several tries before he could finally push past the bruising to his throat.

"He… he took… her," Jason whispered, closing his eyes briefly against the pain. "I… tried to… hold him… told Kali… to… run. I heard…" His voice died as he swallowed painfully.

"What did you hear? Damn it, Jason. What did you hear?" Destin asked hoarsely.

Jason's dazed eyes opened again. It was obvious whatever pain medication Doc had given him was kicking in full force. His eyes started to drift down again, but he forced them open when he heard Destin curse again.

"Scream… I heard her… scream before… before she called my name. Then… then… nothing," he whispered before his head fell to the side as he lost consciousness.

"Damn him all to hell!" Destin roared out in pain and fury. He leaned forward, gripping the side of the bed as a wave of hopelessness washed over him. He rocked back and forth before shrugging off Doc's sympathetic hand and turning to glare at Tim with ice-cold eyes. "As soon as the weather clears, I want a meeting with that alien bastard. If he thinks he is going to use my sister like his blue friend wanted to, then he is about to realize he isn't the only cold-hearted bastard in the galaxy."

"What do you plan to do?" Tim asked as Destin stepped away from the bed and turned back toward the door.

Destin glanced at his friend with steely eyes. "I plan to kill him," he replied. "I want to know where his base is, what type of security he has and where he might be holding Kali. Pull the team together, this takes top priority. If that bastard wants a fight, he is about to get one."

Kali smiled at Chelsea as she shared another amusing tale in her life with Thomas. She nodded as she looked around, paying attention to the conversation just enough to know when an answer was required of her. They had finished a wonderful dinner of steak, potatoes and fresh vegetables almost an hour before. Now, they were sipping an after-dinner hot coffee.

Kali murmured a reply as she turned to look at the new person that entered the mess hall. She stiffened when she recognized the strange blue tint to the male's skin. Her fingers curved around the handle of the spoon she had used to stir the milk in her cup. A part of her wished she had kept the steak knife from her dinner. She would have if Chelsea hadn't grabbed everything and disposed of it before she had a chance.

Icy blue eyes locked with hers. A look of unsuppressed lust flared in them before he remembered to conceal it. It didn't matter. Kali already knew what the male wanted from her. He had made the mistake of expressing his desire to her brother.

She slowly rose from her chair as he approached the table. A muttered curse touched her ears as Chelsea rose from her seat as well. It was obvious that she had no respect for the blue alien either.

"Isn't it a shame that they forgot to take all the trash out, Kali?" Chelsea asked sarcastically. "I bet if they hauled his ass outside no one would even know that his pickle blue ass was getting frostbit."

"You are dismissed, female," Badrick said with a disdainful glance.

"I'm afraid I can't do that, sir," Chelsea snipped with barely controlled civility. "My orders from Doc Patch are to stay close to Kali."

Badrick looked Chelsea's rounded figure up and down. His eyes lingered for several seconds on the satin mocha coloring of her face before traveling down to her ample breasts straining against the blue scrub top she was wearing. A nasty smile played around his mouth for a moment before he returned his eyes to her face.

"You are very unusual," he remarked casually. "A little old, but your exotic coloring and ample figure would be interesting to sample."

Chelsea's normally cheerful expression changed to one of fury. She folded her arms over her chest and tossed her head. Kali had to bite the inside of her cheek to keep from laughing as her new friend slowly looked alien up and down, pausing on his crotch before she raised an eyebrow and returned her gaze to his face.

"Honey, I've seen bigger worms in my Granny's garden," she replied dryly. "Now, unless you want to see what this exotic, old, colorful bitch can do when she kicks your ass I suggest you step away."

Badrick's face turned a darker blue at the slightly veiled insult to his manhood. His mouth tightened and he took a threatening step closer to Chelsea. Kali realized that her friend had just made a powerful enemy.

"Chelsea, I'd like to stretch my legs for a little bit," she said. "Perhaps you can show me around."

"Sure, darling," Chelsea replied, glaring back at Badrick before she dropped her arms. She turned so she could pick up their empty coffee cups. "We'll start with where your *Amate's* office is. I'm sure he'll be happy to see you up and about."

"Sounds great," Kali replied never breaking contact with Badrick's cold gaze. "I'd love to take a cup of coffee with me if you don't mind."

Chelsea glanced suspiciously back and forth between Kali and Badrick before she released a muttered reply. Kali waited until her friend had stepped over to the small bar set up with carafes of fresh brewed coffee. Once she was sure Chelsea was far enough away to not hear what she had to say she stepped closer to Badrick.

"You are a dead man," she hissed under her breath not bothering to hide the loathing in them. "I know what you are."

Badrick's eyes narrowed. "I offered Parks a good sum for you. He should have taken it," he replied in a cold voice. "Though now it won't matter. I have you and have gotten rid of Parks without having to spend a single credit."

Kali refused to show her fear. "What do you mean, you've gotten rid of Parks?" she asked coldly.

Badrick's thin lips curled into a nasty smile. "Now that you are out of the way, Razor has ordered the city to be destroyed. As soon as the weather clears, there will be no more Chicago."

Kali's fist tightened around the curve of the spoon. She had turned it so the handle was sticking out. It would work just as well as any knife if thrust hard enough through vital, undefended tissue such as an eye or throat.

"Kali. Kali, are you ready?"

It took a moment for Kali to realize that Chelsea was talking to her. She nodded her head and took a step back, never taking her eyes off the gloating ones staring back at her with malignant pleasure. She finally broke contact when Chelsea held out her cup of coffee.

"Are you okay, sugar?" Chelsea asked in concern, glancing back at Badrick who continued to stare at them. "That alien is one scary dude. My Thomas said Colonel Baker isn't happy that he is here. None of the head guys like him. Take my advice, Kali, don't go anywhere alone. You keep that Trivator with you. No one will mess with him, including that guy."

Kali gave Chelsea a small smile. "I don't think any of them are safe to be around. I'd like to return to my room, if you don't mind," she added quietly, dropping her full cup of coffee into the trash as they walked down the corridor. "I'm more tired than I thought."

"That's a good idea, sugar," Chelsea replied with concern. "Just make sure you lock the door behind you."

"I will. Thank you, Chelsea. For everything," Kali whispered, hugging the older woman for several long seconds. "You be safe yourself. He isn't a good person to make angry at you."

Chelsea's soft chuckle echoed in her ear. "I wasn't always a nurse, Kali. I was one of Washington, D. C.'s finest. I know how to kick a little ass when it needs to be kicked."

Kali pulled back and smiled. "I just bet you can," she said before her smile faded. "Just be careful. Good night, Chelsea."

"Goodnight, sugar," Chelsea murmured, waiting until the door closed firmly and she heard the lock click. "I hope that alien knows what he's gotten himself into. That little girl is going to keep him on his toes."

Chelsea turned and began humming under her breath as she walked back down the corridor. She wasn't lying when she said she had been one of Washington's finest. She had spent over twenty years with the

FBI before getting her nursing degree. She hadn't missed the way Kali was grilling her for information or the way she was memorizing the layout of the armory. That girl was planning to escape the first chance she got. She couldn't wait to share everything with Thomas later tonight. He was going to love it.

17

Razor paused outside of the door to his quarters. It was almost two in the morning before he was able to quit for the night. Several minor issues had come up, primarily due to the weather. He had also spent a great deal of time researching the fight rings and Spaceports in the Tressalon galaxy.

He inserted his card into the locking device and waited for the light to turn green. Once it had, he quietly pushed open the door. A soft light from the bathroom cast a glow into the room illuminating the bed.

He silently breathed a word of thanks to the Gods when he saw Kali's relaxed face. A touch of guilt flashed through him as he studied her before he quickly pushed it away. Closing the door, he engaged the lock before walking over to the bathroom.

Ten minutes later, he once again pulled the covers to his bed aside. He slid down between the sheets and turned to pull Kali into his arms. A slight smile curved his lips when he realized she came to him with barely a touch. Her sweet scent mixed with the scent of his shampoo and soap flowed his senses. He gently rubbed his mouth against her hair as she snuggled closer to his warmth.

His arms tightened around her as she burrowed closer. He wanted her. This was beyond the normal need for relief. He… needed her. That was something he had never felt toward another female, even with Rainiera. They had both come together simply for relief. Neither one sought the company of the other afterwards. In fact, they had never slept together much less simply held each other for the enjoyment of the act of being close. No, this was something much different, much… stronger.

"Jason," Kali murmured, restlessly moving in her sleep. "Jason, help me."

Pain exploded through Razor at her softly muttered words. This pain was different from any he had felt before. It came from inside him radiating from his chest. He lay stiffly as Kali continued to move restlessly against him. She didn't call for the other male again, but her soft whimpers cut through him with a precision any assassin would be proud of.

After several minutes she finally relaxed, settling into a deeper, calmer sleep. A sense of despair struck him hard, pulling a soft moan from him. Instinctively, his arms tightened around her. He had never been prone to thoughts of doubt or despair before, or even fear. He wasn't sure how to handle them. Drawing in a deep breath, he wondered if he should have talked to Jesse as well. Another moan escaped him as Kali rolled further onto her side. Her left leg pushed between his and her arm wrapped around his waist, laying on his hip. They fit together as if made for one another.

"I will not let you go, Kali," he murmured, staring up at the ceiling. "I can't."

Kali woke slowly. She knew it was still early. She had always been an early bird. It used to drive Destin insane as he was a night owl. There was no talking to her brother before ten in the morning if you wanted either a coherent conversation or to keep your head attached to the rest of your body. Personally, Kali loved the early morning before the sun came up when everything seemed new, reborn and peaceful.

She lay perfectly still. She knew the moment she woke that she wasn't alone. Her gaze ran over the male sleeping peacefully beside her. They were both lying on their sides facing each other so it was easy for her to see him. Asleep, he seemed softer, less threatening. She carefully studied his features, taking her time to really look at him. He wasn't handsome in a classical way, but in a darker, more serious and dangerous way.

With his high cheekbones and olive complexion, he could almost have been a mix of Native American and European descent. He wore his hair cut short instead of longer like most of the Trivator warriors she had seen from a distance. His nose was broader with small ridges along it. He had sharp teeth instead of smooth ones like a human. She thought that would have been a turn off, but it wasn't. He had a strong jaw line that was covered in a five o'clock shadow of whiskers. Overall, he had a surprisingly large number of human characteristics in his features. She knew there were more subtle differences though. He was taller than the average human male, broader, more muscular, and definitely faster. She had seen a few of Trivator warriors in action over the past six years and had a healthy respect for their fighting abilities.

The biggest thing that confused her was her reaction to him. She wanted him physically. The ache inside her grew as did the need to touch and taste him again. She wasn't ignorant of what was happening. It was impossible to live in close proximities like she did and not know about the physical needs between a man and a woman. Hell, as Destin's personal guard, she knew more about her brother's love life than any sister should know. While the desire to explore and enjoy a physical relationship was new to her, she also knew it was because she hadn't found a guy who made her as curious as this male did.

Unable to resist, she reached out to touch his hair. A small smile curved her lips when she found it was just as soft as the first time she had touched it. Threading her fingers through it, she watched as his eyes slowly opened.

"I never got a chance to see if it was a soft as I thought it was," she murmured quietly.

"And what are your findings?" he asked in a husky voice, his eyes darkening with desire as she continued to run her fingers along his scalp. "Is it?"

Kali rose up on one elbow so that she was above him. The move forced him to roll onto his back. She moved with him, curling her fingers in his short hair. She found herself lying partially over him. Her own eyes darkened with desire at his swift intake of breath.

Moving slowly, she slid her leg over his and shifted until she was straddling him. The thin shirt she had found in one of drawers rose up around her thighs. She wasn't wearing her panties as she had washed them out and left them to dry in the bathroom.

"Kali," his thick voice held a thread of warning as she settle down over him, trapping his throbbing cock along her heated flesh. "You are playing with fire. I am not like your human males. I will take you."

Leaning forward, Kali threaded the fingers of her other hand through his hair trapping his face between them. She glanced down at his lips before looking him in the eye again. Hot moisture pooled between her legs, making her want to rub it along the thick shaft pulsing against her.

"I want you," she whispered before pressing her lips to his.

It was as if a switch, one that had been dormant or forgotten for the past six years, had been turned on inside her the moment she met Razor. She had done a little bit of experimenting when she was in high school, but those feelings were nothing compared to what she felt now. After her mom was killed and the alien warships appeared, she had lost all interest in exploring her own sexuality. It was as if her body had been placed in a deep freeze.

She didn't know if her physical attraction to Razor was normal or not. All she knew was she wanted him… badly. For once, she was going to be greedy and take what she wanted, even if it was just for a short time.

Fire exploded like a raging inferno inside him at her whispered words. When he felt her tentative touch it had taken every ounce of discipline in him to remain still. The feel of her fingers scraping along his scalp had finally been too much for him and he knew he had to see her reaction to him being awake. The look of hunger in her eyes took his breath away.

He ran his hands up her bare thighs to her waist. His first thought was to roll over, but some instinct told him to let her take the lead – for now. One thing he realized as he opened to her, he liked the way humans kissed. His hips pressed upwards as he pulled her down against him. He felt as if all the blood in his body was pooling around his cock.

"Kali," he moaned when she pressed tiny kisses to the corner of his mouth and along his jaw. *"Fi'ta,* I will not last long if you continue this."

She pulled back, running her hands along his face down to his chest. This position had her sitting on him. Sweat beaded on his brow as her eyes drooped with desire and she rocked her hips against him.

"What does *'fi'ta'* mean?" she asked in a husky voice.

"It means… fighter. You are my little fighter. The way you defended yourself against the men who opened fire on you… You are my fighter," he groaned shifting his hands to lift her slightly up.

"Razor."

The sound of his name on her lips washed away the doubt he had experienced earlier. It was his name on her lips now. Her eyes connected with his as she lay with him. It was him that she said she wanted.

He lifted her just enough to release his cock. Her eyes widened as he shifted enough to align his hard shaft with her slick entrance. His mouth tightened as he carefully lowered her over it. He didn't want to hurt her. He suspected that Trivator males were larger than human males. There were so many questions he should have asked Hunter!

Razor locked his hands around her waist to keep them from trembling as he slowly impaled her. He had never taken a female this way and wasn't sure how it would work. Everything about this experience was making him feel like a young warrior experiencing his first lover.

He paused when she whimpered. Her eyes darkened with uncertainty and pain. He began drawing in deep breaths through his nose as he fought for control. Everything inside him wanted to thrust upward in triumph at his claim

"Razor, I... you are..." He watched as she drew in a deep, shaky breath. "You're kind of bigger than I thought. I've never done this before. At least, I never got this far before," she admitted.

"I do not want to hurt you," he ground out in a voice filled with frustration and need.

"Just, give me a second," she whispered, closing her eyes and leaning forward.

Razor closed his eyes and tried counting to help relieve the pressure of disappointment inside him. He knew it was possible for a Trivator male to fit with a human female. Hunter and Jesse were proof of that.

Gods, I should have asked Hunter more questions, he thought in despair as his hands fell to the bed and he clenched at the sheet below.

Kali's nails curled on his chest and she rose up on her knees slightly until he was barely inside her heated core. If he lived through this, he would be contacting his younger brother again. This time though he wouldn't let him go until he knew everything there was to know, even if he had to direct some of those questions to his new sister. He didn't care how embarrassed his brother got. He needed to know how Hunter was able to fit with Jesse.

His eyes flew open when Kali suddenly widened her legs and sank down on him all the way. A low moan escaped her and her head fell forward. His hands rose to cup her face, lifting it so he could see it. A shimmer of tears glistened, but none fell.

"You feel so good," she whispered as she moved her hips.

"I hurt you," he choked out in dismay. "You should not..."

Kali laid her fingers tenderly over his lips and shook her head. "It only hurt for a moment. I would have hurt much worse if you had stopped. I told you, I want you."

"Then have me, you shall," he growled in a voice filled with heated passion. "I want to see all of you."

Kali sat back to pull the shirt she had borrowed off. The movement drove him deeper and pulled a choked moan out of both of them. She gripped the bottom of the shirt and pulled it off, tossing it to the floor beside the bed. Razor's hands had already moved from her face to her chest before she even finished.

"Yes!" she cried out when he leaned up and greedily sucked on her right breast. "Oh God!"

"Mine, *fi'ta*," he growled. "You are mine, Kali."

Pleasure washed through him as she rocked back and forth along his long shaft. The nerve endings along his cock reacted to the friction created between their bodies, his hardness against her soft, slick vaginal channel. He rose up to meet her as she came down. The tip of his cock brushed against her womb as the position they were in drove him deeper, bringing with it another rush of pleasure.

He released her right breast with a loud pop and attacked her left nipple like a dying man given a drink of water. He wrapped his arm around her waist as he teased the tip with his sharp teeth. Her nipple swelled in reaction to the combination of pleasure and pain as he nipped her.

"Razor," she panted, moving restlessly on his lap. "I need more. I need you."

Tightening his arm around her waist, he rolled toward the wall. Kali's legs fell apart as he rolled. He pushed his hips forward, determined to keep their bodies locked together as they transitioned to the new position.

He braced his hands on each side of her head as he took over. He pulled almost all the way out of her before driving his cock back in slowly. He wanted to feel every inch of her. A shudder went through his body as she fisted him. He lowered his head to her neck and rubbed against her, leaving his scent on her skin as he continued to stroke her in a slow, determined movement guaranteed to drive them both insane.

"You were made for me, Kali. You, only you," he groaned as his cock swelled.

Her gasp echoed in his ear as she stiffened, and a low cry burst from her lips. A shockwave of pleasure reverberated through him as she shattered around him. A rush of hot liquid surrounded his cock making her slicker than before. The pulsing of her vaginal channel sucked greedily on his cock until he felt his own orgasm explode, pulling a deep cry of satisfaction from his own lips.

He didn't realize he had clamped down on her vulnerable neck until the sweet taste of her blood touched his tongue. He didn't release her as he pushed slightly deeper into her. The combination of their releases felt right. He could feel the connection all the way to his soul.

It dawned on him that this is what his father meant when he explained the difference between a warrior seeking relief and finding his *Amate*. This is what every warrior hoped he would be blessed with if he lived and fought well. Tears burned his eyes that he had been given such a gift.

Releasing his grip on Kali's throat, he ran his tongue over the mark he had left. It would probably leave a scar. The thought of his mark on her skin cause his cock to jerk in response. Her low moan told him she could feel every inch of him as well as he could her.

He shifted enough so he could wrap his arms around her while he buried his face against her bare shoulder. He made sure he kept the majority of his weight off of her. A shudder went through him when she shyly ran her hands along his side before wrapping them around him so she could hold him against her as well.

18

Razor sighed as the weight of what he was about to do washed through him. The last three days had been – incredible. He set the report he was viewing down on his desk and stood up to stretch. The weather was supposed to clear by morning according to the readings. He had ordered Cutter to send a team to each side of the city to meet with the men in charge. If they did not lay down their weapons and surrender to the human military, he would order the city flattened. Anyone remaining after the twelve hour deadline would die.

He walked over to the window, watching as a light dusting of snow continued to fall. His thoughts turned to Kali. A satisfied smile curved his lips. He enjoyed listening to her tales of when she was a child.

He discovered she had broken her arm when she was twelve when she fell from a wall while walking on it. She described how several children in the neighborhood where she grew up learned the art of Parkour. It was the method that she used to move about the city.

"Parkour allows me to move about the city in the most efficient way by using my surroundings. I 'see' the buildings around me and use them," she explained. "It is fun, fast and since not many people can do it, it gives me a measure of safety. Tim, Jason, Destin, and a couple other guys from the neighborhood are the only ones that I know of that use it as well."

They spent the time when he was not working making love and talking. He had been furious when she told him late last night of Badrick's visit to her brother. He promised to investigate the Usoleum's request for women in exchange for weapons. She told him that she wished she had just killed the blue bastard when she had the chance.

"It would have saved countless lives," she had murmured quietly.

During their talks, he discovered she had a unique sense of humor that often left him chuckling. He shared things with her that he never thought about before. He told her of the mischief he and his brothers and sisters had gotten into when they were younger. As the oldest, he was always blamed for corrupting the younger ones.

"How many brothers and sisters do you have?" Kali had asked him as she lay in his arms late last night.

"I have five brothers and three sisters," he had told her. "I'm the oldest. As such, it was always my responsibility to watch out for the others. There are large creatures that live in my world that can be very dangerous. It is important to stay on the paths that have been laid out so that you remain safe when traveling between my home and the city."

He remembered his shock when she had laughed. "It's not like I'll have to worry about that," she had teased before she sighed. "It's nice, listening to you talk about your world. It sounds so different from my own." She had yawned and snuggled down against him.

"You will come to love it," he murmured as her eyes closed.

"I'll dream about it," she mumbled. "Close as I'll ever get to seeing it."

A knock on the door pulled him from his reverie. Turning, he walked back to his desk before calling out the command to enter. He studied the frowning face of Colonel Baker as he stepped into the office.

"Colonel," Razor acknowledged with a nod.

"Razor," Colonel Baker grunted out as he walked over to stand in front of the desk. "Badrick has departed."

Razor raised an eyebrow and waited. He was well aware that the Usoleum councilman had departed. He also knew exactly where the male was headed. Cutter had slipped a tracking device into his transport before it took off.

"I'm aware of the Councilman's departure. Is there another issue that has brought you here?" Razor asked politely, waving toward the chair in front of his desk. "Would you care for a drink?"

Colonel Baker shook his head as he sat down in the seat across from Razor. His eyes flickered to the tablet sitting on the desk before returning to Razor. There were a lot of issues he wanted to inquire about, but he knew he wouldn't get a straight answer out of the bastard sitting behind the desk. Still, he had been ordered to follow through, to find out exactly what plans the brass in Washington should follow.

"Kali Parks," Colonel Baker began.

"Is off limits for discussion," Razor replied in a sharp, but calm, voice. "Next issue."

Colonel Baker sat back in frustration. "Your request to meet with both Allen and Parks."

"Done," Razor replied.

"What if they don't agree to meet with you?" Colonel Baker bit out. "What then?"

Razor leaned forward and stared into the Colonel's eyes. He wanted the human military male to know that he was answering his questions, at least some of them, as a courtesy, not because he had to. The time for involving the human warriors had passed.

"They have twelve hours to either meet with me and surrender, or die," Razor said. "I am aware of your orders to prevent this from happening. I would not recommend trying to stop me, Colonel. Once an order is given, it will be carried out. The Alliance will not continue to waste its resources or that of your planet on those who refuse to move forward. Do I make myself clear?"

"Yes."

Razor's eyes hardened into twin, glowing, molten orbs of gold. He knew from the paling of the Colonel's face that the other male had believed his orders to stop the destruction of the city had been top secret. All communications between the humans had been carefully monitored over the past six years to prevent deception and betrayal on their part.

"Do you have any other issues you would like to bring to my attention?" Razor asked in an icy voice.

Colonel Baker rose on shaky legs. He kept his expression neutral as he gazed back at the golden eyes that reminded him all too clearly that he was not dealing with a human opponent. Stiffening his spine, he bowed his head before he replied.

"No, I believe you have answered most of them," he replied in a stiff voice before he turned and walked toward the door.

"Colonel," Razor called out as Colonel Baker opened the door. "I can only give them twelve hours. I have another situation in a different galaxy that requires my attention. I hope for the sake of the humans living in the area that the two men agree to the peace offerings we are extending."

"You have a strange idea of a peace offering," Colonel Baker replied boldly. "Give up or die isn't much of an offer."

"It is the only one 'on the table' as I believe you humans say," Razor countered. "Enough humans and Trivator warriors have died. It is time for your world to rebuild. What better way than from the ground up?"

Colonel Baker stared at Razor for several long seconds before he nodded his head and opened the door. While he could understand the man's strategic methods, even appreciate them, it still burned that it took an alien to bring the world together. He turned toward his own office located on the other side of the armory. He had a lot to think about and a report to file. It would appear their secure lines of communication were not as secure as they thought.

Kali pressed back against the wall just outside of Razor's office. She had been on her way to see him when the door to his office opened. She heard every word, straight from Razor's mouth. Resting her head against the wall, she bit her lip to keep from screaming at him. Why she thought their relationship would change his mind about attacking the city, she didn't know. She just knew she had no choice but to warn Destin.

Blinking back the tears threatening to blind her, she turned back toward their private quarters. It was time to leave. She knew the layout of the armory. She had taken a fire evacuation map. There were several storage sheds not far from the high fence surrounding the armory. She would use the building's structure and anything else she could find to get over it. It would be dangerous. Not only was there barbwire around the top of the fence, the fence itself was hot. One touch and she would be lucky if it only knocked her out.

Slipping into the room, she locked the door before hurrying to the stash of clothes that Chelsea had given her. She quickly added several layers, making sure she didn't take anything that would be too bulky or inhibit her movements. She glanced around the room once more, pausing on the bed. Hot tears quickly filled her eyes before she brushed at them angrily.

"Thanks for the memories," she whispered sadly before turning to the window and opening it.

19

A nerve throbbed in Razor's jaw as he knelt next to the fresh tracks outside the fence. The indention in the snow where Kali landed was clear in the light from Cutter's torch. He stood and looked over at the other side of the fence where a long metal pipe used for running conduit lay in the snow.

"She is very resourceful. You have to give her credit for that," Cutter said, looking at the same thing before his eyes moved to the top of the shed. "It has to be a good ten feet past the roof of the shed. She is lucky she cleared it."

"She'll be lucky if I don't strangle her when I catch her," Razor growled. "Let's go."

Cutter nodded before he signaled to two other men with them. Thunder and Vice nodded. They were two of the best trackers in the galaxy. He turned back to Razor as the two men disappeared into the growing darkness.

"You're lucky Thunder came back after his last mission," Cutter commented quietly as they moved to follow the men. "It shouldn't take long for him to find her with all this snow."

Razor shook his head and looked up at the buildings. "I'm not sure even he can track Kali. She will go up and use the buildings. If she stayed on the ground, it would be easy with the fresh snow and no other movements but she won't. It is not the way she moves," he said before breaking into a jog when Vice called out to them.

"Her tracks disappear here," Vice said, standing up and looking around with a frown. "It is like she vanished."

Razor looked up. They had only covered a couple of blocks. The moment a building presented itself as a possible way to move higher she had taken it. The narrow alley was cluttered with hidden debris which could trip her or limit her movements, not so on the rooftops.

"She used the fire escape."

Thunder's head jerked up. He frowned as he calculated the distance to the bottom rung. It was at least eight feet. Not a difficult task for a Trivator warrior to reach, but for a human female?

"How tall is she?" he asked skeptically.

"Five foot four, perhaps five," Razor responded as he jumped and grabbed the bottom rung. Pulling himself up hand over hand until he could step on the bottom bar, he turned to look down at the other men. "She would have no problems reaching it."

Thunder watched as Cutter grabbed the metal ladder and began climbing. "What is it with these females? Don't they know their limitations?" he growled under his breath thinking of another human female who had defied the odds by breaking into an encampment in front of a bunch of alien rebels.

"Obviously not," Vice said with a grin. "After you."

Kali turned in a circle, warily trying to keep the three men from surrounding her. Her eyes flashed from one man to the other. She had almost made it to the divide that separated the northern and southern part of the city when she stumbled upon them.

"What's your name, sweet cakes?" one of the men called out.

"I think she's a keeper. What do you think, Ralph?" another male with a goatee and no front teeth snickered.

"Shut up. She goes to the boss man," the largest of the three ordered.

"Now Mitt, you know he don't like girls," Ralph whined. "He likes them boys."

"I said shut up, Ralph. This is Kali Parks. He'll want her," Mitt snapped.

Kali gauged the distance to the wall behind the three men and the height of the open window on the second floor of the building. If she could get a running jump, she could be up and through the second story window before they knew what happened. She just needed a lucky break.

"Oh no you don't, lady. I've seen what you can do," Mitt said coldly.

"I have to get to my brother," Kali demanded. "It is a matter of life and death."

"Maybe if you're real sweet, Colbert will exchange you for your brother," Goatee joked. "I heard he has a crush on him."

Kali jerked back another step as they moved closer. "You don't understand!" she said angrily. "This affects Colbert as well! The Trivators want my brother and Colbert to surrender. If they don't, they are going to flatten the city like they did Mexico City!"

"Yeah, maybe Colbert would like one of those huge asses to fuck when they try it," Ralph laughed.

"Please," Kali begged, turning her gaze to the only one in the group who seemed to have any brains. "Mitt, I'm serious. Razor has given them twelve hours. If they don't lay down their arms and surrender within twelve hours he has ordered the Destroyers in. Hundreds of thousands of innocent people will die!"

Mitt shook his head. "You can tell him yourself, lady. Colbert said if anyone ever found you on this side of the divide that we better bring you in or we'll be feeding the fish."

Kali shook her head in frustration. She couldn't back up any further. She had no choice. It was either fight and have a chance of escaping, or be taken prisoner. If she went down, she would rather go down fighting. Making a fake to the left, she turned to the right and pushed past Ralph, knocking him to the ground. She twisted as Goatee reached for her, elbowing him hard in the stomach.

She was almost to the wall when pain exploded through her back. Her muscles stiffened as a wave of shock from Taser hit her in the back. Even her jaw clenched, smothering the cry of agony that went through her at the powerful assault to her nervous system. She fell forward, unable to protect herself. Her forehead struck the unforgiving brick of the building as she collapsed.

Darkness was a blessing. At least the terrifying agony disappeared as she lost consciousness. She faintly heard a nervous laugh as she was turned over.

"Damn, Mitt. I think you killed her. Look at all the blood," Ralph said.

20

"Do you want me to take the shot?" Tim asked quietly as he lined the largest Trivator warrior in his site.

"No," Destin said coldly.

He carefully watched as the small group of four males knelt in the narrow alley three hundred yards from them. He adjusted the night vision binoculars to zero in on them. They had been tracking the men for the last few blocks.

They had to move carefully. They were in enemy territory now. So far, they had to detour twice on their mission to the National Guard Armory. Destin had cursed the last four days. It would have been suicide if they had tried to get to the Armory during the storm. He and Tim left as soon as it cleared enough for them to travel under the cover of darkness.

They had discovered the small group of Trivator males about ten minutes earlier. It looked like they were tracking someone, namely Kali if Destin had to guess. Dread twisted his gut when he saw one male touch the wall of the building, then lift his hand to his nose.

"Shit! What happened?" Tim asked when a ferocious roar echoed through the empty streets. "Something has really pissed him off."

"I don't know, but I think it's time I introduced myself," Destin said, standing up.

Tim's head jerked around in surprise. "Dude, I don't think that is a good idea. Those bastards have been wanting your hide for the past two years."

Destin's eyes hardened with determination. "Yeah, well they are about to find out what happens when they get what they want. Take out the one that roared first if shit goes down. I'm pretty sure he's the leader," Destin ordered as he threw his leg over the side of the ledge of the parking garage.

Tim watched as Destin disappeared before turning his eyes back to the warriors across the street. It didn't take long for Destin to get down the two levels. Tim followed his friend and leader as he moved with a grace born of determination and confidence.

"I sure hope you know what the fuck you're doing," he muttered under his breath as Destin's movements caught the attention of the men.

"Razor," Cutter's quiet voice said.

"It's Kali's blood," Razor bit out, curling his red stained fingers into a fist.

"We'll find her," Vice said. "Whoever took her can't have gotten far."

Thunder's head jerked up and he sniffed the air before turning in a crouch, his hand pulling the laser pistol at his waist. The low rumble of warning from him had the other men turning as well. His eyes scanned the darkness as he opened his senses and breathed in the scents carried on the frigid air.

"We've got company. I smell one, possibly two distinctive scents," Thunder growled.

Razor turned, scanning the area. He jerked his head slightly to the right, signaling Cutter and Vice to spread out. He froze when a voice called out for everyone to freeze.

"I wouldn't," the deep voice echoed in the narrow alley. "Your main man is targeted. You move, he dies."

"Human!" Vice snarled.

"Calm," Razor said coldly as he turned toward the voice at the end of the alley. "Where is she?"

Destin took a step closer, keeping the rifle he carried firmly aimed at the alien male. He stopped when he was almost ten feet from him. His eyes flickered to the other three males who stood in a semicircle behind him. They were slightly taller than the one in front but there was something about the way the bastard in front stood that warned Destin he was probably the most deadly of the group.

"Who?" Destin asked, already knowing the answer.

"My *Amate*! Kali Parks," the male snarled, flashing his teeth in a way that reminded Destin of a male lion. "I will rip the answer from you before I kill you."

Destin's mind swirled at the hostile tone and fury behind the male's threat. Something was wrong. Unless Kali killed one of them when she escaped, he couldn't see this type of reaction coming from the male unless…

"What does *Amate* mean?" Destin asked with growing anger. "So help me, if you've raped my sister, I'll blow your fucking balls off first."

The human's voice faded on the last word. The anger, pain and grief in it combined with the word 'sister' registered as the man took another step closer. A glimmer of shadowy moonlight offered enough light for him to recognize the face of Destin Parks. He reined in the rage he was feeling when he realized that this human cared about Kali as much as he did.

"I have claimed her as mine," Razor replied quietly, watching the fury build again in the man's eyes.

"You bastard," Destin choked out. "She's not a fucking whore!"

Razor lifted his hand when Cutter shifted to throw himself in front of him when Destin's hand tightened on the grip of the weapon he was holding. He stared into the other male's eyes, willing him to hear the truth in his words. Humans could not scent the deceit the way a Trivator could. He would have to proceed slowly. He raised his hands up, palms forward, to show he was unarmed and meant no threat.

"No, she is not," Razor replied calmly. "She is my *Amate*. She is my life. I have sworn to protect and care for her. An *Amate* means the world to a Trivator warrior. We do not take one lightly, as it is for life."

Razor could see the indecision flash through Parks' eyes as he took another step closer. He knew that the male didn't believe him. His eyes flickered to the markings peeking out from under the end of the sleeve of his jacket. He carefully pulled one sleeve down so that the dark markings were visible.

"I am Razor. I belong to Kali as she belongs to me. Forever will I tie my life to hers. I will care for, protect and give my seed only to her. She is my *Amate*. She is my life," Razor said quietly. "These are the markings that bind my life to your sister. I need your help. She is hurt. Her blood is on the wall."

Destin's eyes widened, not only from what the warrior said, but who he was. This was Razor. The Destroyer. His throat worked up and down as he swallowed. His mind raced through everything he had heard, knew for a fact and what the male was telling him.

"Destin, I swear on my life I have not harmed Kali," Razor insisted stepping close enough that the barrel of the rifle pushed against the center of his chest. He continued to keep his hands raised. "I need your help. She is hurt. I fear Colbert's men may have captured her. Every minute we delay our search for her means another minute she is in danger."

He saw Destin's eyes flickered past him to the other three warriors who remained frozen in silence before turning back to him as he waited for Destin to make up his mind. He watched as Destin slowly raised his left hand high and fisted it before holding up two fingers. Only when he lowered the rifle did Razor release his breath.

"You better be telling me the truth," Destin warned in an icy voice. "Tell me what happened."

Razor nodded, recognizing the same calm focus and edge of barely suppressed civility in the human male that made him a strong leader. He glanced over as another human male approached. It didn't take long to relate Kali's escape and their search for her.

"They'll take her to Colbert's headquarters," Destin replied, turning to Tim. "Get the team together. And Tim, let them know we are finishing this tonight."

"I'll let Mason know," Tim replied, looking with a touch of caution and a lot of curiosity at the Trivator warriors who stood to the side. "What are you going to do?"

Destin's lips curved into a menacing smile. "I'm going to go have a chat with Colbert. It has been a long time coming."

"And them?" Tim asked under his breath.

Razor turned, shooting Tim a look that sent a shiver of dread down his spine. His cold eyes made Tim hope that whatever happened tonight would resolve the need for the Trivator forces to move in. He had no desire to face off against them.

"We will accompany him," Razor said.

"Tim, make sure everyone is ready. If anything happens to me, you are in charge," Destin said quietly before nodding to Razor. "Let's go.

We'll move faster along the rails. Colbert moved his headquarters a few days ago to the old Central Station."

"How can you be sure that is where he is?" Razor asked.

Destin's lips curved up in a confident smile. "Because Kali followed one of the bastards back when they used a tunnel we didn't know about. Mason found a few more accesses and sewer tunnels that were on the original blueprints, but not on the updated ones in the city building archives," Destin replied. "We'll go topside until we get closer then move underground. My men will be there."

"Cutter," Razor called out. "Contact the advance troops. I want them in position. This will be a ground assault."

"The Council isn't going to like this," Cutter replied quietly. "I received a report before we left. Badrick has them believing you are compromising your position because of Kali. He is asking for your removal and wants Kali transferred to his personal security forces so he can interrogate her."

"They will not agree. Why does he want Kali so badly?" Razor bit out in a harsh voice.

"I'll tell you why. The same reason he struck a deal with Colbert. He is collecting any female between the ages of fourteen and forty and shipping them off planet," Destin informed him bitterly. "He wanted Kali for himself. He offered weapons in exchange for her and any other women we supplied for him. I told the bastard I'd kill him and any other one of you sons-of-bitches before I let any of you take a female under my protection."

"Kali did not tell me," Razor responded quietly. "I will deal with Badrick once I have Kali back."

"Sure you will," Destin muttered. "What about the women Colbert gave to him? Will you deal with that too?"

Razor's eyes flash with a cold determination. "Yes," he promised. "I will send a team to find and return them."

Destin studied the hard features and steady gaze before he slowly nodded. Holding out his hand, he waited until Razor gripped it firmly with his own. A man was only as good as his word. He planned on doing everything in his power to make sure that this Trivator warrior kept his.

"You better not be fucking with me," Destin said, dropping his hand to his side. "Keep up. We are going to be moving fast and the tracks are icy so watch where you step."

Razor watched as the human took off at a steady pace. He glanced at Thunder and Vice who had been silently listening to their conversation. He nodded to the two men. When this was over, he would send them after the females that had been taken.

21

"You promised to keep that bastard away from Chicago," Colbert said, sitting back and staring moodily at Badrick. "Why should I believe you now?"

Badrick kept the bland expression of calm on his face even as he seethed in anger. His private security team had discovered a tracking device that had been planted on his transport. He knew exactly who had ordered it placed there. It was time to depart this horrid planet before Razor discovered the extent of his deceit. His hope of using the unusual female population to repay some of his debtors had seemed a good plan until Razor was brought into the conflict.

"If your men had killed him like they were supposed to he wouldn't be an issue," Badrick pointed out. His eyes flickered to the unconscious female that had been brought in just minutes after he arrived. A small smile curved his lips. Perhaps he could have a limited amount of satisfaction before he left. "I have submitted my recommendation that he be removed from his position to the Alliance Council."

Colbert straightened and stood up. He stepped down from the raised platform where a single chair sat. He liked being higher than those that came in. It gave him an advantage that he wielded with an iron fist. He was the top dog of the group of men who followed him.

Colbert's eyes flickered to Kali's unconscious body. Blood covered her forehead and down the left side of her face from a small cut. Resentment boiled inside him. She was the reason Destin chose not to join him. Destin's desire to protect her, shelter her from the real world of the streets, tore them apart. Without Kali in his life, it would have been easy for Destin to embrace the life that Colbert had followed. They could have ruled together, even before the presence of the aliens. He had been moving up the ranks, graduating from the local street gangs to the harder core men who really ruled the city.

"I don't have a lot of faith in your recommendations," Colbert replied sarcastically, walking past him to a small table where several blueprints were spread out across it. "My sources say that the bastard isn't easy to kill."

"He would be dead if not for the interference of Kali Parks," Badrick threw back at him. "She rescued him."

Colbert threw another disgruntled glance at Kali's limp body. "Why am I not surprised? Kali has always managed to land on her feet. Even as a kid, she was a thorn in my side."

"I can remove that thorn… permanently," Badrick responded with an insincere smile. "I must return to the my planet. She could no longer hinder your plans if she is no longer on yours."

Colbert's dark chuckle echoed in the dim lower level of the former metro station. He knew what the bastard really wanted. He wanted Kali. Colbert's eyes narrowed as he thought about it. It was true, if Badrick took Kali he wouldn't have to worry about her inference any longer. He could offer a peace treaty with Destin, console him in his anger and grief. With Kali somewhere far, far away there would be no way of her ever coming between them again. Yet…

"I need a way to defeat the Trivator forces if they attack," Colbert said, turning and leaning back against the table. "I want some way of making sure they don't use those Destroyers on the city. I also want complete control of Chicago. You give me that, I'll give you Kali."

Badrick's mouth tightened into a straight line as he studied the smug human male. His long fingers curled before he relaxed them. He could make a hundred promises and the male would never know that he was powerless to provide them. By the time Allen found out, he would be light years away from this world, with Kali Parks as an enjoyable distraction.

"That is simple," he replied with a wave of his slender blue hand. "Join with Parks and agree to rebuild the city. That is the only thing the Alliance wants. If you do this, the Trivator will not attack. I will document that you are to have control over the area in appreciation for your cooperation."

"Simple," Colbert repeated in a suspicious voice. "What guarantees can you give me that they will accept your documentation giving me control?"

Badrick's eyes flashed in fury. "I am a member of the Alliance council," he growled in a low dangerous voice. "I have favors owed to me, thanks to some of the females you sent. There will be no questions as to the approval."

Colbert threw his head back and laughed. As he stood straight and walked over to Badrick. It was a shame the bastard was a little too dangerous for his taste or he might have enjoyed getting to know him a little better. He made a rule to never have sex with anyone capable of killing him in the middle of it. Something told him this guy would like it rough. Colbert's eyes flickered to Kali. She was tough. She might actually live through it, the first time.

"Deal," Colbert said, holding his hand out.

Badrick glanced down in distaste before he held his own hand out and limply gripped Colbert's hand. He cursed when Colbert suddenly tightened his hold and jerked him forward. A shudder went through him when the human male ran his lips up along his jaw to his ear.

"You better be fucking sure you aren't trying to screw me," Colbert whispered in his ear. "Because if you do, I'll tie your ass up and fuck it before I kill you."

Badrick stepped back and smoothed the sleeves of his jacket before he raised his eyebrow at Colbert. A fake smile curled the edges of his tightly pressed lips. He gave a brief shake of his head to his Security guard when the warrior stepped forward after Colbert released him.

"Perhaps if our paths cross in the future, I'll take you up on the first part of your threat," Badrick replied in a mild voice. "But only if I get to do the same."

Kali lay still listening to the conversation between Colbert and Badrick. Her pounding head made it easy to pretend she was still unconscious. She silently cursed the bastard who had Tasered her. The stinging in her back, along with the tenderness, made lying there in the awkward position she had been dropped even more excruciatingly uncomfortable.

She cracked her eyelids open just a fraction so she could get a bearing on where everyone in the room was located. Badrick and Colbert were about ten feet away while two of Badrick's personal guards stood stoically near the door. She opened her eyes a fraction more to see how many men Colbert had with him. She counted three, including one of the bastards from the alley.

She quickly closed her eyes when Colbert turned toward her again. Keeping her breathing steady, she listened as he walked across the concrete floor. In her mind's eye, she pictured Colbert. He was left-handed and always wore a pistol tucked into the back of his pants where he could grab it easily. If, and it was a big if, he leaned over her to check on her, she could grab him by his arm, roll and come up with the pistol. She would need to keep his body between her and his guards, otherwise she would lose her advantage.

Just as she hoped, he reached down to turn her onto her back. The moment he touched her, she grabbed his extended arm and rolled. Her right hand held onto his left while she reached behind him for the pistol. His loud curse echoed in the room as she twisted around pulling him up at an awkward angle so he was still off balance. She held the pistol firmly to the back of his head while holding his left arm behind his back.

"Don't," she muttered in a dark voice. "I'll do it, Colbert. I'll end this now."

"You'll be dead too, Kali," Colbert bit out harshly.

Kali jerked on his arm, ignoring the growing panic inside as she felt her own body tremble. She still wasn't up to her full strength and it wouldn't take much for Colbert or any of his men to overpower her. Pressing the end of the pistol into his scalp a little harder, she jerked up on his arm until they were both standing. Because of their differences in height, she redirected the gun to the center of his back.

"Yeah, well, I've got to die someday and taking you out first might just be worth it," she snapped back in frustration, watching as the other men stepped closer. "I wouldn't if I were you. I've got this gun pointed right in the center of his back. One shot and you'll be looking for a new boss."

Badrick's chuckle drew her attention to him. "I understand what you mean now about a thorn in your side," he commented dryly. "Unfortunately, I do not have time for this. My starship is prepared for departure. Kill him, I have no further use for his services."

Colbert's mouth tightened into a straight line as he glared back at the Usoleum Councilman. "You bastard! Kill them all!" he ordered, flashing a look at his three guards.

Kali stumbled forward when Colbert jerked hard to the left as his men opened fire on Badrick. The force of his sudden move, combined with her shaky limbs, almost sent her sprawling. She caught herself at the last minute as she lurched forward.

Colbert spun around and kicked out. His booted foot caught her in the side, knocking the wind out of her as he connected with her ribs. This time she wasn't able to prevent herself from hitting the floor. The pistol she had taken from him flew out of her hand as she hit the unforgiving concrete.

She rolled away from Colbert as gunfire and laser blasts lit the large open area of the former metro station. She crawled toward a stack of crates in an effort to find some form of protection. A harsh cry ripped through her as one of the blasts from the laser cut a path along her right thigh. It stung, but she was pretty sure it was just a glancing blow as she tumbled behind the crate and leaned back against it.

Kali glanced down at the wound and breathed a sigh of relief that it was just a thin slice; more like a long scratch from a branch than a deep wound. Her hand trembled as she pushed her hair back. From the sound of the fighting, others had joined in.

Her eyes swept the area to see if there was any possible way to escape. She was boxed in. The crates offered her protection, but if anyone decided to come looking for her she was toast.

Leaning her head back, she was about to close her eyes in resignation when she saw the rungs that led up to the exhaust vents. Hope soared inside her as she calculated how fast she could make it up them. She was still weak from the Taser and her head injury, but she felt confident she could make it. She moved her wounded leg to see how bad it felt.

Not bad at all, she thought as she looked up again.

Biting her lip, she gave a nod. It was good. She had run with worse. Twisting around until she was on her feet again, she crouched and listened to the exchange of gunfire. If anything, it sounded even louder. Turning on her heels, she placed her hands on the floor and breathed deeply in and out as she imagined the route she would take.

"Jump on the crate, push off the wall, grab the second rung and use the back wall to walk up," she murmured as she forced everything else going on away from her mind until all she saw was the crate, wall and metal rings. "One, two, three!"

Kali exploded upward with the graceful motion of a gymnast. She jumped up on the crate, used her forward momentum to push off the wall with her feet and twisted in midair where she captured the second rung. Before her body could hit the wall, she was using her feet against it to push her up, while her hands grabbed the next hand grip.

She didn't stop until she had reached the top. She swung over the side railing onto the narrow platform high above the fighting. It was only as she glanced down that she saw men that she had fought beside day after day, month after month for the past six years.

Her eyes widened when she saw her brother fighting side by side a Trivator warrior that she knew all too intimately. From her vantage point, she could see everything going on. The Alliance councilman was lying in a puddle of dark blue blood as were one of his security men. Three of Colbert's men were dead. Unfortunately, more had appeared when they heard the gunfire. Now, they battled her brother and other Trivator warriors. While her brother's forces were outnumbered, the Trivator warriors fighting beside them were drastically evening the odds.

Kali couldn't contain her cry of dismay when she saw William in the mass of bodies that had fallen. The old man who had livened up the small world she lived in lay to one side, a deep red stain coating his chest. She bit her fist when the sound caught the attention of Razor who was cutting through the two men attacking him.

Her eyes locked with his for a brief moment before he turned when another one of Colbert's men tried to thrust a knife into his back. It almost found its mark. The shift of her gaze and the look of horror had him twisting to deflect it in time.

"Destin," Kali breathed when she saw her brother was in trouble.

Not stopping to think, she ran down the narrow catwalk to the end. A long chain, used to hoist heavy equipment, hung from a pulley. She jumped over the edge of the railing, grabbed the chain and slid down it. Right before she hit the bottom, she let go so that she landed on the backs of the two men that had Destin cornered.

"Damn it, Kali," Destin cursed out as she rolled to the side as one of the men struggled to get up. "Get the fuck out of here!"

"Not happening, Destin," she yelled back as she kicked the man closest to her in the face as Destin killed the second man. She reached for the gun at the male's waist. It was empty. "Damn."

She gasped as Destin reached down and hauled her up to her feet. He pressed one of the knives he had taken off one of the dead men into her hand. His look of rage and warning told her he didn't like what he was seeing.

"Are you okay?" he grunted out as they pressed back against one of the curved pillars for protection. "You've got a shitload of blood on your face."

"That happens when you hit a brick wall with it," she snapped, yanking him back as a bullet flew mere inches from his head. "What are you doing here with Razor?"

"You and I need to have a serious talk!" Destin growled under his breath. "The guy claims you are his *Amate!*"

"Oh shit," Kali muttered.

"Yeah," Destin bit out. "What the fuck were you thinking?"

Kali didn't know how to answer her brother's coarse question. She glanced around the side of the pillar and watched as Razor cut a deadly path through those that stood in his way. The way he was looking around told her he was looking for her. She pulled back with a grimace. If she thought she was trapped before, it was nothing to what she was feeling right now. She turned to Destin just as another figure rounded the pillar.

"Destin, look out!" she cried out in warning.

She pulled him backwards at the same time as Colbert struck. Pain exploded through her as the knife aimed for Destin struck her instead as she stepped protectively in front of her brother. The force pushed her back into Destin.

"You son-of-a-bitch!" Destin roared in rage, striking back at Colbert. He hit him hard in the jaw, knocking him backwards several steps. "Why? You were like a brother to us. Why?"

"I was never your brother," Colbert choked back as he tried to defend himself from Destin's vicious attack. "I didn't want you as a brother."

Destin struck hard again, knocking the bloody knife out of Colbert's hand as he hit him in the jaw again with his fist. He rammed his knee into Colbert's stomach before he struck him again. The force of the blow knocked Colbert off his feet. While Colbert might have been the taller of the two men, Destin was more thickly built from working out continuously over the years. That strength was only enhanced by his rage.

Destin stood breathing heavily over the man he used to care about like he was family. No more. Colbert's jealousy of Kali and his desire for power made Destin sick to his stomach.

"This ends here and now," Destin said in an emotionless voice. "The city needs to heal. You're through, Colbert. Get out before I kill you."

Destin turned away from the prone, bleeding figure lying on the ground. Kali needed his help. Her white face stared back at him in shock and pain. He started to take a step toward where she was sitting against the pillar when the expression in her pain filled eyes changed from pain to horror. He deftly palmed the switchblade he carried strapped to his wrist. Flicking it open, he turned and threw it in a single graceful arc. The long, sharp blade cut deep as it embedded itself in Colbert's chest.

Destin watched with regret as the life faded from his old friend's eyes. For a brief moment, he saw the small boy he and Kali had befriended when they were just kids. The look of fear and confusion tore at him almost as much as the tears in Colbert's eyes.

"I love you. I always have," Colbert whispered faintly as the life faded from his eyes.

Destin pushed back against the grief threatening to overwhelm him.

He wanted to cry out against the unfairness of the world. He wanted to roar out his pain, but he couldn't. He was now the leader of Chicago. He had too much responsibility and too much to do to give in to his own feelings of grief, pain and despair.

Turning on his heel again, he walked toward Kali who stared back at him with dark, sad eyes. He knew she could feel his pain and sorrow. Her own eyes reflected it as she watched him walk toward her.

"How bad is it?" he asked in a husky tone as he knelt beside her.

"Not so bad," she whispered even as the tears coursed down her cheeks. She raised a trembling, bloodstained hand and gently touched his damp cheek. "I love you, Destin. Together, we will rebuild our home."

Destin turned and stood up as Razor stepped around the pillar. He studied the huge Trivator's face as the alien knelt in front of Kali. A frown crossed his face for a moment as the male pulled a small pouch out from his waist. Razor pulled a thin piece of cloth-like material out of it and pressed it against Kali's neck. Even as he watched, the look of pain faded from her eyes and she began to slide to the side.

"What did you do to her?" Destin asked in a voice thick with emotion.

"I gave her a pain patch," Razor replied stiffly as he bent and scooped Kali's lethargic body up. "She needs immediate medical attention."

"No," Kali said with a weary shake of her head. "Doc can stitch me up. He's done it enough times."

Destin studied Kali's mutinous face for a moment before he looked back at Razor. His mouth tightened as he pushed his personal feelings aside. He had made a deal. Razor would protect Kali and keep her safe in exchange for the Trivator's help in defeating Colbert. It was one deal he hoped he didn't live to regret and one that he hoped Kali would one day forgive him for making.

"You promise to protect her?" Destin demanded in a hard voice. "You will keep your promise to let me rebuild the city."

"You have my word. I agreed to assist you in defeating Colbert in exchange for Kali. I will instruct the Alliance council to give you the governorship of this city. Trivator troops will help you maintain order while the city is being reconstructed."

"What?" Kali mumbled, looking back and forth between Razor and her brother. "Destin, I… I'm coming with you. I have to protect you."

Destin's face softened as Kali's head fell back against Razor's shoulder. He stepped closer. Lifting his hand, he gently stroked her short hair. She reminded him so much of their mother. She was a free spirit. She deserved to live a long and happy life; not one filled with uncertainty and constant danger.

Tears burned the back of his eyes as he realized he might never see her again. His eyes turned down to the blood soaking her shirt. Memories of their mother lying in a pool of blood flooded him for a second. He couldn't risk losing Kali. It was better to know that she was alive somewhere out in the universe than to watch her die here on Earth.

Razor had pointed that out in the alleyway. Razor swore that if Destin agreed to his taking Kali with him, he would protect her. Now, he realized that the Trivator was right. If Kali remained on Earth, she would more than likely end up like their mom, a victim of the violence that held the world in its greedy grasp.

He stepped back away with a firm nod to his face. "Take her. She's yours," Destin said, turning away. "Let's move out. We have a lot to do."

"Destin?" Kali whispered, confused. "Destin!"

"Take her, damn you," Destin bit out without turning around. "Take her before I change my mind."

"I will protect her with my life," Razor replied, turning away.

"No! Destin! Please, no," Kali cried out, weakly fighting to break out of the strong arms carrying her. "Destin! Damn you! You can't do this! You need me. You promised you'd never leave me. You promised."

Destin kept his back to her. He didn't want her to see the tears streaming down his face as he walked away. He hoped if there was a God out there that he forgave him because he wasn't sure that Kali ever would.

Destin paused as he saw William's sightless eyes. The crazy old man had refused to remain behind. William was determined to help him find Kali. Kneeling beside the old hot dog vender and former bookie's body, he carefully lifted the snarled hands and laid them across William's chest.

"Thank you, old friend," Destin murmured. "I hope you find that heaven you were talking about. If you do, tell my mom I said hello and to please forgive me. Please, tell her I'm sorry I didn't do a better job of taking care of Kali."

Destin knelt on one knee with his head bowed and let the pain and grief wash through him. The fading sound of Kali's hoarse pleads echoed around him as members of the Trivator and his forces started cleaning up the dead and wounded. His shoulders shook for a moment as the pain of losing so much ripped through him. Throwing his head back, he breathed in deep, gulping breaths as he begged for the pain to ease. After several long minutes, he felt Tim's hand on his shoulder. Turning tortured eyes to his friend, he nodded.

"Make sure he gets a decent burial," Destin said gruffly, standing up.

"I will," Tim replied, motioning to two men. "Kali?"

"She's gone… she's gone. Hopefully to a place where she will be safe." Destin replied thickly, looking over his shoulder toward the dark tunnel they had come through a short while before.

22

Razor held Kali's silent form tightly against his chest. She had finally quit fighting against him. He knew every move she made must have hurt her. He knew she was still conscious from the occasional movement of her head.

He nodded to Cutter who stood to one side as he approached one of the attack transports that had arrived with the troops he had ordered. He ducked his head as he stepped inside the back of the transport and continued down the long open back where the troops normally stood ready for departure to the front. He carefully laid Kali down on one of the medic cots that folded down from the side of the transport.

"Lift off," he ordered to the pilot. "Notify Patch that I need his presence at the landing site."

"Yes, sir," the pilot said, immediately opening communications with the main base.

"What about Councilman Badrick?" Cutter asked. "The council will have questions about why he was not transported out."

Razor's eyes glittered with barely suppressed rage. "Let them," he snapped. "Badrick is dead. Usoleum custom is to immediately incinerate the body. Have it done."

His head turned when he felt slender fingers wrap around his wrist. He threaded his fingers through Kali's short dark hair as he leaned forward. Her soft, warm breath caressed his cheek as he bent to hear her faint words.

"You promised… to find the… women he took," she reminded him.

Razor pulled back and shook his head in wonder. She was bleeding, bruised and exhausted and she was more concerned about the women Badrick had taken than her own wounds. His fingers tightened in her hair when she tried to pull away.

"Send Thunder and Vice to Badrick's apartments to search it and confiscate his Starship," Razor ordered, never breaking the contact between him and Kali. "I want them to find the women that were taken."

"I'll notify them immediately," Cutter replied quietly, turning toward the front of the transport.

Razor relaxed his fingers when Kali released his wrist. He watched as she licked her dry lips several times. Leaning forward again, he bent so he could hear her again.

"You are totally on… my shit… list," she whispered, closing her eyes as she gave into the medication of the patch and her exhaustion.

Razor sat back on his haunches and smiled down at her relaxed face. Dried blood coated one side of her face and dirty tracks from her tears stained the creamy skin, but he had never seen anything more beautiful in his life. He raised a trembling hand to stroke her cheek.

Lowering his head, he rested it next to hers and listened as she breathed in and out. Closing his eyes, he wondered how she was going to react when she realized what his plans were for keeping her safe. After what just happened… a shudder went through his body as he remembered seeing the knife piercing her body.

He pulled back so he could cup her warm cheek in his hand. The feel of her warm skin, her soft breath, the slight rise and fall of her chest reassured him that she lived. When he had seen Colbert strike her, his blood had run cold. From the angle he was standing it looked like it had gone into her heart. Destin's roar of rage had only re-enforced his fear. He had fought his way over to her in a desperate bid to get to her as she slid down the stone pillar.

"You have caused me to feel more fear in the few weeks that I have known you than I have felt my entire life," he murmured as he gently stroked her hair. "Your brother thinks you will not forgive either of us for wanting to protect you. I would rather have your rage than to lose you and so would he. You do not understand how precious you are, my *fi'ta*. For a Trivator warrior to find his *Amate,* only to lose her is a pain no warrior wants to endure. You are far too brave, far too proud, far too precious for your own good. I hope you forgive us for… for loving you enough to want to keep you safe from harm," he whispered.

He loved her! That was what the feelings were that were driving him crazy. He had heard about it, even seen it between his father and mother, and Hunter and Jesse. For a minute he was stunned. He leaned forward and pressed a light kiss to Kali's slightly parted lips.

"I love you, Kali," he whispered in wonder, looking at her with a growing determination. "I will not let you expose yourself to danger. I can't. You are my life." He picked up her wrist and pressed another kiss to the inside of it, over the dark markings claiming her as his. "I am Razor. I belong to Kali as she belongs to me. Forever will I tie my life to hers. I will care for, protect and give my seed only to her. She is my *Amate*. She is my life." His voice faded on the last word.

My life, he thought as he turned to look up at Cutter who was walking through the doorway.

"Thunder and Vice are heading over to Badrick's apartment," Cutter informed him as he glanced at Kali. "Jag just arrived with the *Star Raider*. He heard the message and sent a team over to the Usoleum Starship. It has been seized."

"Good," Razor commented, standing. "You will remain on Earth to oversee the rebuilding and the withdrawal of the troops. I must return to Rathon but there is another matter that requires my attention before I do."

Cutter nodded. "Chicago was the last major city not under control. Except for some smaller bands of rebels in remote locations, the transition should go smoother now that Parks is in control."

Razor nodded, looking down at Kali again. "Yes," was all he said. He had formed a compromise on their way to Allen's stronghold with Kali's brother. He had offered to support him in exchange for Kali. At first, Parks had resisted. It wasn't until Razor pulled Kali's brother to the side and asked him how many times she must almost die before he would agree that Razor had a better chance of keeping her safe.

It was not a part of Razor's personality to negotiate or even care if Destin Parks agreed. As far as Razor was concerned, Kali already belonged to him. But, there was some instinct deep inside that told him he needed Parks' alliance if Kali was to come to accept him as her *Amate*.

While it was highly unusual, there were cases where a female taken by a warrior later rejected him. In their race, the women held the power over a male. If she rejected him, his mark could be removed from her, but hers would forever tie him to her. A warrior did not give his mark easily or to just any woman. He knew instinctively when he found his *Amate*, not so the female. She was not tied to the male as he was to her.

"Did you notify Patch I needed his assistance?" Razor asked.

"Yes, he is waiting at the landing site," Cutter said, nodding toward Kali's unconscious form. "What makes them so different? They are so fragile yet they fight with a fierceness that any warrior would be proud to stand beside in battle."

"I don't know," Razor admitted, glancing at Cutter as they began their descent. "I don't know."

~

Fifteen minutes later, he was once again laying Kali on the bed in the makeshift medical unit set up at the National Guard Armory. He had to press his lips tightly together to prevent the coarse words he wanted to unleash on Patch. The healer was muttering under his breath about what a sorry piece of work Razor was for not taking better care of his *Amate*. Cutter, who had followed them in, didn't bother hiding the chuckle that escaped.

"Just heal her!" Razor barked out.

"Why? So you can let her get beaten up again?" Patch retorted angrily as he pulled the medical tray closer. "Maybe if I don't, she can remain safe here in medical."

"Darling, that girl is going to find trouble no matter where she is," Chelsea said as she walked into the room. "She's got too much fire to be tied down."

"Well, put the fire out," Razor growled, glaring at Chelsea as she slipped a blood-pressure cuff around Kali's arm. "What are you doing?"

Chelsea raised an ebony eyebrow at Razor and pursed her lips together. She didn't break eye contact until he shifted from one foot to the other in agitation. Only then did she refocus on the task at hand.

"I'm checking her vitals the old fashion way," she snorted. "I don't like those odd things Doc Patch uses."

"I told you they didn't know when not to fight," Cutter muttered to Razor under his breath.

Chelsea's chuckle echoed in the room as she heard Cutter's remark. She shook her head as she recorded the results. These Trivator warriors were good at fighting, but clueless about human women if they thought they would just let them walk all over them.

"Honey, I've tangled with kids high on drugs, dealt with bank robbers, raised three kids, all of them girls, and not a one of them ever got the best of me," Chelsea commented. "You growl and snarl all you want. All it will get you is my foot across your tight-looking ass."

"Tight-looking ass?" Patch repeated, looking at Chelsea in surprise before looking at Razor who scowled at him in frustration. "Now that is an image that I never thought of before."

Chelsea's infectious laughter pulled the tension from the air. She shook her head. This is what she loved about her new career. She met all kinds of people still; but now, they usually weren't trying to kill her.

"You know what you boys need?" she commented as she took a warm, damp cloth and began cleaning the blood off of Kali's face.

"No, but I suspect you will inform us," Patch replied dryly as he ripped open the tear in Kali's shirt covering her wounded shoulder and applied cleanser to the cut.

"You're right, I'm going to tell you," Chelsea said, looking specifically at Razor with a knowing eye. "You need to go have a talk with my Thomas about women. Bless his soul, after being in a house for over thirty years with us, he knows a thing or two that might help save you a lot of headaches, not to mention heartache."

"I think that is a wonderful idea," Cutter announced thinking of one female he was still looking for. "Does he know everything about them?"

Chelsea just shook her head again and muttered 'stupid men' under her breath. "He can tell you all you need to know," she promised.

Patch paused as he finished sealing the wound on Kali's shoulder. He glanced from Chelsea to Cutter to Razor. A gleam of interest brightened his eyes.

"Don't meet with him until after I'm done taking care of the wounded. I want to hear what he has to say," Patch said, returning to the task at hand. "There is another transport coming in with wounded, so it will be a couple of hours."

23

Razor stared at Thomas Cuddles in disbelief. He rubbed his left ear as the man sat back in his seat and raised his beer bottle up to take a deep swig from it. He shook his head. No, his hearing was fine.

"Are you serious?" Patch asked in disbelief. "That's it? That is the answer to the women of Earth?"

"Yep," Thomas replied, wiping his hand across his mouth and grinning. "You follow those rules and you'll live a long and happy life."

"You are not serious," Cutter remarked with a frown.

"Oh, I'm very serious," Thomas said, nodding his head. "I've been married to Chelsea for thirty-one years, four months, and fourteen days. We've had three daughters, all of them married now. Let me tell you, I gave their husbands the same advice."

"This is impossible!" Razor growled sitting forward. "How can these things make her happy?"

"How can they not?" Thomas asked, pointing his beer bottle at Razor. "You've got to accept her as she is and not try to change her."

"But she keeps trying to get herself killed!" Razor retorted, setting his beer down on the table with a thud and running his hands through his hair. "I can do the others. I can kiss her and cuddle her and… wash the dishes. But…"

Thomas shook his head slowly back and forth. "There is no 'but'. You have to accept her. If you try to change her, then she isn't the woman for you. Let me explain," he said, leaning forward again. "When I met Chelsea I was studying accounting at Washington U. She had just been recruited by the FBI. I knew this was important to her even it if scared the hell out of me. Over the years there were a few close calls. She was shot twice. Once when our daughter Lettie was only a year old. I wanted her to quit and we had a huge argument. I finally realized that she wasn't trying to prove how big and bad she could be. It was more than that, it was who she was. She was born to help and to serve others. It was because of that part of her that I fell in love with her. She was an amazing agent, but she was also an amazing wife and mother. When I finally accepted that, our relationship became stronger than ever before and I fell more in love with her every day because every day was a special one."

"Why?" Patch asked curiously. "Why would every day be a special one?"

Thomas sat back again and looked at Patch before turning his gaze to Razor. He knew what the male was going through. He felt a pang of sympathy for him. He had gone through the same thing and Chelsea had shared her talks and insight about Kali Parks with him.

"Because I never knew if it would be our last," Thomas replied in a quiet voice. "I made sure that I made each day a special one. Most importantly, I made sure to let Chelsea know how much I loved her."

"How could you stand by while she placed her life in danger over and over again?" Razor asked in a low voice. "Why would she do that to you?"

"I could stand it because I finally accepted that when it is our time to die then it really doesn't matter if you are an FBI agent or someone driving to work. Death doesn't care what your job is," Thomas explained. "Yes, her job was dangerous, but she was smart, well-trained and took precautions to reduce that danger. I had to trust her, just as she learned to trust me that I would take care of our girls. A relationship is about being a partner. Not a part-time one, but a full-time, 24/7, 365 days a year partner."

"I will not leave Kali behind," Razor said, standing up. "She will be by my side."

Thomas looked up at the huge warrior's dark, determined face and smiled. "As long as she is beside it and you don't expect her to walk behind you," he remarked.

"Is that when, as Chelsea so eloquently told us, she would 'put her foot across our tight-looking ass'?" Patch asked curiously.

Thomas' deep chuckle shook his slightly rounded frame. "Oh yeah. And let me tell you, it only takes once to learn not to let her too far behind you," he laughed. "You'll do fine. Just trust her."

"Trust her, accept her, love her," Razor repeated with a short nod. "I will remember."

Thomas sat back in his chair and watched Razor as he left the mess hall. He shook his head. The man was hard-headed. He was going to have to learn the hard way. He just hoped he didn't screw things up too bad or both he and Kali Parks were in for a difficult journey.

"Do you think he will follow my advice?" Thomas asked distractedly, sipping his beer.

Cutter glanced at Razor's departing back. "Yes," Cutter replied, standing and stretching. "Yes, but it will not be easy for him. He is used to giving orders and expecting them to be followed."

Patch sighed when his comlink pinged. He was needed in medical. Setting his own beer to the side, he rose as well. He turned and gave an apologetic smile to Thomas.

"Thank you for your insight," Patch said. "I'm afraid I must return to medical."

"I've got to go as well. Jag is supposed to have a report on his findings to me in ten minutes," Cutter said with regret. "Thank you for your wisdom, Thomas. I will think on it as well."

Thomas watched as the two Trivator warriors hurried away. His eyes lit up with love and delight when the figure of his beautiful wife appeared in the doorway. A huge smile curved her lips when she saw him. He stood up and opened his arms for her.

Maybe he should have told them a few more pointers, he thought as he gave Chelsea a long, deep kiss.

Razor stood outside the bathroom door in his apartment. He discovered that Kali had woken shortly after he had left medical. Chelsea had helped her back to his room as the medical unit was filled with mostly wounded human males from the fight at Allen's former headquarters.

Colonel Baker had insisted that Kali be moved for her own safety. He was thankful for that, but irritated that he wasn't immediately informed that she was awake. Now she was refusing his request to open the door.

"It is dangerous for you to be alone," he growled. "You lost a lot of blood."

"That happens when you get stabbed," she retorted.

"You were still recovering from the last time you lost a lot of blood," he reminded her. "Kali, open the door."

"I'm not talking to you," she called out.

"Yes, you are," Razor replied, confused. "I hear your voice."

"Well, I'm not talking to you anymore," she argued back.

"But, you are still speaking," Razor said in frustration, clenching his fist and leaning against the door. "Kali, I demand that you open this door."

Silence greeted his demand. He banged on the door in frustration. His brow creased in worry when there was still no response. What if she had fallen unconscious again? What if she had hit her head when she fainted? What if she was in the shower and drowned? All kinds of horrible thoughts flowed through his mind.

"Kali," he called out, the edge of desperation making it deeper and louder than before. "Kali? Answer or I will break the door down!"

He was about to follow through on his threat when he heard the lock turn and the door cracked open a couple of inches. Kali's tear-stained face peeked up at him. Her bottom lip trembled and she angrily brushed at another tear as it escaped to run down her cheek.

"What?" she snapped. "I want you to leave me alone. I want you to... to just go away!"

"You are hurting? I will call Patch. He will give you something for the pain," Razor murmured in concern as he studied her red eyes. "Come, I will help you to the bed."

"I am not hurting, at least not where Patch can help me," she replied. "I don't want to... to lie down."

"What is wrong, *fi'ta*," Razor asked in a husky voice. He raised his hand and captured another tear as it fell. "Why do you cry?"

"I 'cry' because I'm so mad I want to hurt two of the stupidest men on the Earth," she growled in frustration. "I want... to 'cry' because... because... because I just want to cry."

Razor's eyes softened when she sniffed. He remembered Thomas' advice about cuddling. Earth women liked to cuddle. He pushed the door open a little further so he could tenderly pull Kali closer. Wrapping his arms around her, he breathed a sigh of relief when she buried her face against his chest.

"Who are the two stupidest men?" Razor asked gently.

"He gave me away? I thought he loved me! I'm family. You don't give family away," she whispered in a choked voice.

Razor bent and carefully picked her up. He turned and carried her over to the bed and sat down on the edge of it. The same confusing feelings he felt before threatened to drown him again, only this time he knew what it was. Thomas said to trust her. To be honest with her. That she would know. Thomas said that women didn't smell a lie like a Trivator. He explained that they knew instinctively when a male was being deceitful.

"He does love you, Kali, just as I do," Razor replied in a quiet voice. "He did not give you away. He gave you to me. I am now your family."

Kali rested her head against his chest, her ear pressed against his heart. It was strange how similar he was to a human man, but also so different. It skipped a beat when he said he loved her. She lay still for several minutes as he held her close to his warm body.

She didn't know if what she felt for him was love or lust. All she knew for sure was that her body ignited into molten lava whenever he was around. She had never had a reaction to anyone the way she did to Razor.

Okay, whenever I even think of him I short circuit, she thought. *But still, is that love or infatuation?*

She had no experience with what she was feeling and it had been so long since she had talked to another woman about feelings, she had no idea what to do. Maybe she should talk to Chelsea. She seemed like she would know. After all, she had been married for a long time and had three daughters who were also married.

"Why did he tell you to take me away?" she asked in a quiet voice.

"Because I couldn't stand by and watch you die like mom did," a husky voice said from the doorway.

Razor's eyes connected with Destin's for a long moment. His arms tightened possessively around Kali when she started to sit up. He hadn't realized that the door to his living quarters was still ajar. When he had entered his rooms early and found the bed empty, his first thought was that Kali had escaped again. It wasn't until he heard a sound coming from the bathroom that he realized that she was there.

"Destin!" Kali exclaimed in a tear-choked voice.

Destin studied Kali's red, swollen eyes. He didn't plan on coming to the National Guard Armory. He had fought against it, but he couldn't leave her. He couldn't let her go without telling her he loved her. That she was his Kali. His wind sprite, his baby sister, his family. When Razor stopped him in the narrow alleyway, he had almost killed the bastard. At least, until Razor asked him how many times did Kali have to almost die before Destin realized that it was time to accept the Alliance's help in rebuilding the Earth.

He licked his lips and stared back at Razor. "May I come in?" he asked quietly.

"Yes," Razor replied.

Destin would have to have been blind and deaf to miss the possessive way the Trivator warrior was holding his sister or to miss the warning in his voice. Razor was making it clear that Kali belonged to him and he was not going to let her go. In that, they were still in agreement. Destin realized that Kali would always put herself in between him and danger.

Destin slowly walked into the room. He grabbed one of the chairs by the table as he walked by and positioned it next to them. He sat down and gently picked up Kali's left hand. He ran his thumb over the dark symbols circling her wrist as he thought about what to say to her. Drawing in a deep breath, he looked up into her swollen eyes.

"Kali, everything is going to be alright now. I… I need you to know that I love you. It is because I do that I want you to stay with Razor." His eyes locked with Razor's darker ones. "He has sworn to protect you. Earth is not such a good place to be right now, especially Chicago. It may be selfish of me, but I *need* to know that you are safe."

"I can help you," she murmured. "I have stood by your side and protected you for the past six years."

Destin's eyes returned to her. "I know and I love you even more for that. Now it is my turn to protect you. It isn't like I won't ever see…." Destin drew in a deep breath before he tightened his grip on her hand. "We'll see each other again, but for now I need for you to go with him. I need to know that you are safe and protected. I need to be able to focus on rebuilding our home so that when you return, it will be ready for you."

"Destin," Kali started to argue in confusion. "Why? Why are you suddenly so concerned about me getting hurt? Why are you wanting me to leave when there is still so much that needs to be done?"

"Because you are carrying our babe," Razor replied suddenly, looking back at Destin. "I gave my seed to you and Patch confirmed that it has taken hold in your womb."

Kali jerked forward, almost falling out of Razor's lap as she twisted. Only his arms and Destin stopped her from sliding off onto the floor. Her mouth hung open like a fish out of water as she looked at Razor in shock before shaking her head in denial.

"How can he tell so soon? I mean we've only…" She blushed a deep red and glanced at her brother. "It's only been four days," she mumbled.

"Yes, and we have been together frequently over those four days," Razor pointed out, ignoring her deepening blush. "He picked up a change in your blood and did a scan. It confirmed that you are pregnant with my child."

"But… but…," Kali stared at him in shock. "How? I mean I know *how* but… how can it be possible?"

Razor's eyebrow rose as he looked at her pale face. "It is possible. My brother and Jesse have proven that it is possible for a child to be created between a human and a Trivator."

"What… will the difference between us cause any problems? I mean, I've heard that people with different blood types here can have problems," Kali whispered with a worried frown.

"I talked to Patch about that," Razor admitted. "He explained that our blood types were compatible. There is no danger that we are aware of at this time. Lyon, Hunter and Jesse's son, is very happy and healthy. My biggest concern is the trauma you have endured and the amount of blood you have lost. Patch wants to monitor you to make sure everything will be well for both you and the babe. He also wants you to get plenty of rest. You need to let the healing process complete and give your body time to recuperate from the blood you have lost."

"I'm happy for you, Kali," Destin added with a smile. "You deserve to be happy."

"Yeah, but… a baby!" she exclaimed in a dazed voice as she sank back in shock. "I… I don't know anything about babies."

Razor slid his arms around her and pulled her protectively closer to his body. He felt the trembling in her slender frame as shock and fatigue washed through her. He would talk to Patch again before he retired tonight. He wanted Patch to check Kali one more time to make sure she was going to be alright.

"We will learn together," Razor whispered in her ear as she sank back against him. "I will be there for you, Kali. This is a gift no warrior would want to miss."

What little energy Kali had seemed to desert her as she sank back in Razor's arms in stunned disbelief. She listened as the men talked quietly about what happened after Razor took her. Most of the men who were under Colbert surrendered and pledged to work under

Destin. The few that continued to resist were slowly being hunted down by a combination of Trivator and Destin's forces.

After a short time, her eyes grew too heavy to keep them open. The combination of blood loss, her body healing from its injuries and her crying had exhausted her. Soon, their quiet voices lured her into a light sleep.

"You promise you'll keep her safe?" Destin asked as he watched Kali breathing evenly. "She loves to run and explore. I really don't see her slowing down much. If she becomes real quiet, just be there for her. She is working things out on her own. She needs her space. She can't stand being cooped up. She hates broccoli and peas, but loves spinach with cheese in it and egg drop soup."

"I will make sure I download the ingredients and how to prepare them before we leave," Razor replied. "Is there anything else I should know?"

"She loves mint tea, but hates mint," Destin said with a chuckle. "It relaxes her."

"I will get a crate of it," Razor assured him.

"She also likes to hog the covers when she's cold. Razor," Destin started before releasing a deep breath and staring into the other male's eyes. "Please, keep her safe. She is everything to me."

"I swear on my life, I will protect her. She is my life, Destin," Razor murmured, holding Kali's relaxed body closer to his. "I will do everything I can to protect her."

"But remember to let her fly," Destin said, rising out of his chair and bending to brush a kiss across Kali's cheek. "She is a free spirit. She needs to fly."

"I will be right beside her when she does," Razor assured him as Destin picked up the chair and replaced it by the table. "Cutter will make sure you have all the support you need."

Destin looked over his shoulder at the huge male holding his sister.

They looked – right. A small smile pulled at his lips and he bowed his head in acknowledgement before walking out the door. For the first time since their mother's death, a huge weight felt like it had been lifted off his shoulders. Standing tall, he nodded to Tim, who was standing waiting for him further down the hall.

"Everything good?" Tim asked quietly as Destin walked up to him.

"Yeah," Destin replied, glancing over his shoulder at the closed door before turning back to Tim with a small smile. "Yeah, everything is good."

"You know Jason is going to be pissed," Tim commented casually. "He wanted Kali."

Destin chuckled. "After the beating he got, I don't think he is going to try to tangle with that huge bastard again. He'll get over it. She didn't love him like she does Razor."

Tim grinned. "I hope he knows he is one lucky bastard then," he said as they stepped out into the frigid air. "Kali is one very special gal."

Destin looked up at the stars in the sky. It was hard to believe that one day soon Kali would be up there flying through the solar system. Life had changed a lot for them, but change could be a good thing. Perhaps one day he would get a chance to go see it for himself. Until that day, though, he had a lot of work to do.

"Yes, she is," Destin agreed, pulling his sock cap on. "Let's go. We have a lot of work ahead of us."

24

Kali fumbled with the comlink that Razor had given her right after they arrived on board his Flagship. The *Journey* was an experimental prototype warship that he was overseeing. Razor explained that while it was smaller than most of their other warships, it was much faster and was equipped with the latest advancements in Trivator weaponry. All Kali knew was Razor's definition of small and hers were not the same. She had spent the last three days exploring and she still hadn't seen a quarter of it!

It was going to take a while to get acclimated to what was happening. Everything was so foreign to her and she was feeling more than a little intimidated by it. Hell, she was still trying to get oriented to the feeling of being in an enclosed area. She was used to being able to step outside and feel the sun on her face and the wind in her hair any time she felt like it.

To make matters worse, she hadn't seen much of Razor since they arrived. She understood he was busy with the preparations for the departure and everything, but it wasn't much comfort to her growing unease. The problem with him being gone so much during the past three days was she couldn't help but wonder if she was making a huge mistake. After all, it wasn't like she could just hop on the metro, if it had been working, and go home.

As the view of the Earth began to fade from the viewport she was looking out of an hour ago, her doubts and fears escalated. It had taken everything inside her to keep from screaming out that she had changed her mind, that she wanted to go home.

There were so many things that could go wrong, she thought as she fumbled with the comlink attached to the collar of her shirt. *All I have are the few things that Destin brought me before we lifted off. I don't know anything about spaceships and alien planets and…*

She groaned in frustration when the metal clip holding the comlink on caught on the button holding her collar down. She was about ready to just rip the thing off.

She wanted to run. She wanted to feel the cold wind on her face and the thrill of moving through the ruins of the city. She thrived on the challenge of finding the best way to maneuver through the only place she had ever known. Here she couldn't even figure out how to take off a stupid communication's device!

"Do you need some assistance?" Razor asked as he walked into the bedroom of their living quarters.

Kali looked up with a tight smile. "I've got it twisted and can't figure out what is going on. Are you here to stay or are you leaving again?" she asked, as he carefully removed the comlink and set it down on the bedside table.

Razor bent and brushed his lips across her slightly parted ones. "I have finished what needed to be done for the moment. I did not mean to leave you alone for so long. Some critical information came in that needed my attention," he murmured in a husky voice filled with need. "I want you. I cannot stop thinking about you. Even when I was reviewing the information and meeting with Hammer, you were in my thoughts."

"I was thinking about you too," she admitted softly. "I... Razor, are you sure about this? Maybe it would be better if someone took me back. I mean, you have a lot to do and...."

She gasped when he suddenly wrapped his arms around her and lifted her off the floor until she was pressed against his hard body. His lips claimed hers in a passionate kiss that left her shaken and dazed by the intensity of it. She held on to his shoulders as he continued to press hot kisses along her jaw before rubbing his nose back up the curve of her neck to her ear.

"Never!" he growled in a low voice. "You are mine and you will stay by my side. I have apologized for leaving you."

"You don't have to apologize for doing your duty," Kali whispered, pulling back so he could see the sincerity in her eyes. "I understand duty and the need to place it before all else. I also understand that having a distraction can be dangerous, even deadly. I don't want to be the cause for either. There are things back on Earth that I can do to help Destin that are not as dangerous. When you are finished with whatever you are working on you can come back for me."

Razor rested his forehead against hers. A deep sigh escaped him as he realized that he was to blame for her feeling like he did not want her. The past three days had been filled with meetings and preparations. The mission to the Tressalon galaxy was filled with danger. Even with the *Journey's* capabilities, it would be a challenge to get in, find Trig and Jordan, and get out again in one piece. He hated that there was even the slightest chance that he might be risking Kali and his unborn child. He had no choice after talking to Hunter again last night.

Trig had finally responded to Hunter's continued attempts to contact him. Jordan was with him. From the look on his younger brother's face, the meeting hadn't gone very well.

"I'm going to kill him," Hunter had said as an opening line.

"I take it Jordan is with him," Razor had responded.

"Yes, that bastard refuses to return her. He says she threatened to go on her own if he didn't take her," Hunter had grunted out. "The trouble is, she would. I never knew Jordan could be so stubborn. She has always been the quietest one of the group."

"Trig will protect her," Razor assured him. "He is deadly. He will not allow any harm to come to Jordan."

"Even he is no match for the number of cutthroats on the Spaceport," Hunter pointed out tiredly.

"Are you alright, Hunter? Something else is bothering you," Razor observed, his eyes narrowing on the lines of fatigue around his brother's eyes and mouth. "Have other problems developed that need my attention?"

Hunter shook his head and glanced over his shoulder to make sure he was still alone. When he turned back, there was a slight glint in his eyes. A small smile tugged at his lips.

"Jesse is expecting our second child," he shared quietly. "She has been sick and I've been getting up with Lyon, who has more teeth coming in. I'm worried about her. She has been very sick this time, but she never complains. Yesterday, the healer came and recommended she remain in bed for a short time. It tears me up to see her like this."

Razor's stomach had twisted in fear. His thoughts had immediately turned to Kali. What if his child made her sick as well? What if…

"I want Patch to examine you," he said suddenly, tightening his arms around Kali.

Kali frowned in confusion. "What does Patch examining me have to do with you sending me back to Earth?" she asked, puzzled.

Razor's face darkened at her insistence to be returned to her planet. "I am not sending you back to your world! You will remain here. It is too dangerous to send you back."

"Too dangerous? I already told you I can do things for Destin that aren't dangerous," she pointed out.

"No!" he growled. "You need to rest. I will have Patch come here to see you. No, I will carry you to him. That way he will have any equipment he needs when he checks you," he murmured distractedly.

"Whoa, we are definitely on two separate pages here," Kali replied with a confused shake of her head. "What are you talking about? I don't need to see Patch."

"Yes, you do," Razor said, suddenly anxious as his mind flooded with all the things that could go wrong. "You could become very sick, even worse."

"Razor, look at me," Kali said gently, cupping his face between her hands. "What are you talking about? I'm not sick. I'm fine. What is going on?"

Razor buried his face in her neck again and groaned. A shudder went through him when he felt her thread her fingers through his hair. Ever since he met her, one thing or another involving her seemed to send him careening out of control.

"Tell me what's wrong?" she murmured quietly as she stroked him. "I'm a lot stronger than I look. Tell me."

He drew in a long, shaky breath before he slowly lowered her to the floor and gripped her hands in a fierce but gentle hold. Staring down into her upturned face, he realized that she was strong. She had proven time and time again that she wasn't as delicate and fragile as she appeared, starting when she risked her life rescuing him from the helicopter.

"I talked to Hunter," he said gruffly.

Kali tilted her head and waited. When he didn't continue, she squeezed his hands in encouragement. Whatever they talked about had really shaken Razor up. She had never seen him so… vulnerable.

"He's your younger brother, right?" she asked.

"Yes, he has taken a human female as his *Amate* as well," he said, carefully studying her face.

"And," she encouraged.

"Jesse is expecting their second child. She is very sick. Hunter is worried about her. The healer has placed her on bed rest," he added.

Kali's mouth opened in an 'O' as the light came on. Razor was worried about her. He was afraid that she was going to be the same way.

"Razor, each pregnancy is different for a woman. Even if a woman has more than one child," she said in a gentle voice. "Just because Jesse is sick doesn't mean I will be. I mean, I will be, but it might not be as bad. I remember some of the girls who were pregnant and had babies. It isn't often that a woman dies during childbirth anymore."

"Die?" he repeated, latching on to her last word. "You will not die. I will not allow it."

Kali laughed and shook her head. "I don't plan on dying, but there are no guarantees in life. Is this why you don't want me to go back home?" she asked.

"Yes. No." He let go of her hand and rubbed his own across his face in frustration. "Yes, I don't want you to return to your world. The medical treatment there is not good. Patch can care for you much better."

"And the no?" Kali said, trying not to grin.

Razor's eyes softened as he wound his hand around the back of her neck and pulled her close enough so he could rub his nose against her cheek. He loved the feel and smell of her. When he touched her, it felt so – right. It was as if she had been created just for him. She... completed him.

"I do not want to be away from you. I can't be away from you," he admitted huskily. "The past three days have been torture. The only thing keeping me sane was watching you on the vidcoms."

"You were watching me?" she breathed out. "How? When?"

His eyes flickered to the comlink. "It tracks you. I used the onboard systems to locate and watch you. I never left your side," he confessed.

"Oh Razor," Kali said, her heart melting at the silent plea in his gaze. This warrior, a man stronger and more powerful than she had ever met before, loved her. She could see it in his eyes and hear it in his confession. She reached up and touched the corner of his bottom lip. He was so different, but so perfect. He was a combination of the darkness and light. "I love you."

In that moment, she knew that she did. Everything that he had done in the short time since they had met flashed before her. His insisting that she leave him in the helicopter because he feared for her. His grabbing her and holding her when she almost fell. The exasperated humor in his eyes when she played with his hair. The way he made love to her like there was no other woman in the universe but her. So many clues came together all the sudden, including the one time he told her he loved her. He had meant it.

"You love me," she breathed out, looking up at him in wonder. "You really do."

A soft groan escaped Razor as he cupped her face in his hands and claimed her lips with his. He poured every ounce of his feelings into it. The kiss turned to desperation when her hand slipped between them to cup him through his trousers.

"I love you, Kali," he murmured. "I love you. I need you."

"Yes," she cried out when his hand cupped her breast and pinched her nipple through her shirt.

"I want you," he muttered as he reached down and grabbed the bottom of her shirt and pulled it over her head. "Now!"

Kali giggled as her hands went to the clasps holding his shirt on. She felt wild and… free. Her eyes glittered with amazement. She didn't need to run. She just needed Razor!

"I need a shower," he grunted. "I…"

Kali laid her fingers against his lips. "Then, we'll get a shower together."

Razor's eyes flared with desire. He quickly finished undressing. He knelt in front of her when she cursed as her left pant leg got caught around her foot. He gently took her hand and placed it on his bare shoulder to steady her as he loosened the bunched-up fabrics and pulled it off of her.

"You are so beautiful," he whispered, staring up at her.

It was true. She was beautiful. It was more than the physical attraction he felt for her. It was the warmth and humor and love in her eyes when she looked at him. She glowed from the inside out with a beauty that surrounded him with the pureness of it.

He closed his eyes as she tenderly ran her fingers along his cheek. Breathing in the heady scent of her arousal, he pressed his face against her flat stomach. It wouldn't be flat for long. Pressing a kiss to her skin, he prayed to the Gods that she would be alright. For the first time in his life, he realized that he needed someone, he needed Kali, to make his world richer. She brought color into it that he hadn't realized was missing. He slowly opened his eyes to stare up into hers and what he saw took his breath away.

"So are you," she whispered, pulling him up. "So are you, Razor."

25

Razor rose to his feet. He swept Kali into his arms, enjoying her husky laughter as he turned her around in a circle before he walked toward the bathing room. It was larger than the one back on Earth, but not by much. He still couldn't wait to get her into the one at his home on Rathon.

He set her on her feet so he could program the mist controls. Instead of wasting precious water, the *Journey* used a cleansing mist that condensed like water before evaporating. He pulled her into the rounded bathing cylinder and closed the door.

He enjoyed her giggles as he ran his hands over her slick body. The mist surrounded them, making their bodies slick. The feel of her silky skin against the rough palms of his hands sent an explosion of heat through him. He bent, running the tips of his fingers over her sensitive nipples at the same time as he nipped at her throat.

Her hands were driving him wild. She was running them up and down his chest. With each stroke, she went lower and lower. His lips crushed hers when her hands wrapped around his throbbing length. The kiss turned more and more desperate as she stroked him.

His hands slid around her damp skin and he ran them along the line of her ass. His breathing grew heavy when she arched as he ran his fingers along it. He slipped his right hand down between her legs to make sure she was ready for him. His fingers pushed past her swollen lips and slid into her. A low moan greeted his exploration. Cupping her ass with his left hand, he pushed deep into her.

"I want you bare for me," he muttered. "I want to taste you, devour you."

It took a moment for Kali to understand what he was wanting. When she did, a wanton feeling of desire scorched through her pulling a deep moan from her as it shot down through her. Razor's muttered curse told her he could feel her body's reaction to his suggestion. She knew other women back on Earth shaved their pubic areas. Hell, she had even tried it when she was sixteen after hearing some of the girls at school talking about it.

"Do it," she whispered, raising her hands to cup his face. "Shave me."

She watched as Razor's eyes widened before they turned a dark, dark yellow gold that left her pulsing with need. She was ready to come just from him touching her. She didn't know if she would make it through him shaving her as well.

"Wait here," he grunted as he pulled his fingers from her. A wicked smile curved his lips as he raised them to his mouth and sucked on them. "That is what I want."

Kali leaned weakly back against the wall of the shower as he opened the door and stepped out for a moment. Her eyes greedily roamed his body. She wasn't sure her legs would be able to hold her up, but she would damn sure try. Her mouth parted in a gasp when the shower door opened again. This time she was given a full frontal view that left her own mouthwatering. The man was built. There was no denying that he was a fully aroused male. His cock was long, thick and throbbing up and down. The head was larger around than a human male and she knew she felt small ridges circling it.

"Razor," Kali breathed wondering how on Earth she was able to fit him inside her before. He looked massive now. "I..."

"Spread your legs for me," he growled.

"I..." Kali moaned as she grasped his shoulders for balance as he lifted her left leg and slid it over his shoulder. "Razor... that feels so good."

Razor didn't say anything. He couldn't. The view of Kali spread open for him sent his heated blood straight to his cock. Right now, he felt like his balls were about to explode if he didn't release the pressure. He quickly flicked on the shaver he used. The laser would remove the hair and keep it off for several weeks before having to be redone. He had never opted for a permanent removal as it had never been necessary. If Kali liked the feel of being bare, he might see if she wanted it to be permanent. For now, he just wanted to taste her.

He carefully ran the laser over her swollen mound. Within minutes, her smooth, soft folds begged for his lips. He ran his hands over her, enjoying her cries as he touched the ultra-sensitive flesh. His fingers caressed the narrow slit, stopping at the swollen nub near the top of it.

"I love this," he murmured, rubbing it gently.

"I.... Oh God, I'm going to come!" Kali cried out hoarsely as he continued to rub her. "Razor!"

Razor watched as Kali's body exploded around his fingers. He leaned forward and clamped down on her. His teeth pinched the soft nub. Kali's hoarse scream echoed in the bathing unit as she came hard. Razor ran his tongue along her slit until he could push it up inside her and drink as she continued to pulse around him. Only when she started to slide down along the shower wall did he release her. Pulling her leg from around his shoulder, he rose on shaky legs to catch her around the waist.

He twisted and turned off the mist. Wrapping his arm around Kali's limp body, he slid the door open again. This time when he stepped out, he took Kali with him. He bent and lifted her in his arms. Turning, he quickly walked back into their sleeping quarters and laid her down on the large bed.

"I need you now, Kali," he said hoarsely.

"Whatever you want, big guy, I'm still soaring right now," Kali said with a satisfied grin.

She gasped when he rolled her onto her stomach and wrapped an arm around her waist so he could pull her up onto her hands and knees. A loud moan escaped her when she felt his other hand guide his throbbing cock to her slick entrance.

"Oh God," she groaned as he pushed into her with one thrust.

"Yes, sweet Goddess," he groaned with her. "You wrap around my shaft like a fist, Kali. I love your heat."

"Razor," Kali whimpered.

"Yes, my *fi'ta*."

Razor closed his eyes as he began rocking back and forth inside her. He could feel every delicious inch of her against his cock. The muscle in his jaw throbbed as he clenched his teeth in an effort to bring her to another climax. He wanted to feel her shatter around him. Just the thought pulled at his control and he felt the small spurt of pre-cum.

A shudder escaped him as he fought to control his release. Opening his eyes, he gripped Kali's hips and began moving faster. The view of her slender back bowed as she tangled her fingers in the covers drove him to the brink.

Turning his head to the side, his eyes widened as the mirror on the wall caught their entwined bodies. In fascination, he watched as he drove into her. The movement of their bodies was an exotic mating dance between a male and his female.

Feelings of possessiveness, pride and the primitive male triumph of claiming his mate washed through him like a tidal wave. He slowed his rhythm so that he could watch as his cock slid back and forth into

Kali's slick channel. Her breasts swayed as they came together. Reaching around, he captured one taut nipple between his fingers. Rolling it between them, he was rewarded when she lifted her ass even higher and threw her head back.

Her face was tense with emotion. Her eyes were closed, her lashes lying like crescents against her flushed cheeks. Her lips were swollen from his kisses and slightly parted. She looked like a woman caught in the thrones of passion.

Kali turned her head and opened her eyes. For a split second as their eyes locked, it was as if he could see the stars from the universe opening to give him a glimpse of what it meant for a new world to be born. He felt like that. He felt like he was being reborn and being given a chance at a life that he had only dreamed about before.

As he pushed deeply into her, his body exploded. His orgasm triggering hers. The combination of the two of them shattering, mixing, becoming one took his breath away. He wrapped his arms around her, cupping her breasts and pulling her tighter against his body.

There in the mirror, they continued to stare into each other's eyes; their bodies locked together as one. Razor bent and pressed a kiss to her shoulder before he opened his mouth and bit down on the curve of her neck. The chemical in his saliva would numb the pain as he marked her and help with the healing.

Watching as her eyes widen and her body reacted to his claiming stiffened his cock and he rocked into her as she exploded again. Her hot core, already slick from her orgasms and his seed, pulsed around him as he drove into her again and again as he held her submissively against him as he took her. He didn't release her until his seed was once again filling her womb. His scent was now a part of her own.

He reluctantly released her neck, licking the small marks he had left against her creamy skin. He slowly bent forward until she was lying flat as he covered her sleeping figure. He made sure to keep his upper body up enough to keep from crushing her.

It took several minutes for his breathing to return to normal. He carefully pulled out of her. Kali moaned but didn't wake from the deep, exhausted sleep she had fallen into. Razor rose and walked to the bathroom. Returning, he cleaned Kali up before crawling back into bed with her. He drew her against him, sighing as she snuggled closer to him.

Razor looked up at the ceiling. His mind was swirling with all that had happened over the past few months. A smile curved his lips as he thought of the female in his arms. She was everything a warrior could dream of and more.

26

Two weeks later, the comlink next to Razor's side of the bed chimed, waking Kali from a sound sleep. She lay quietly as he reached for it and tapped it. Her hand slid across his flat stomach as he carefully rolled out of the bed. Her eyes lit with desire as she eyed his firm ass.

"I can feel you watching me," he murmured in amusement.

"How can I resist?" she replied, sitting up and letting the sheet pool around her waist. Her nipples hardened in the cooler air. "I'm not the only one looking."

"You are going to be the death of me," he muttered, as his body hardened with desire. "I can't get enough of you."

Kali pulled the covers up to cover her exposed breasts. She chuckled when his eyes followed the movement and he released a sigh of regret when his comlink chimed again. She rose from the bed, grabbing her wrap and slipping it on so she could follow him into the other room.

He glanced up at her as she stood in the doorway in indecision. A smile softened the frown on his face and he held out his hand to her.

The moment their fingers touched, he drew her up against him even as he answered the call.

"Speak," he said.

"We passed into the Tressalon galaxy eight hours ago. We will arrive at the moon furthest from the Bruttus Spaceport in less than an hour," Hammer stated.

"I'll be on the bridge in fifteen," Razor replied. "Out."

Kali rested her head against his shoulder after he turned and pulled her closer. "Is this where you think Jordan might be?" she asked.

Over the past two weeks, Razor had shared the mission they were on. He had told her more about Hunter and how his brother had taken Jesse as his *Amate* two years before. Jesse's two younger sisters had been embraced in their family. Kali liked how Razor referred to all the women as his new sisters.

She had learned a lot about Razor and what life was like on board a Trivator warship. She learned that to have a family was the greatest gift a Trivator warrior could be 'blessed' with. It was something they all hoped to one day find. While they had relationships, just like the men and women back on Earth, when a warrior recognized his *Amate* he gave up all others and devoted his life to caring for and protecting her. It was just going to take Razor a little while to accept that she had every intention of caring for and protecting him as well.

"Yes, I must leave for a short time. It would be dangerous for Trig, Jordan and Dagger, if they are there, for a Trivator Warship to be seen. We have come in cloaked so they are not aware we are here. Unfortunately, it is too dangerous to bring the *Journey* in any closer where it could be seen. There is too much traffic arriving and departing from the Spaceport to take a chance," he explained before pressing a kiss to her forehead and releasing her. "Why don't you try to get some more rest. You were sick yesterday morning."

Kali pressed a hand to her stomach and nodded when it turned. She had her first bout of morning sickness the day before. She had to beg, then threaten Razor when he started demanding that Patch be called. Thankfully, it had only lasted for about half an hour, then she was fine.

"I think that is a good idea," she said with a tired sigh. "How long will you be gone?"

"Hopefully just a few hours," Razor said, pulling on a pair of dark brown trousers and a matching vest. He grinned when he saw Kali's raised eyebrow at the unfamiliar clothing. "We will try to blend in as much as possible. Hammer is known here."

Kali had met the commander of the *Journey* just once. That had been one time too many. The man made her think of a caged lion who hadn't been fed in a while. He was quiet and his eyes had followed her with a look of suspicion in them, as if he was trying to figure out what power she had over Razor.

"Is that a good thing or a bad thing? Hammer being known," she added with a grin when he raised his eyebrow in question.

A deep chuckle escaped him as he finished fastening his shirt. He stepped closer to her and brushed a kiss across her lips. That was another thing he loved, her sense of humor. She always knew what to say to release the tension.

"Both," he admitted. "More good than bad, I hope."

"Oh, that is sooo reassuring," she drawled before turning more serious. "Just be careful."

Razor paused as he pulled on a pair of soft, leather boots that matched his trousers. His expression softened when he saw the slight worry in her eyes, but the smile on her lips. Thomas' words came back to him when he talked about Chelsea and her work as an FBI agent.

He suddenly understood what Thomas was trying to tell him. It wasn't just him accepting Kali, but her accepting and trusting him to do what needed to be done. He straightened and held his arms out. He inhaled her sweet scent as she stepped into his arms. Resting his cheek against her hair, he wondered how he had ever survived with the emptiness in his life before.

"You are an amazing female, Kali," he whispered, enjoying the feel of her in his arms. "Your scent is changing. It is slightly sweeter, more exotic."

Her body shook as she laughed silently into his chest. She wasn't so sure that was the best compliment she had ever received in her life; but then, it had to be the most unique. She tilted her head back and offered her lips to him. For a guy who thought kissing was rubbing his nose against her, he had picked up the human way of kissing very quickly. She moaned as he pulled away.

"I'll return in a few hours. Go rest," he encouraged. "Hammer and I will be careful."

"I know," she whispered.

A deep sigh escaped her as he picked up a leather belt filled with weapons as he walked by the table near the door. She didn't turn back toward their bedroom until the door sealed behind him. A yawn escaped her as she climbed back into the large bed. Within seconds, she was fast asleep.

27

Kali bit her bottom lip again as she looked around the bridge. This was her second trip up to it in the past two hours. The silence that greeted her this time told her something was wrong. Something was very, very wrong. She recognized the looks. God, she had given it enough times over the past six years to know what it meant.

I'm sorry, Ed. It happened so fast. Tracy didn't have time to get out of the way. I'm sorry, Cindy… Craig was a good man. I'm so sorry Elaine… Todd fought hard. How many times had she had to say that to the men and women back home? Dozens? Hundreds? Each one took a little piece out of her soul until she had to force the bile back.

She reached out and grabbed the arm of one of the men working on the bridge as he walked by. She made sure she had her best 'give me answers or die' look on her face. It must have worked because the warrior swallowed and looked nervously past her to another male for help.

"What is going on? I'm only going to ask you once," she gritted out through her teeth. "Where are Razor and Hammer?"

"I…" the warrior started to say before he released a relieved sigh when Patch stepped onto the bridge.

"Kali, I need to speak with you," Patch said grimly. "I'll take it from here."

"Yes, sir," the warrior replied, stepping back and turning once Kali released his arm.

"Patch, where are Razor and Hammer?" she asked bluntly.

Patch's mouth tightened and he nodded toward the Commander's office to the left of the bridge. Kali nodded and walked toward the room with her head held high. She would not show how frightened she was. She needed facts, not sympathy or pity.

Once they stepped through the door and it closed behind them, Patch stepped around her and headed for a small bar to the side. He lifted a cup and looked at her. He grunted when she shook her head.

Kali waited impatiently as Patch fixed himself a hot drink. She knew what he was doing. She had done it herself numerous times when she was trying to think of how to relay the bad news. For her, she would rather he just spit it out. She would deal with it afterwards.

"Just tell me," she demanded. "Is he dead?"

Patch's eyebrow rose at her calm, intense look. "No, neither one of them are dead," he replied. "At least, not yet."

"What is the situation? I need complete details," she said, stepping toward the long table. "Start at the beginning."

Patch's lips twitched before he nodded and sat down at the table. Touching the keypad, he brought up a hologram of the space station. With a touch, he turned it so the section with the two red forms were facing them.

"Earlier today, Hammer and Razor took a nondescript transport and docked it with the space station. They were following leads trying to locate Trig and Razor's new sister, Jordan," Patch said looking at the holographic map.

"Did they find her?" she asked, focusing on the two dots and the outline of the buildings.

"We don't know for sure. Hammer communicated that they were following a possible lead. That was the last transmission we had from them," he replied. "We know they are alive. Both were implanted with a tracking device before they departed."

"So, this is where they are," she commented, studying the detailed image. "How do you know they are in trouble? Besides the lack of communication," she added. "I agree it would seem strange for both devices to stop working at the same time unless there was some type of electronic interference. How do you know that they aren't hunkered down?"

Patch's lip curved upward. He shook his head in amazement. This is what continued to surprise him; the way human women looked at things like a warrior would. Chelsea had done the same thing when the wounded started pouring in. She had divided the most critical to the least and organized it so he and the human doctors could care for them in the order of their injuries.

"This location is called *The Hole*. It is where the fight rings are," Patch explained before pointing to the twin location of the dots. "And this, is the dungeon below it. There is no place for them to hunker down there."

"So, what are the plans to get them out?" Kali asked as she enlarged the diagram.

Patch sighed, staring at the image. "Sword wants to take a team in," he said reluctantly. "The problem is, the minute we send in forces, the owner of *The Hole* will more than likely order them to be terminated."

Kali stared at the diagram in deep thought. She thought back to some of the strategies she and Destin had used against Colbert and his men. Colbert was used to the methods of the street gangs.

Understanding that, she and Destin had decided to do the unexpected. Sometimes, they struck hard and fast, then disappeared. Other times, they would use the street gang approach. One thing they never wanted to be was predictable. Since they were outnumbered, they had to keep Colbert and his men off-balance.

"Tell me about the owner of *The Hole,*" she murmured. "What does he like? What does he hate? I need anything and everything you know about him."

"Why?" Patch asked with a frown.

Kali turned and smiled at Patch. "Because he has something I want and I am going to get it back," she replied.

"You know, if Arindoss doesn't kill us, that Razor will," Sword muttered under his breath.

Kali ignored the huge Trivator security chief. He had been arguing and bellyaching since Patch informed him of the new plan to rescue Razor and Hammer. For the first five minutes after listening to Kali explain their plan of attack, he had opened and closed his mouth like a fish out of water. In truth, the poor man had been speechless that not only was Kali in charge but that Patch had agreed.

"Razor is not going to kill us," Kali replied.

"Maybe I should rephrase that," Sword grumbled. "He is going to kill me for letting you off the *Journey* and Patch for agreeing to this crazy plan."

"It is not a crazy plan," Kali assured him as she rolled her eyes.

"You don't think just walking into *The Hole,* demanding to speak with Arindoss and telling him to release Razor and Hammer is crazy?" Sword asked in disbelief.

"No, I think it is ingenious!" she replied with a grin as she swerved around another merchant and his cart of goods. "Everything I heard about Arindoss kept coming back to the same thing, the man appreciates and respects unusual things."

"Arindoss doesn't appreciate or respect anything," Sword growled. "This is a suicide mission. You don't have a clue as to what you are up against or what you are doing. I'm taking you back to the *Journey*."

Kali twisted as Sword grabbed her left arm. She pushed into him, taking him by surprise, as she shoved him into a narrow alley and up against the wall. Fear had heightened her adrenaline levels, making her stronger. The other two warriors with them followed in surprise.

"Don't disparage me," she hissed. "I'm not some rookie who doesn't know how to defend herself. I was in charge of my brother's security back on Earth. This will work. If you can't handle it, then go back to the warship. I won't jeopardize my life or that of the other men with us with your doubts. You are either in or out. Do I make myself clear?"

Sword looked down in surprise at the fierce expression on the human female's face. The look in her eyes showed she meant every word she said. The knife in his belly told him she knew what she was doing. For a moment, the doubt resurfaced before he pushed it away. The plan was so preposterous it might just work.

"I'm in," he replied quietly.

"You'd better be," Kali growled as she slipped the knife back into the sheath attached to her wrist. "You damn well better be or I swear I'll kill you before Razor gets a chance to."

Turning on her heel, she stepped back out into the busy corridor that made up the main market area of the Spaceport. Each side of the narrow passage was lined with bars, carts and creatures from a wide variety of star systems. Kali glared at a large brown barrel shaped creature that was checking her out. It must have decided she would be too much trouble because it quickly shifted its gaze when she didn't look away.

"I think I'd rather deal with Razor, if you asked me," Race murmured. "Something tells me she would take her time killing you."

She ignored Race's quietly spoken words. If she wasn't so worried about Razor, she would have laughed. Instead, she focused on the huge glowing sign at the end of the corridor. That was where Razor was. Nothing else mattered at that moment, but getting to him.

28

Razor paced back and forth in the small confines of the cell. Hammer was sitting on the stone slab that made up the 'beds' for the fighters. He winced as he rubbed the back of his head. A small knot just behind his left ear was evidence of the blow he had taken from behind.

"Are you alright?" Razor asked as Hammer sat with his head bowed.

Hammer raised his head and nodded. Dried blood from a deep cut on his cheekbone and another from his lip showed he had fought hard. Unfortunately, the ten males that had attacked them had come with stunners as well. The long rods sent a bolt of electricity through their bodies.

One powerful bolt had knocked him to his knees. He had been attacked from behind before he could rise again. At least, he and Hammer took five of the bastards down first.

He turned as two armed men came down the corridor with another prisoner. One of the men pushed the male into the cell across from him. He took a step closer to the bars as the male turned.

Razor watched as the male kicked out, catching the guard in the groin with his foot. The guard fell backwards through the opening of the cell with a grunt of pain. Before he could attack again, the other guard pushed a stunner through the bars and hit him in the side with it. The male dropped to his knees on the hard floor. His head fell forward as the guard shot another bolt of electricity into him.

Razor and Hammer both watched as the guard who had been kicked slowly rose from where he had fallen and shut the door to the cell. A moment later, the corridor was empty once again. Razor reached out and gripped the bars of his cell as he stared intently at Trig's bent head.

"Where is Jordan?" he demanded.

Razor watched as a shudder went through Trig's body as he fought the effects of the powerful bolts of electricity he had received. He slowly pushed himself up until he was sitting. His dark, savage eyes held a haunted look in them.

"I don't know," he ground out, looking from Razor to Hammer and back again. "We got separated during the attack."

The muscle in Razor's cheek throbbed as rage built inside him. His mind pulled up the delicate, quiet features of Jordan Sampson. Her long brown hair framed her heart-shaped face and her hazel eyes had always seemed so much older than her years.

He knew that Jesse and her sisters had been through a lot before his brother found them. He couldn't imagine how they had survived for so long with the turmoil Earth had been in at the very beginning. His eyes darkened as he thought of how difficult it had been for Kali. Now, Trig had exposed the young female to even greater danger. He was going to kill the bastard.

"When?" he bit out, knowing that every minute meant a greater possibility that Jordan had been captured and possibly sold to a…. "When?" he demanded again.

"Two days ago," Trig replied, standing stiffly and running his hand down his bruised face. "We had been to one of the fights. Dagger was there."

A low curse exploded from Razor's lips. His eyes swept over to Hammer, who had come to stand next to him. Hammer nodded. They needed to get the hell out of there.

"What happened?" Razor asked harshly.

Trig stepped closer to the bars and looked down the empty corridor before returning his attention to Razor. He threaded his arms through the bars and leaned forward so he could stretch the cramp in his side from where he had been hit.

Two days ago, he and the young human female had attended a fight in the rings three levels above. He had been against it, but the human female was a tenacious little thing. She had disappeared while he was relieving himself. He had finally found her waiting outside the doors to *The Hole,* two tickets for the event in her hand. He didn't bother asking her how she made it through the crowded Spaceport without trouble, much less how she was able to obtain tickets to the sold out event.

She had kept the hood of her cloak over her head and moved with a natural grace as they weaved through the crowded stadium. It was the third and final event of the evening that had shaken them both. The lights had dimmed and a spotlight had shone down on a three-head Serpentian. The creature's sharp teeth, hard reddish-green scales and foot-long claws dug into the metal floor, producing a loud screeching sound that had most of the audience screaming and yelling. It was when the light shifted to the other cell that he heard Jordan's faint cry of horror.

Dagger had stood in the caged area. He wore a pair of dark brown leather trousers, dark brown boots and nothing else. In his hands, he held two six foot swords. His head had been bowed, but Trig would have recognized his younger brother anywhere.

Dagger's chest and arms were covered with deep scars from previous battles. The roar of the crowd had been deafening when the doors to the cages opened. The two adversaries had circled each other, striking with a precision that resonated above the crowds cheering.

"What happened after the fight?" Hammer asked quietly when Trig's voice faded. "Did he win?"

Trig looked up at Hammer and nodded. "Yes, he won. After the fight, six guards came in with stunners. He killed two before the other four knocked him out. If he hadn't been exhausted from the fight, he would have killed them all."

"I can't believe Arindoss would be stupid enough to have purchased a Trivator warrior for the fight rings," Hammer muttered in a deep voice. "He has to know that we would come after him once we knew for sure."

Trig shook his head. "Arindoss was killed a week ago. A Drethulan has taken over. Those bastards only care about profit. They'd sell their own offspring to the whore houses if it meant making a credit."

Razor's mouth tightened. The Drethulans lived on the edge of the Alliance boundaries. The single planet in their Solar System was a dry desert and the Drethulans lived underground due to the scorching temperatures above. They returned only to breed. Trig wasn't kidding when he said they would sell their young if they could make a profit.

"We need to find Dagger and Jordan and get out of here," Razor said, studying the bars again. "Do you know where are they keeping him?"

Kali was almost to the entrance of *The Hole* when a small, cloaked figure stepped out of the shadows in front of her. She started to push past it, thinking another merchant was trying to pawn their wares on her, when a pair of hazel eyes locked with hers. The very human face of a young woman about her age stared back at her.

"Jordan?" Kali asked in a husky voice.

A hint of a smile lifted the girl's lips before they tightened. Jordan's head nodded once before her eyes darted to the three men standing slightly behind Kali. They widened before shifting back to Kali.

"Yes, come with me," she murmured, turning back toward the back alley.

Kali glanced at Sword. He nodded to her before murmuring quietly to the warrior named Cannon. Cannon turned on his heel and disappeared into the crowd.

Kali looked back at the figure who was waiting in the shadows. She took a step forward knowing that whatever was happening could not be good if the girl was alone. Kali, Sword and Race silently followed Jordan down the dark alley. Several minutes later, Jordan pushed aside a fabric covering a doorway and disappeared inside.

"Wait," Sword said quietly, placing his hand on Kali's arm. "Let me go through first."

Kali wanted to argue, but knew he was right. It was important to know when to lead and when to follow. She would let Sword make sure everything was safe before she entered.

"Come," he called out quietly after scanning the small room that was bare except for a pallet on the floor and Jordan. "Race, keep watch."

Kali stepped through the entrance and stopped. Her eyes took in the tiny area. Except for the makeshift bed and a small container for water, it was empty.

"Who are you?" Jordan asked quietly. "Did Hunter send you?"

Kali smiled at the stubborn look that crossed the girl's face. She could totally relate to what the girl was feeling. She had no intention of leaving without Razor so she could understand Jordan's determination to save Dagger.

"No, I am here to find my *Amate*, Razor," Kali said with a reassuring smile. "He was looking for you and Trig. Hunter did send him."

Jordan's face softened at the mention of Hunter. "I knew he would be worried. I had to come. Dagger…" Jordan drew in a deep, steadying breath, but Kali could still hear the tears in her voice. "Dagger has been lost for too long. After… after seeing what he has been through, I can't leave him now that I've found him again."

Kali took a step closer and gently gripped Jordan's hands in her own. She squeezed them in comfort. Jordan's lip trembling and a tear escaped to slide down her pale cheek. Kali pulled the young woman into her arms and they held each other tightly.

"It will be alright," Kali murmured. "We'll get them all out. I was going to go have a 'talk' with Arindoss."

Jordan shook her head. "Arindoss was killed a week ago."

Kali pulled back and looked at Jordan with a frown. "How do you know that?" she asked.

Jordan pulled away and wiped at her damp cheeks. She gave a nervous glance at Sword who was standing silently by the door, listening to everything. Releasing a shaky breath, she wound her arms around her waist.

"Trig and I saw him. One of his security guards turned on him in the lower markets. Shortly after he was killed, a strange looking creature came and ordered the man to get rid of the body," she explained.

"What did the creature look like?" Sword asked.

Jordan's eyes flashed to his before she looked down at the floor and bit her lip. The creature had scared her. Its eyes had been large and black. No emotion at all shone from them. Its skin was hard and yellow with touches of black and red in it.

"A Drethulan," Sword cursed. "I wish the Alliance would have let us kill the bastards when they refused to join."

"He is the one that has been bringing in the creatures for those… for the fighters. He said it is more exciting and profitable, according to the information he has been sending out," Jordan whispered. "Dagger and two other men are the only ones who have survived the fights so far this week."

"He will need to replenish his fighters," Sword commented.

"From what I've seen in the past couple of days, the... Drethulan, has been sending teams of men out to find new fighters. Two days ago, they attacked Trig. They didn't want me as I was too small but Trig fought them."

"That may be why they attacked Razor and Hammer," Sword said. "Trivator warriors are fierce and will fight until the death."

Kali's mind turned with ideas. Her eyes flickered to Sword before turning back to Jordan. They needed warriors, she needed to get inside. A smile curved her lips.

Men always underestimated a woman, especially ones that were small and fragile looking, she thought as she bit her lip.

"Jordan, how good are you at sneaking around?" Kali asked as a plan began forming in her mind, taking root and growing. "Can you get inside *The Hole* unseen?"

"Yes, I've been searching for Dagger and Trig. I stole an access key from one of the kitchen workers," she replied. "I have a good idea of where they are being kept."

Kali watched as Jordan pulled a small tablet from a pouch at her waist. She swiped her finger over it and tapped in several codes. Before long, a schematic of the huge complex appeared. She stepped closer looking at it. It was the plans from the original construction of the building.

"Where did you get this?" Sword asked in surprise.

"I hacked into the Space Station's building archives," Jordan murmured as she moved through the diagrams. "There are three levels under the complex that are used to hold the fighters. The first one isn't in use right now. The second and third one are. I think that's where they are holding the men."

"Jordan, you are a genius," Kali laughed in delight.

Jordan shook her head. "No, I'm desperate. I've been studying and learning the coding so that I could find Dagger. He's there. I have to help him before… before they put him back into that cage again."

"We will," Kali said with determination. "I have a plan."

Sword winced at Kali's words. If her plans involve what he was thinking, he was definitely going to be a dead man. Not only would Razor kill him, but Dagger and Trig, for exposing the women to danger. He knew the brothers well enough to know that they were very protective of those they cared about.

Yes, he thought as he listened to Kali. *And it is going to be a very long and painful death.*

29

"Lady Kali," Cannon murmured as she tightened the cuffs around his wrists and neck. "Are you sure this is a good idea?"

"Yes, I'm sure," Kali said, looking at the three other creatures that he had returned with. "Are you sure we can trust these guys?"

Cannon glanced over at the Raftian, the Trusset, and the Jawtaw. Each male was dressed in the dark uniform of *The Hole's* security personnel. Cannon knew each of the males from previous missions. The Raftian, a small but fierce reptilian species, was working undercover on a slave trading issue. The other two were working on missions as well.

"We can trust them," Cannon said.

"If you say so," Kali murmured. "Now, Jordan will lead Sword down to the lower cells and release the prisoners there, while Race takes care of making sure the transport is ready to leave the moment we get out. I've captured you and need to sell you so I can return to my home world."

"The Drethulan will not believe that you captured a Trivator warrior," the Jawtaw grunted out.

"Yes, he will," Kali replied.

She tightened the strap holding her switchblade. She would have to remember to thank Destin for this small gift. It had been his, but she found it in the items he had packed for her before she left Earth. A sense of comfort came from knowing that a little piece of her brother was with her in this upcoming mission.

"How? You are too small and weak," the Raftian hissed out. "You could not overpower a Trivator."

"No, I couldn't," Kali replied. "To defeat an enemy, sometimes you need to use your brains over brawn. Never underestimate the power of a woman on a mission. Just make sure you follow the plan and we might just make it out of this alive."

"Might?" Cannon snorted. "Even if we do, Razor, Trig and Dagger are going to kill us for bringing you here. Not to mention Hammer just for the fun of it."

"Quit belly aching," Kali muttered as her own stomach fluttered at the thought of Razor's reaction to what she was about to do. "He'll understand."

"He will understand what?" Cannon asked as he rolled his neck.

"Nothing," Kali muttered before turning to the other three men. "Are you ready?"

The Trusset grinned. Well, its lips opened to reveal rows of jagged teeth so she assumed it was a grin. The creature didn't really speak as much as make a series of clicking and popping noises that the other men appeared to understand. The translator in Kali's ear didn't so she was left to communicating through the other men.

The group stepped out of the small area Jordan had been using and moved down the narrow alley toward the entrance to *The Hole*. Kali hoped that Jordan and Sword were able to get down to the lower sections. If everything worked out tonight, *The Hole* might be shut down permanently before it was over.

"This way," Jordan said in a quiet voice. "There is one guard at the far end. He runs the controls for the lower levels."

"How do you know that?" Sword asked.

Jordan turned dark, haunted eyes up to his. "I delivered food to him yesterday."

"You…." Sword bit off what he really wanted to say. "Stay here."

"No," Jordan said, pressing her hand to his chest to stop him. "I'll go. He will sound the alarm if you do."

She glanced around. Seeing a small discarded tray that had been left by one of the cell doors, she picked it up, ignoring the dust and what looked like dried blood that covered it. Instead, she wiped it off as best she could with the end of her cloak and placed a dented cup on it.

"I'll take care of him," she whispered in a trembling voice.

"Jordan," Sword hissed, but she had already stepped around the corner and was walking down the long corridor.

Jordan's hands trembled as she carried the tray. She knew the guard had seen her. He rose out of his chair in the small control room and stretched. Her fingers tightened around the small laser pistol she held in her hand as he stepped out of the door. She had never killed anyone before and the thought of doing so made her sick to her stomach. The only thing keeping her going was her memories of Dagger locked in battle in the cage. She couldn't let him go through that any longer.

"What do you want?" the guard demanded.

"I… I brought you refreshments," Jordan responded hesitantly. "I was told by the man in the kitchen to bring it."

She lowered her eyes when the filthy male rubbed the front of his pants before rubbing his hand across his mouth. She knew what she would see, the same look that was in his eyes yesterday when she had delivered his food. If it had not been for a small group of guards bringing two other men down, she didn't want to think of what the male would have done to her.

"No interruptions today," the guard sneered. "I want something more filling."

A shiver of distaste ran through Jordan at his lascivious laugh. Her hands trembled so violently that the cup on the tray rattled. When she felt like she was close enough, she dropped the tray. The laser pistol shook as she pointed it at his chest and fired.

The guard roared out in pain. Her hands had been shaking so badly that she hit him in the shoulder instead of his chest. In rage, he reached out and gripped the pistol. He twisted it away from him at the same time as his other hand wrapped around her throat.

"You shouldn't play with weapons if you don't know how to use them," the guard growled. "What type of species are you? I have not seen your kind before. It doesn't matter, I'll show you what happens when you miss."

Jordan's slender hands desperately gripped the man's wrists as he lifted her by her neck and slammed her back against the hard, stone wall. She choked and tried to kick him, but everything was beginning to turn dark. She stared into the furious eyes, fighting to break away from the long, forked tongue that slowly slipped out from his mouth.

"Lucky for me, I don't miss," Sword said as he slid a long blade through the male's side. "And I know how to use a weapon."

Jordan slid down the wall as Sword jerked the body of the guard away from her. Her hands went to her bruised throat even as she watched Sword turn the male and slice through his neck. She turned her head and closed her eyes as blood splattered outward.

She jerked when she felt a pair of warm hands tenderly grip her fore-arms. She looked up with frightened eyes at Sword as he knelt in front of her. Her bottom lip trembled and her eyes filled with tears before she determinedly brushed them away.

"Are you alright?" he asked quietly.

"Ye... yes," she forced out. "Tha... thank you."

Sword's eyes softened and he held out his hands to her to help her up. He noticed the way she kept her eyes averted from the guard's body. He also felt the trembling that shook her slender frame. The thing that really moved him was the determination in her eyes. He glanced down at her wrists. They were bare of any markings. He did not know if this female belonged to Dagger. Her insistence on finding him made Sword believe that she might. If she didn't, he might claim her for himself.

"There are no other guards that I could tell from here on," Jordan whispered hoarsely. "The guard here controlled the locking mechanisms to each section."

"I will take care of it," Sword said.

He guided Jordan into the small room containing the control station for the holding cells. Within minutes, he returned with the keys to the locking devices for all three levels. Fortunately, the cells used an older model that did not require a passcode to unlock. It depended on a manual release. Unfortunately, it meant he needed to go to each level and pull the release on specific cells at the end of each corridor. It was a double safety standard in case the prisoners escaped, they would be unable to get out of the lower levels.

He flicked through the vidcom until he found the cells holding Razor, Hammer and Trig. They were on the second level. All the other cells were empty except for two other males. He flicked down to the third level. Each cell was empty except for the very last one. A dark figure sat in the shadows. Only his hands were visible. The rest was hidden in the darkness. Dagger.

"I've found them," Sword murmured. "I'll go to level two and release Razor, Hammer and Trig first."

"Dagger?" Jordan asked in a fearful voice.

"He is in the last cell on the left on the third level," Sword replied, glancing at Jordan. "I won't leave him."

Jordan glanced down at the screen to the vidcom. She saw the dark figure. His hands clenched and unclenched as he sat shrouded in the shadows.

"I'll go release him," she said.

"I don't want you down there alone. Jordan, he has been held for over two years. He… he might not be sane after what he has been through," Sword said hesitantly. "It might be necessary to knock him out."

Jordan watched the figure rise up. Dagger stepped into the dim light and glared at the camera. A long scar ran along his right cheek. Cold hatred glared back at her.

"Go, do what you have to," she murmured. "I'll make sure that you aren't trapped down there."

"Stay here. Lock the door in case anyone comes. I will return in ten minutes," Sword said, stepping out of the room.

"I'll be okay. Go. I want to get out of here," Jordan replied as her eyes flashed over the dead body of the guard. "Just… free them."

Kali waited silently outside the thick double doors; a confident mask of calm on her face. She was thankful she had learned to hide her true feelings. Cannon would have bundled her up and had her back on the *Journey* before she could say her name if he knew how scared she was under it.

"He will see you now," a heavyset female grunted.

Kali ignored the nasty grin on the female's face. The receptionist had the face of a toad complete with large moles and bumps that looked a lot like warts. Kali strode into the main office of the Drethulan, not turning around as the wart-face bitch closed the door behind them, sealing them inside.

She noted that there was another male besides the Drethulan in the room. He was tall and thickly built with black hair and brilliant dark violet eyes. His features were surprisingly humanoid. He watched them as they entered, a speculative look in his eyes as she stopped and held his gaze in challenge. The trace of a smile curved his lips upward as he bowed his head.

"I will leave you for now, my lord," the man murmured, straightening up.

The Drethulan ignored the male as he walked out of the room. His eyes were assessing Kali and the four males behind her. The dark eyes blinked slowly as she folded her arms across her chest.

"I heard you were looking for fighters," Kali announced in a determined voice.

"And you have one to sell?" the Drethulan replied, his dark eyes following Kali's hands as she placed them on her slim hips and tossed her head.

"Yes!" she hissed. "The bastard thought I wouldn't care if he cheated on me!"

The Drethulan glanced at Cannon's pained expression. He noted the stun collar around his neck and the ones connected to both wrists. His eyes flickered back to him and then to the three guards that stood behind him. All three belonged to *The Hole's* security team. He did not know each of the guards yet, but knew that they would never have been able to get into the building without an access key.

"You expect me to believe you captured a Trivator warrior on your own?" he hissed in distrust.

"Kali," Cannon began.

Kali swiveled and looked up at Cannon's face. "Don't you, Kali me! I *saw* you! I saw you and her!"

"Kali, I don't…" Cannon began, but stopped when Kali turned her back on him.

"I drugged his drink last night," Kali cried out in rage and hurt. "He thought he could sleep with me after being… after being…" She lowered her head and sniffed before raising angry eyes to the Drethulan. "No male will treat me like that and live."

For a moment, silence froze the room before the sound of a rusty chuckle slowly built. The Drethulan stepped closer to Kali and ran his eyes up and down her. He dismissed her as being a profitable commodity. She was too fragile to be used as a whore and too dangerous to keep for himself. Though maybe the Kassis warlord would be interested. He focused his gaze back on the cuffed male standing behind her.

The Trivator warrior was a different story. With four of them, his profit level would substantially increase. He walked around Cannon with a slow, measuring look. He liked the fire in the male's eyes. He would be deadly. He might even be able to sell his body to some of his more affluent female customers.

"A hundred credits," the Drethulan said.

"Two hundred," Kali countered. "I have to pay to get off this rock."

The Drethulan's mouth tightened before he nodded. "Two hundred," he agreed, knowing he would get his credits back with interest from the fights.

Kali held out her hand for the credit chip. The Drethulan snorted and returned to his desk. He inserted a chip and transferred the credits onto it. Walking back around the side of his desk, he handed Kali the disk.

"What species are you?" he asked with an assessing frown. "I have not seen your kind before."

"No, you haven't," Kali replied over her shoulder as she turned back to Cannon and ran her hand up his chest. "I'm not from around here. Goodbye sugar, I hope you get what's coming to you."

Kali knew this part of the plan had been the hardest for Cannon to accept. Kali slipped the key into the lock of the cuff around his neck at the same time as he pulled the key for the ones on his wrists from the waistband of her pants.

The Raftian had warned her that the cuffs would be scanned to make sure they were active before Cannon would be allowed into the complex. In fact, it had been checked twice. Once upon entering and again by the wart-faced receptionist who insisted on testing it. The bolt, even on the lowest setting, had knocked Cannon to his knees with a low groan.

They could not take the chance of Cannon being disabled and defenseless. The plan was for Kali to release the cuff around his neck while he freed his hands, then find a safe corner while Cannon and the other men killed the Drethulan. She had been more than happy to stand back when she found out the damn guy could shift into a large deadly worm creature when angered.

"Good luck," Kali whispered as she brushed her lips next to Cannon's ear in a display of affection. "He has a pistol in the left drawer of his desk."

She still had her arms around Cannon's neck when the double doors to the office burst inward. Her eyes froze on Razor's furious face. Time stood still as they gazed at each other before speeding up as the Drethulan roared out in rage.

Kali felt her body being lifted at the same time as Razor, Hammer, Trig and Sword swept into the room with a terrifying war cry. Cannon swung her around and tossed her toward the Trusset who caught her and set her gently in the corner with a wink. Kali pressed her back up against the wall as the Drethulan started shaking and expanding.

This was nothing like what she was used to fighting. Her hand went to her stomach as it turned when a putrid smell poured from the creature. She covered her nose and mouth trying to minimize breathing it in. It was no use, her stomach rolled in rebellion.

She turned at the same time as the wart-faced bitch came through the door with a laser pistol. Kali opened her mouth and threw up all over the woman's arm. The female screeched and stumbled sideways.

Kali fell back against the wall as another wave of nausea swept through her. She had to get out of the room. The other woman snarled at Kali as she shook her arms. A look of disgust twisted her ugly face before she switched the laser pistol to her other hand.

"I am going to kill you," she screeched.

Kali was too sick to care at that moment. She leaned forward as her stomach heaved again as more of the nauseous odor filled the room. She lifted her hand in a feeble attempt to stop the woman. Her eyes closed when the Trusset saw what was happening and grabbed the female by the arm. He lifted her up and tossed her at the Drethulan.

The sound of bones breaking and the woman's screams was too much for Kali. She stumbled forward and out of the doors of the office desperately gasping in fresh, untainted air. Sliding her hand along the wall, she slid down it just on the other side of the doors.

Soon the room grew quiet. Kali sat on the floor with her head on her knees uncaring if the world stopped at that moment. In fact, she hoped it did because it was spinning like a tilt-a-whirl on steroids. She moaned when a pair of hands tenderly cupped her face and forced it up. She closed her eyes to keep from seeing the room.

"Kali, *fi'ta,* are you alright?" Razor's deep voice asked urgently.

Kali slowly opened her eyes and gave him a weak smile. She didn't have the energy to respond verbally. She laid her cheek against his hand and closed her eyes.

"Jordan?" she finally whispered with her eyes still closed.

"Gone," Razor said quietly. "Along with Dagger."

30

Almost a month later, Kali stood looking out of the viewport at her new home. The planet was slightly larger than the Earth. Where the Earth looked like a large blue and white marble, Rathon was a dark green with the swirls of white. Over half of the planet was covered by an emerald green ocean.

They had left the Tressalon star system shortly after discovering that Dagger had stolen Arindoss' personal starship. Since there was no current new owner to *The Hole* and the starship had probably been stolen from its previous owner, there was no reason to stay once Trig had finally been able to talk with Dagger. The conversation must not have gone very well as Trig looked pissed and Razor infuriated. Razor finally told her that Dagger said he would return Jordan to Rathon… when he was ready.

"Do you think it is safe for Jordan to be with Dagger right now? I know Sword and Cannon were worried about his mental stability after being held for so long," she had asked as Razor ordered the *Journey* to return to Rathon.

She remembered Razor's aggravated sigh before he responded. "I do not believe he will harm Jordan. From what Hunter has told me,

Dagger is very protective of her. It is obvious from her determination to find Dagger that Jordan feels the same. He refused to tell Trig where he was going, but I imagine it is to a safe place. I cannot see him putting Jordan in danger."

"But, if he isn't thinking straight," Kali said before her voice faded and a small smile curved her lips upward. "You're right. Jordan can handle him."

Razor's eyes narrowed at the look on Kali's face. "Why do you think that?"

"Because she loves him," Kali replied, tilting her head to the side.

Razor shook his head. "I am not sure even that will save him," he had responded quietly.

Kali turned as the door slid open behind her. A smile lit up her face when she saw Razor standing silhouetted in the doorway. He had been busy all morning with Hammer in preparation of their arrival so she hadn't seen much of him.

"It's time," Razor told her with a returning smile. "Now, I will take you to our home."

"I'm looking forward to it," Kali replied, glancing back down at the planet. "It looks so beautiful from space."

"It is beautiful down there as well," Razor commented. "Come, the shuttle is ready."

"You said that there are dangerous animals that roam the forests," Kali said as she threaded her fingers through his. "Will we be living near them?"

Razor nodded his head. "Our world is different from yours in many ways, yet similar as well. We have only a few larger cities, such as Julumont which my brother Hunter oversees. Our ancestors believed that for future generations to survive, it was important to live in harmony with our environment. The Trivator males are not much different from the creatures that roam the forests. A part of our primitive ancestors still live within us."

Kali laughed. "So you are still beating your chests and hopping up and down when you are angry," she teased.

"No," Razor replied, flashing his sharp teeth. "We hunt down and rip out the throats of those that annoy us."

Kali's breath caught at the reminder that Razor was not human. A shiver of desire swept through her as she remembered what those teeth felt like against her skin. The low rumble from Razor showed that he felt her reaction.

"I cannot wait to get you to our home," he murmured as they passed by several warriors. "I have been dreaming of you naked in my bath."

Kali blushed as two warriors walking toward them grinned. She silently cursed the Trivator's enhanced hearing and shot Razor at warning glance. She was going to have to think of a good payback when she saw him grin even bigger.

An hour later, she wasn't thinking of payback, but of murder as she stood stiffly glaring at the tall, elegant female that was standing in what was supposed to be the bedroom of her new home. Kali's mouth tightened as the woman looked her up and down. The disdain on the woman's face was enough to make Kali curl her fingers into a fist. It was hard to resist clawing the woman's eyes out as she turned those same eyes to Razor who stood frozen in the doorway behind Kali.

"Razor, I have missed you," the woman said, taking a step toward him and tilting her neck seductively.

Kali knew the bitch was expecting him to run his nose along it. She'd break it if he even tried. She didn't journey halfway across the universe to be set aside while he had fun with his fuck-bunny. Kali had no doubts that was exactly what the woman was in her tight fitting gown and with her perfectly made-up, I'm-ready-to-be-fucked, face.

There is no way I will ever sleep in this room, Kali thought infuriated.

"I wouldn't go any closer if I were you," Kali growled in a low tone. "Who are you and what are you doing here?"

Rainiera's eyes narrowed at the warning in Kali's voice. "I am Razor's… mate," Rainiera responded. "And who are you?"

Kali refused to let the pain raking through her show. She reached for the calm mask that she had perfected, but she knew that the fury still showed in her eyes at the woman's raised eyebrow.

"I'm obviously in the wrong place," Kali snapped back.

"Yes, you are," Rainiera replied in a haughty tone, looking at Razor. "Who is this female? Is she the new house help? I thought I told you I would take care of maintaining it while you were away."

"Oh, fuck no," Kali snarled, turning to glare at Razor. "Who is she and what is she doing here?"

Razor looked back and forth between the two females. His former lover stood looking back at him with a look of quiet challenge while his *Amate*, while Kali… looked like she was ready to disembowel him. He silently cursed Rainiera. This was not the way he wanted Kali's first impression of his world to be like.

"Rainiera, leave," Razor ordered, never taking his eyes off of Kali.

"Why? I am your lover. She is… whatever she is. We had an agreement," Rainiera stated coolly. "We had discussed joining when you returned. I will agree to it."

"Joining," Kali repeated, glaring at Razor. This time, she knew that the mask hiding her true feelings had slipped. She stumbled back a step when he started forward. "Joining, as in this?"

Rainiera's eyes widened when she saw the dark markings around Kali's wrists as she lifted her arms and slid the sleeves of her shirt back. Bitter disappointment and rage at being denied such a powerful position as being Razor's *Amate* flooded her. She reached out and wrapped her hand around Kali's wrist so she could read the markings.

"Don't touch me," Kali snapped, jerking her arm away and stepping closer to the door leading to the large bathroom. "Is it true? Did you promise her you would 'join' with her when you returned?"

"No," Razor said, ignoring Rainiera's outraged gasp. "We discussed it, but I made no promises."

"Well, obviously she thought you had," Kali said bitterly, tears of hurt and anger making her eyes glitter. "How could you? How could you bring me here, knowing she was waiting for you?"

"I brought you here because this is my... our home," Razor said in a quiet, intense voice. "I did not know Rainiera would be here. I sent her a message stating that I no longer wished to consider joining with her."

"You broke up with her through an email?" Kali whispered in shock and disbelief.

Razor growled in frustration, shooting a menacing look at Rainiera. The self-satisfied look on her face proved that she had planned this. When he had contacted her before, she swore she would not make his decision easy on him. He had underestimated her desire for revenge.

"Get out," Razor snapped in fury.

"Razor," Rainiera whispered, paling at the cold look of rage on his face.

"Now before I do something I might not regret, Rainiera. You've had your revenge. You can smell her pain," Razor growled. "You are fortunate that I do not kill you for that."

Kali's eyes flashed at his mention of her pain. She *hated* that they could smell so damn well. Well, neither one of them could smell her if she was not there.

"Don't bother. I'll take my smell and leave you two love birds alone. You both deserve each other," Kali interrupted through clenched teeth.

"Kali, my *fi'ta,*" Razor said in exasperation as she moved to step around him.

"Don't," Kali whispered when he reached for her. "Just... don't."

"Razor, if she wishes to leave, let her," Rainiera said. "Surely you see now that you are back that such a weak creature could never stand by your side the way I could."

Kali might have been able to ignore the comment if Rainiera had kept her disdain and satisfaction to herself. Her hands clenched into fists again. This time, though, she didn't do it to keep from clawing the woman's eyes out but to punch her. Kali rubbed her fist as she glared down at the woman now lying on the floor with a bloody lip.

"That, bitch, is just a taste of how weak I am," Kali growled in a low, menacing voice. "If I ever see you again, you'd better run the other way or I'll show you what happens when I really get pissed."

Without another word, Kali turned sharply on her heel and strode from the room. She didn't stop until she was out the front door. She picked up speed as she ran down the steps. As soon as she hit the long pathway leading up to the front of the house, she started running. She didn't have a clue where she was going, but it wasn't going to be here.

She turned the corner of the path and skidded to a stop to prevent running into an older couple coming up the path. The old man's strong arms steadied her when she almost fell on the loose gravel. She pulled in a deep breath to apologize. Her eyes flew up to meet a set of dark gold eyes similar to Razor's. A low sob exploded from her as she swayed from the pain washing through her.

"Oh child," the woman's soft, sympathetic voice was too much for Kali.

She turned into the woman's open arms, uncaring that she was a stranger. Harsh sobs escaped Kali as her heart broke. She should never have come to this suddenly horrid world.

~

Razor stood stiffly over Rainiera. He didn't help her to stand as she struggled to get her feet under her. He daren't, for fear he would wrap his hands around her neck and snap it. He wanted to follow Kali, but first he needed to get Rainiera out of his home and out of his life once and for all.

"I told you we were over," he said harshly.

Rainiera touched her bottom lip and winced as her fingers came away with blood. She glared at Razor for a fraction of a second before paling when she realized that she had never seen him so angry. At that moment, she feared she had pushed him too far.

"You did not mention you had taken an *Amate*," she whispered defensively. "I… I thought you were simply unsure of how I could fit in your life."

"You do not 'fit' in it at all," Razor replied brutally. "I told you that we were over and not to return to my home."

"Razor, I apologized for disobeying you, but do you really believe that… that creature is better suited for you than I am?" Rainiera whispered.

Razor lifted his arms so that Rainiera could see the markings surrounding his wrists. His face was set in stone as he fought to contain his temper. Each second he delayed making sure Rainiera understood her mistake meant a second longer Kali thought he did not want her.

"She is my *Amate*, my life, not a creature," Razor hissed out. "The question is not whether she is fit to stand at my side, but if I am fit to stand at hers! She is a warrior. She saved my life not once, but twice. She is the mother of our unborn child. *Kali* is my family!"

Rainiera shook at the intensity of raw emotion in Razor's voice. His words left no doubt to his feelings and commitment. The markings around his wrists eliminated any hope that she had of ever winning him back.

"I… forgive me, Razor," Rainiera choked out in a hoarse voice.

"Get out."

Razor stood stiffly as Rainiera nodded. His eyes followed her as she grabbed her wrap and walked by him. She bowed her head when he glared in warning at her when she hesitated as she did. Only after he heard the front door seal behind her did he release his breath.

He briefly closed his eyes as the picture of Kali's pain filled eyes flashed before him. Turning on his heel, he quickly left the room praying Kali hadn't gone far. The thought that she might have veered from the protected paths pushed him forward. He swept through the front door only to come to a sudden stop when he saw his father sitting on the top step waiting for him.

"I can't…," Razor began.

"She is with your mother," Scout informed him.

"Where?" Razor asked in relief.

"Your *Amate* refused to return to the house so your mother took her to Hunter and Jesse's," Scout replied.

"Kali told you who she was?" Razor asked.

"Your markings did," Scout replied dryly. "She is not happy with you right now."

"No, I imagine she is not," Razor replied heavily.

"Did she give Rainiera the bloody lip?" Scout asked, a glint of humor in his eyes as he stood up.

Razor's lips twitched. In spite of the heaviness he felt at causing Kali pain, his relief combined with her punching Rainiera in the mouth drew a reluctant chuckle from him. He would have to remember that Kali threw a wicked right hook.

"Yes," Razor admitted. "Rainiera called her weak."

Scout chuckled and slapped Razor on the shoulder. "I bet Rainiera doesn't do that again."

"No, I hope she never comes near Kali again," Razor agreed following his father back down the path to where his transport was. "I just hope Kali will listen when I explain that I had no idea Rainiera would be here."

31

"Kali, please talk to me," Razor begged in frustration outside the bedroom Hunter and Jesse had given her. "Please, my *fi'ta,* please let me in."

It had been two days since the incident with Rainiera. Two days since he had seen Kali. She refused to talk to him, to see him. The sounds of her quiet sobs tore through him like knives.

He splayed his hands flat against the outside of the bedroom door. His mother had made him promise not to break it down. Leaning his forehead against it, he closed his eyes as another smothered sob escaped from Kali.

"I miss you, Kali. You are my *Amate*. You are my life," Razor said quietly, knowing that she could hear him. "I would never cause you pain. I… I love you so much, Kali. Please, let me in."

Emotion choked him when her tortured cry sounded through the door followed by silence. He turned when he felt a gentle hand touch his shoulder. He turned his anguished gaze to look into his mother's sympathetic eyes.

"Go," Shana instructed quietly. "I left you a plate on the table. Go eat. I will see to your *Amate*."

"She will make herself sick," Razor whispered. "What can I do to prove to her that I see no other but her?"

Shana's eyes softened at the pain and grief in her eldest son's face. "I will talk with her," she said. "Go, have a drink and eat. Your father is waiting."

Razor turned back to stare at the closed door for several long seconds before he nodded his head in resignation. He ran his hand down his face. He hadn't eaten or slept since they returned to the planet. The idea of sleeping in the same bed that he had shared with Rainiera sent a wave of distaste through him. It had been so bad that he had pulled the mattresses off and burned them.

It hadn't relieved the ache inside him. He had moved into a guest bedroom, but even there he couldn't sleep. He missed the feel of Kali's warm body wrapped around him. In frustration, he had contacted the building department and requested a new home be built on property he owned closer to the ocean. Construction was supposed to begin today.

This home would be for Kali. A new home where they could start fresh, as a family. A home built just for her.

"Please, tell her... tell her I love her more than life itself," Razor requested as he turned away.

Shana watched as her eldest son walked away. A small smile curved her lips as she shook her head before she straightened her shoulders. Sometimes it took a mother's touch to help bring two stubborn individuals to their senses. Her son had learned a very valuable lesson. He would not take his *Amate* for granted. Now, it was time to help Kali understand just how much power she held over Razor.

"Kali, this is Shana. May I come in?"

~

Kali wiped at the tears that still kept escaping. In truth, she was tired of crying! All it had given her was a headache, a stuffy nose and red eyes. She sat curled up on the bed with her arms wrapped around her pillow as she listened to Shana.

"So he couldn't cheat on me?" Kali asked.

"No, child. Razor could never cheat on you. He would have no desire to. You are his *Amate*. When he said you were his world, he was not saying that lightly," Shana assured her.

"Why was Rainiera there, then?" Kali sniffed.

Shana shook her head and her mouth tightened. "Rainiera has always been very spoiled. She wanted my son because he holds a position of great power and prestige, not because she had feelings for him," Shana replied.

"Well, if I ever see her again, I'm going to rip all her hair out," Kali growled on a hiccup. "I'll do more than punch her in the mouth if she comes near Razor again."

Shana laughed and covered Kali's left hand. "I would have loved to have seen that. I've wanted to do that a time or two when she attended functions we were at."

"I'm not going to be running into her all the time, am I? I don't think I could handle that," Kali said, looking down at their joined hands.

"No, Razor would not do that to you," Shana assured her. "Not to mention, I believe Rainiera would want to keep her hair."

The image of a bald Rainiera pulled a giggle from Kali. Within minutes, she and Shana were laughing hysterically as they made up all kinds of ways Kali could get back at Rainiera. After ten minutes, Kali released a deep sign.

"He really does love me," she murmured, fingering the marking on her left wrist.

"Very much," Shana said. "Why don't you get cleaned up. Perhaps, you can find it in your heart to forgive my son. Men do not realize what they do sometimes. It is good that Razor has learned just how much he needs you."

Kali smiled at Shana. "Thank you, Shana."

"No, thank you, Kali. I feared Razor would never know the joys of having an *Amate*. I could not have chosen a better mate for my son," Shana replied before she bent and brushed a kiss across Kali's forehead. "I will send him in after Scout has finished with him."

Kali laughed again as she rose from the bed with renewed vigor. It was time she let Razor know that she was the only woman in his life from now on. The knowledge that he missed her as much as she missed him wasn't lost on her.

"I need him as much as he needs me," she whispered into the mirror. Her hand dropped to the slight swell of her stomach. "We both do."

Razor looked up as his mother walked into the kitchen and smiled at him. A wave of relief flooded him and he stood up so fast that his chair fell backwards, hitting the hard surface of the floor behind him.

"Go to her, but be patient, Razor," Shana cautioned him. "She has been hurt very deeply."

"I will. Thank you," Razor said hoarsely. "I… thank you."

"Good luck, my son," Shana whispered as she watched him rush out of the room.

"I believe Razor will have his hands full with Kali," Scout chuckled, wrapping his arm around Shana's waist and rubbing his nose along her neck. "Just as I have my hands full with you. I think it is time to return to our home."

A shiver went through Shana at the slight growl in Scout's voice. When his hand slipped up to cup her breast, she moaned and rubbed back against him. A wave of desire hit her hard as he nipped her neck.

"Yes," Shana gasped out as Scout turned her and scooped her up in his arms. "I love you, Scout."

"Not as much as I love you, my beautiful *Amate*," he replied.

Razor stood in Kali's bedroom looking out the window. The door to the bathroom was closed and he could hear her as she stepped out of the shower. He thought of joining her, but remembered his mother's word of caution to be patient. He did not want to make any more mistakes. The last two days had been hell and he wasn't about to mess up again.

As he stared out at the darkening sky, he discovered he was feeling another foreign emotion – nervousness. His hands trembled as he thought of how close he had come to losing the most precious thing in his life through his own stupidity. He should have known that Rainiera would try to change his mind. If he had told her he had an *Amate*, it could have avoided so much heartache.

He turned when the door opened. His breath caught at the sight of Kali silhouetted in the doorway. Her wet hair was slicked back away from her face. A few droplets of water glistened on her bare shoulders. Only a towel covered her.

Mesmerized by the image and desperate to touch her, he took a hesitant step forward. He swallowed past the lump in his throat when he saw the shimmer in her eyes. He didn't care if he had to get down on his knees and beg, he had to touch her. Lifting his arms until they were opened for her, he waited to see if she would accept his peace offering.

A low cry escaped Kali as she rushed into his arms. A relieved sigh escaped him as he captured her tightly against his chest. A shudder went through him when her arms circled his waist to hold him in return.

"I'm sorry, Kali," Razor whispered. "I am so sorry for hurting you."

Kali just nodded, burying her face in his chest and breathing in his scent. She had missed him. She had missed his warmth, his scent, his voice, everything.

"Kali," Razor groaned when her hands moved to work at the clasps on his shirt.

"I want you, Razor," she whispered. "I want to touch you, feel you.... I want to love you."

Razor's lips desperately captured hers. Her words were music to his ears. He tugged the towel away from her, letting it drop to the floor as he swept her up in his arms. Crossing over to the bed, he gently laid her down. He quickly removed his clothing.

He wanted to worship her. He placed one knee on the bed next to her and his hands on each side of her head until she was caged below him. Bending over, he brushed his lips across hers until she was gasping and arching toward him.

Moving lower, he tenderly pulled one taut nipple into his mouth. He sucked on it until it stood rosy and swollen before moving to the next one. Her moans and pants fanned the flames burning inside him.

His lips trailed down her stomach, pausing on the slight swell. He shifted his weight so he could cup her stomach. His eyes locked with hers as he pressed a gentle kiss to it before he continued his journey. A satisfied smile curled his lips when her legs fell apart. Her bare mound rose to meet his lips.

"Oh God," Kali moaned as he ran his tongue along her clit. "I... More."

"Mine, Kali," Razor murmured against her. "You are mine."

"Yes," Kali hissed out as his warm, moist breath caressed her sensitive skin. "Razor."

Razor heard the need in Kali's voice. It was a need only he could assuage. He lapped at her, focusing on the swelling nub with his tongue while he slid three fingers into her.

"Yes," Kali cried out as she bowed under him.

Hot come flooded his senses as she came hard around his fingers and tongue. He continued lapping at her until she cried out again. Rising up, he aligned his cock with her slick entrance and pushed forward. The sight of watching as his engorged penis penetrated her was enough to tighten his balls to the exploding point.

He fell forward onto his elbows to keep from crushing her as he began moving. His eyes locked with hers as he pushed deeper and deeper with each stroke. He could feel the tingling begin to build at the base of his spine. He wasn't going to be able to control his release.

"Kali," he groaned out, his face tensing as he fought for control. "Kali, I love you."

He watched as her face tensed before her eyes closed and she moaned loudly. Watching as she came, he released the tight hold on his own body. The feel of her body pulsing around his as he came drew shuddering gasps from him as he fought to keep from collapsing on her. He pushed upward as he poured everything he had into her. His seed, his hopes, his dreams, his soul, he gave her everything.

"Kali, my *Amate*," he cried out in ecstasy as he stiffened. "I belong only to you, my *fi'ta*. Only you."

He rolled, keeping them connected until Kali was lying draped across him. He held her tight against his body. For the first time in days, he felt peace settle around him.

32

Kali grinned at Taylor as she moved around the room like a small tornado. It had been eight weeks since they left the Tres-salon star system and returned to Rathon. Jesse and Taylor were excited because Jordan had contacted them last night to let them know that she and Dagger would be returning later that evening.

"I can't wait to see her!" Taylor exclaimed in excitement. "I wonder where they've been. She was so secretive about it. I bet it was some totally cool place with lots of beaches and these little umbrellas in a glass."

Jesse laughed and shook her head. "I doubt they were on a beach in Hawaii or Tahiti, Taylor," she said, bending to pick Lyon up as he pulled on her skirt.

"Let me," Hunter murmured, sweeping Lyon up in his arms. He grinned as Lyon giggled and wrapped his arms around his neck. "You should be resting."

"Hunter, I'm not going to break," Jesse said with a shake of her head. "I'll rest if I get tired."

Kali turned and smiled as Razor stepped into the room with Saber. Her eyes twinkled with amusement when Saber's eyes immediately went to Taylor. Razor caught her gaze and smiled.

She flushed as he ran his eyes over the swell of her stomach. Since she began showing, he had become even more protective and, well… horny. He said that her new scent was driving him crazy. He also loved to feel the baby moving inside her as he held her and made love to her.

They had talked a lot over the past several weeks, spending time to really get to know each other. She had feared he would be furious with her involvement with the rescue mission, but he never said anything negative. In fact, he had commended her on her plan. He often talked to her about the different things that were going on during the day when he was at work.

She also had a chance to talk to her brother the week before and found out that construction back on Earth was going well. Destin was fascinated by all the new methods and composites that were being used. The new council member from the Usoleum star system was very helpful. When Kali teased her brother, asking him how helpful. He had turned red and muttered that he didn't want to talk about it.

"Are you happy, Kali?" Destin had asked instead. "I mean, really happy?"

"Yes," Kali had replied. "This is amazing, Destin. I wish you could see it. Rathon is beautiful. There are parts that are still wild and untamed but they live in harmony with it."

"I'm happy for you, Kali," Destin replied with a sigh. "I miss you though."

"I miss you too, Destin," Kali said with a tearful smile. "Have I mentioned that you are going to be the proud uncle of a baby girl in a few months?"

"A girl, you didn't tell me that part!" Destin laughed. "I have a feeling that Razor is going to be more protective than ever. Especially if she is anything like you."

Kali smiled as she remembered their conversation. For the first time in a long time it had been about them and not about the world around them and surviving to the next day.

"Are you feeling well?" Razor asked as he slid his arms around her and laid his hands across her stomach.

"I'm fine," she replied, laying her head back against him. "Just thinking of Destin. He seemed happy."

"I am glad," Razor grunted before rubbing his nose against her neck. "I want to return to our home."

"Sounds good to me," she murmured as he pressed a hot kiss against her neck. "As long as Rainiera doesn't show up this time."

She bit her lip to keep from chuckling at Razor's flinch. She wasn't sure she would ever let him forget the incident the first night they arrived on Rathon. In some ways, it had made their relationship stronger. She now understood what it really meant to be an *Amate*. She also realized just how much Razor truly loved her. Their new home was a testament to his desire to start fresh with her.

"She will never bother us again," Razor promised. "She has been transferred to another location."

"Far, far away?" Kali asked in a husky voice.

"Very, very far away," Razor swore.

"Didn't you say our new home is ready for us?" she asked in a husky voice. "If so, I can pick up my clothes tomorrow."

Razor grinned. Finally, he would get her to his home; to their new home! For the past eight weeks he had been supervising the construction of their new home along the cliffs. He hadn't let her see it. He wanted to be able to carry her across the threshold as was the tradition according to Taylor.

"We must be going," Razor called out. "Kali is tired and I wish to get her to our new home before dark."

"Oh, you're leaving, Kali?" Taylor asked before she paused to answer the comlink that pinged at her collar. "Yes? Sure, ten minutes? Great, see you then. Buzz, one of the guys from school, is coming to pick me up. We'll be back before it gets dark. I want to be here when Jordan and Dagger arrive."

"Where are you going?" Saber demanded.

Taylor looked at him with a raised eyebrow. For the past two years, he had treated her like she was a child. She wasn't a child any longer. She was studying Physical Therapy and working at the local medical clinic. Her eyes moved to the cane that he was leaning heavily on. He still refused to do the Physical Therapy that would help him.

A low growl drew her attention back to his face, which had turned darker. She could see the rage that always seemed to be simmering under the surface. She missed the Saber of old who used to joke and tease her and the others.

"Buzz is taking me out," she replied with a shrug as she grabbed her jacket off the back of the kitchen chair and started to walk by him. "We've been hanging out on and off."

Saber put his hand out to stop Taylor from walking past him. He was breathing heavily and a dark regret burned in his eyes. He stared down into Taylor's flushed, upturned face. There was so much he wanted to do and say, but he was not the male for her. She deserved a male who was whole. A male who could protect her the way she deserved to be protected.

"It is probably the way it should be," he muttered.

"Why?" Taylor asked softly, ignoring everyone else in the room.

"Because you deserve a male who is whole," Saber bit out, dropping his arm so she could pass.

Anger glittered in Taylor's eyes for a moment before it was replaced with a sly grin. She reached down and cupped the front of Saber, ignoring the shocked gasp from her sister and the smothered, choked chuckle from Hunter's mom and dad. She squeezed him, empowered by the quick swelling of his cock at her touch.

"I don't know," Taylor said thoughtfully, "you feel pretty damn whole to me."

Without another word, Taylor ran her hand across the bulge one more time before she turned and walked out of the front of the house. A feeling of triumph swept through her. Saber wasn't immune to her touch and she damn well planned on touching him a lot more.

"Did she just…?" Jesse asked in a choked whisper.

"I think it is time for us to leave," Razor muttered.

Kali's eyes glittered with a touch of mischief as she brushed her hand across the front of Razor. Yep, Razor wasn't immune to her touch either.

~

Later that evening, Kali lay back against Razor's bare chest. Her breath had been taken away by the beauty of their new home. Far below, the sound of the waves crashing against the cliffs echoed softly through their bedroom. A light breeze blew the curtains around the tall doors that lead out onto the balcony.

They had finally made it to the bed. They started making love in the entry way and had made it to the thick rug in front of the massive fireplace the first time. The second time had been in the huge bathroom. The tub was the size of a small pond and they had made love slowly, exploring each other; one touch, one kiss at a time. They finally fell into an exhausted sleep several hours ago.

Kali rose silently from the bed, glancing down at Razor's relaxed face. In the dim light from the moon, he looked almost like a Greek god with his chiseled features and muscular build.

Sweeping a silk wrap up off the footstool, she slid it on and tied it at the waist. She stepped out onto the wide balcony. The marble under her bare feet felt cool and smooth. She glanced at the wide balcony. Biting her lip, she glanced behind her before deciding once wouldn't hurt.

Using the thick corner pillar as a brace, she climbed up onto the banister circling the patio. She wrapped her arm around the pillar and raised her face to the gentle breeze. For a moment, as she looked out over the diamond spotted ocean, she felt like she could fly.

A pair of strong arms circled her waist and tenderly lifted her off the edge of the balcony. She melted back against Razor's warm body. Opening her eyes, she smiled up at him.

"You're supposed to be sleeping," she whispered, lifting a hand to run her fingers along his jaw.

"So are you," he replied in a husky voice. "What were you doing?"

"Flying," she said.

Razor's eyes darkened at her simple explanation for nearly giving him a heart attack. For a moment, vivid imagines of the first time they met flashed through his mind. Her concern, the way she held his face and kissed him for hurting him, her curiosity about the softness of his hair. All of it.

"I love you, Kali," Razor whispered. "I love your strength, the beauty you see in the world around you, the touch of your fingers against my skin. You make me feel like I can fly whenever you look at me."

Kali's fingers threaded through his hair. "Kiss me, love me," she begged. "Never let me fall."

"Never, my *fi'ta*. You are my *Amate,*" he said. "I am Razor. I belong to Kali as she belongs to me. Forever will I tie my life to hers. I will care for, protect and give my seed only to her. She is my *Amate*. She is my life."

"I am Kali. I belong to Razor as he belongs to me. Forever will I tie my life to his. I will care for, protect and cherish him as he cherishes me.

He is my *Amate*. He is my life," Kali whispered at the same time as he spoke his vows to her. "Forever, Razor."

"Forever, my *fi'ta*."

To be continued.... **Dagger's Hope**

USA Today Bestseller! New York Times Bestseller!

Dagger is a Trivator warrior who feared nothing until he met a young, delicate human female who awakened his heart. It's been a few years since Jordan Sampson was brought to the Trivators' home world Rathon with her sisters, and she is slowly adjusting to her new life, but when Dagger is captured during a mission, Jordan's all-consuming need to find him and bring him home may cost them both their lives. The star system is a dangerous place for a young human female and a damaged Trivator warrior.

Check out the full book here: books2read.com/Daggers-Hope

Or try a new series! S.E. Smith recommends:

Capture of the Defiance, A Breaking Free novel

A thriller mystery that stands on its own as danger reveals itself in sudden, heart-stopping moments.

With some time before the next semester at her university, Makayla Summerlin travels to Hong Kong to join her grandfather Henry in his voyage around the world on the Defiance. The reunion goes well until Henry is kidnapped and the Defiance disappears! Her team of allies grows as they slowly unravel the reason Henry and Makayla have been targeted, but will they discover the truth before time runs out for Henry?

Check out the full book here:
books2read.com/Capture-of-the-Defiance

ADDITIONAL BOOKS

If you loved this story by me (S.E. Smith) please leave a review! You can discover additional books at: http://sesmithfl.com and http://sesmithya.com or find your favorite way to keep in touch here: https://sesmithfl.com/contact-me/ Be sure to sign up for my newsletter to hear about new releases!

Recommended Reading Order Lists:

http://sesmithfl.com/reading-list-by-events/

http://sesmithfl.com/reading-list-by-series/

The Series

Science Fiction / Romance

Dragon Lords of Valdier Series

It all started with a king who crashed on Earth, desperately hurt. He inadvertently discovered a species that would save his own.

Curizan Warrior Series

The Curizans have a secret, kept even from their closest allies, but even they are not immune to the draw of a little known species from an isolated planet called Earth.

Marastin Dow Warriors Series

The Marastin Dow are reviled and feared for their ruthlessness, but not all want to live a life of murder. Some wait for just the right time to escape....

Sarafin Warriors Series

A hilariously ridiculous human family who happen to be quite formidable... and a secret hidden on Earth. The origin of the Sarafin species is more than it seems. Those cat-shifting aliens won't know what hit them!

Dragonlings of Valdier Novellas

The Valdier, Sarafin, and Curizan Lords had children who just cannot stop getting into trouble! There is nothing as cute or funny as magical, shapeshifting kids, and nothing as heartwarming as family.

Cosmos' Gateway Series

Cosmos created a portal between his lab and the warriors of Prime. Discover new worlds, new species, and outrageous adventures as secrets are unravelled and bridges are crossed.

The Alliance Series

When Earth received its first visitors from space, the planet was thrown into a panicked chaos. The Trivators came to bring Earth into the Alliance of Star Systems, but now they must take control to prevent the humans from destroying themselves. No one was prepared for how the humans will affect the Trivators, though, starting with a family of three sisters….

Lords of Kassis Series

It began with a random abduction and a stowaway, and yet, somehow, the Kassisans knew the humans were coming long before now. The fate of more than one world hangs in the balance, and time is not always linear….

Zion Warriors Series

Time travel, epic heroics, and love beyond measure. Sci-fi adventures with heart and soul, laughter, and awe-inspiring discovery…

Paranormal / Fantasy / Romance

Magic, New Mexico Series

Within New Mexico is a small town named Magic, an… unusual town, to say the least. With no beginning and no end, spanning genres, authors, and universes, hilarity and drama combine to keep you on the edge of your seat!

Spirit Pass Series

There is a physical connection between two times. Follow the stories of those who travel back and forth. These westerns are as wild as they come!

Second Chance Series

Stand-alone worlds featuring a woman who remembers her own death. Fiery and mysterious, these books will steal your heart.

More Than Human Series

Long ago there was a war on Earth between shifters and humans. Humans lost, and today they know they will become extinct if something is not done....

The Fairy Tale Series

A twist on your favorite fairy tales!

A Seven Kingdoms Tale

Long ago, a strange entity came to the Seven Kingdoms to conquer and feed on their life force. It found a host, and she battled it within her body for centuries while destruction and devastation surrounded her. Our story begins when the end is near, and a portal is opened....

Epic Science Fiction / Action Adventure

Project Gliese 581G Series

An international team leave Earth to investigate a mysterious object in our solar system that was clearly made by someone, someone who isn't from Earth. Discover new worlds and conflicts in a sci-fi adventure sure to become your favorite!

New Adult / Young Adult

Breaking Free Series

A journey that will challenge everything she has ever believed about herself as danger reveals itself in sudden, heart-stopping moments.

The Dust Series

Fragments of a comet hit Earth, and Dust wakes to discover the world as he knew it is gone. It isn't the only thing that has changed, though, so has Dust...

ABOUT THE AUTHOR

S.E. Smith is an ***internationally acclaimed, New York Times*** **and *USA TODAY Bestselling*** author of science fiction, romance, fantasy, paranormal, and contemporary works for adults, young adults, and children. She enjoys writing a wide variety of genres that pull her readers into worlds that take them away.

Made in United States
Troutdale, OR
11/04/2024

24446371R00137